A pit village scholar [illegible] be a coal miner. After assorted [illegible] went to university in Manchester and London, then joined the professional middle classes as an industrial psychologist and later as a research/clinical psychologist. Now returned to his native Yorkshire, he continues his trade as a psychologist in Ilkley, supports Doncaster Rovers Football Club, and writes novels.

Don Bannister

Sam Chard

Pan Books London and Sydney

First published in Great Britain 1979 by Routledge and Kegan Paul Ltd
This edition published 1980 by Pan Books Ltd,
Cavaye Place, London SW10 9PG

ISBN 0 330 26083 9
Made and printed in Great Britain by
C. Nicholls & Company Ltd, The Philips Park Press, Manchester

to my village

The market square was empty save for the three men sitting on the Corn Exchange steps. The pubs round the square had closed an hour and were shuttered and dark. The man sitting in the middle was small and hump-backed. He fumbled in the poacher's pocket of his overcoat and brought out a quart bottle of beer, drank from it and passed it along.

'There's none left after that.'

The bottle was handed to and fro.

In front of the Corn Exchange the steel pens of the cattle market cast a trellis of shadows in the street lights. There was a clatter of hobnailed boots as someone walked along the fold that ran behind the covered market. The tall man, sitting on the right, slowly set and reset a row of empty beer bottles, paying great heed to them. He sprawled back, resting his head on the top step and frowned at the blackened sky. Clambering to his feet, he traced his way carefully down the steps and walked slowly across to the low fence by the canal side. The older man followed him and they leaned against the fence and watched the younger man weave his way through the empty market stalls. He climbed on one of the stalls and hung for a moment or two, swinging from the tie bar. He climbed down and stood behind the stall, arms waving, mimicking a trader shouting.

'Riiiiiipe tomaarrerrs.'

His voice boomed and echoed across the square.

'All luvverleeee, all sowwwwwwned, riiipe tomaaarerrs.'

He braced his hands on the edge of the stall, swung his body out and straight, balanced on his elbow, held for a moment, then lowered himself slowly down. He called across to the other two.

'Ah want some more beer.'

He was silent for a few moments, hugging the side post of the stall.

'Dost hear me.'

'Cum ovver 'ere.'

The young man came across to them, walking a fancied tight

rope, see-sawing his arms as if about to fall off. The tall man put his arms round the shoulders of the other two and gazed at the ground.

'We'll go to Ma Bamford's. Wek her up and mek her give us some beer.'

'She'll not sell us owt this time o'night.'

'The old bitch'll sell owt any time if she's paid reight.'

He swung them to face along the narrow path that skirted the warehouse wall by the canal and they began to walk, lurching a little, playing falling in and out of step.

A faded Off Licence sign was painted on the door. The tall man thumped on it, his head resting on the wood and his hand pounding above his head. He lurched forward as the old woman opened it and cuddled her to him. She struggled and swore at him, a kind of vicious hissing making her words hard to hear.

'Bloody big sot. 'Sa want. Geroff. Tek thi hands off. Silly bugger.'

'Beer mother, mi old love, mi sweetheart, tha bad-tempered old bitch.'

The mauling and the argument went on for a while with the other two men staring silently at the pair. Then the old woman yielded and they trooped through the off licence and into the kitchen behind.

A tall woman was sitting by the fire, long, white, well shaped legs stretched out in front of her. Her blouse was unbuttoned and lay loosely over large breasts. She smiled at the tall man as he swayed into the kitchen.

'Sam Chard. How art tha love.'

He stood for a moment looking at her then slumped into a chair by the table. The other two fitted themselves in beside him.

'Madge Vallance. Ah'm well enough. You've come back then.'

'I got fed up of Lancashire and Harry Vallance. Are tha really well.'

'You know. Middlin' fair. Dost know mi mates. The little feller is Jack Camn and the young'n is Diddy Adams.'

The old woman fetched three quart bottles of beer and thumped them down in front of the men. She mumbled bitterly over the money and sat down by the fire across from the young woman.

'What's up wi' your Harry then.'

'He still commercial travelling, Leigh to Brum and back.'

'And the kid.'

'Wi mi Mam.'

The older man made his way into the talk.

'You local then.'

'Newcastle.'

'My father come from Hexham. 'Ave you ever been there.'

'Not to remember.'

Sam fetched a glass from the scullery and poured Madge some of his beer. She raised the glass to him and smiled.

'You look grand Madge.'

'Thank you kindly.'

The young man started to say something about she could have some of his beer if she wanted but tailed off.

The talk rambled on but was hard to hear because of the rattle of the poker which the old woman was viciously jabbing and banging at the bars of the fire-grate.

'Do stop Gran and go to bed.'

'Bitch,' the old woman muttered. 'Bloody bitch. Soon as I'm off, know what you'll be up to. Legs oppen for anybody.'

'I shan't ask you, Gran.'

The old woman spat into the fire and scurried out of the room. They could hear her muttering as she clattered up the stairs. She banged her bedroom door to, several times.

'The old cow's got an idea though. Had you thought of stayin' the night Sam.'

Sam shook his head, smiling.

'It's a nice thought Madge but I'm due down pit at six, Sunday shift.'

'There's a lot could be done between now and six, lad.'

'Aye, and I'd be in grand shape for work.'

'Ah'm not working tomorrer – today,' the young lad said suddenly, blushing and choking on his words.

The woman giggled and said 'You cheeky young bugger.' There was a long silence. Sam refilled her glass, pouring the beer very slowly at a tilt.

'He's a nice enough young chap, Madge, you could do worse.'

The lad scowled and started to rise.

'Ah can speak for miself, Sam Chard.'

He looked round and waved his arms.

'Anyway, I'm goin'.'

'Hod on a minute,' Sam's voice was friendly.

The lad stood shuffling his feet and looking at the floor.

'Ah tha givin' me away, Sam Chard,' the woman said.

'It's not that. Just that he's a bit green an' you'd make him a wiser feller.'

The woman stood, stretched and walked to the stairs.

'Are you comin' then.'

The lad turned to Sam, his face reddening.

'Is she serious.'

'Now you ask me that question, and it's up to you to make up your mind if you're serious.'

She went out of sight up the stairs. After a while Sam spoke.

'I should not wait too long Diddy, unless you'd sooner sit and sup beer.'

The lad moved slowly to the foot of the stairs, hesitated a moment, then went up out of sight. Jack Camn puffed air out in a long sigh.

'Bloody hell, Sam. The young sod. I wish she'd nodded at me. I'd been that quick.'

'She'd swallow you first go mi old son.'

'You were bein' a bit generous, weren't you. Passin' her to t'lad.'

'Nowt like. It were Diddy she fancied from t' minute we came in.'

'She asked you.'

'Aye, but that was just for old time's sake. It was Diddy she was eyein'. I was just a way of dropping the hint.'

'She's a bit free with it, in't she.'

'No, she's not really. Just now and again the fancy teks her and tonight's one time.'

'What she like then. On t' nest.'

'She reight keen. She'll make a good boy of young Diddy. She has a way of squeezin' it without moving her legs. Brings tears to your eyes.'

'Be walkin' bow-legged tomorrer then.'

'Aye. But happy with it. Sup up lad, I'm for off.'

'I think I'll sit a bit and see if I can hear owt goin' on.'

'You mucky old bugger, Jack.'

Sam rose, finished his beer, tied his white scarf and moved to the door.

'I'll see you then.'

'Reight.'

'Goodneet.'

The old man nodded and moved to the chair by the fire.

Sam felt his way through the shop and into the street. He walked down the snicket into the main road, along to the clock tower and up onto the bridge. He stood for a few minutes watching the black water swirl over the weir. Then he started the five miles back to the village at a steady walk, singing quietly, 'Little Grey Home in the West.'

The taller of the two lads walked to and fro under the tree, staring up into the branches looking for walnuts. He held the heavy, foot-long stick by one end and threw it upwards so that it spun in flight. It thumped against the end of a branch and the other boy scurried round collecting the walnuts that came tumbling from the tree, stuffing them down the front of his shirt. The taller lad caught his stick as it cannoned out of the tree and stared upwards again.

'Dost want a nut, Ron.'

Ron Widowson nodded and the boy began to crack some of the walnuts against a root of the tree, using the heel of his boot.

'Don't smash 'em to smithereens. An' keep lookin' out for Poteye. If he catches us he'll half-kill us.'

'We seen him at top o' t' bridle path, Ah'll bet he's still theer.'

'Tha daft.'

The two lads began to box each other round the tree, using their hands flat and slapping, cartooning a fight with gross bobbings and weavings, sliding to their knees on the grass with noisy grunts of pretending pain. After a while they stopped and squatted at the foot of the tree, eating the walnuts.

Iverson watched them from the shelter of some elderberry bushes at the field edge. He sat astride his bike, his wooden leg thrust forward into the stirrup that had replaced one of the pedals. Squinting his one good eye he guessed the distance from himself to the tree and from the tree to the boundary fence on the far side of the field.

He had lost the leg and the eye on the same day at Passchendaele. Unscratched from the beginning of the war he had been caught by mortar bombs as he struggled through the barbed wire and a strand had whipped the eye out. Then, shuffling back to the aid station, arms on the shoulders of the man in front of him, a piece of shrapnel had severed his left leg above the kneecap.

It seemed to Iverson that the lads were nearer to the church side of the field than they were to him. He pulled his bike round, rode slowly in a half-circle and stopped. He was now hidden by a ridge near the path that edged the church side of the field. He slid a heavy beechwood cane from its straps on the cross-bar of the bike and balanced himself carefully before thrusting with his good leg and pedalling strongly up over the ridge and down the slope towards the walnut tree in the middle of the field.

The smaller lad was throwing the stick up into the tree, with the older lad showing him how to make it spin into the branches, when Iverson came across the ridge. The keeper was halfway to the tree before they saw him. The smaller lad screamed 'Poteye' and ran head down for the nearest fence. The older boy started to run square away from him and then saw Iverson swing his bike into a circling track that would cut him off. He spun round and raced back to the tree, jumped for the lowest branch and heaved himself on to it and up into the tree. Iverson turned his bike towards the smaller lad and swept past the tree. He drew level with the lad, forty yards before the fence and rode alongside him, thrashing him across the shoulders with the cane. The lad wailed and sobbed but kept up a wobbling run, trying to dodge away from or round the keeper. Iverson used his fixed gear pedal to hold his bike to the lad's speed and turned into him so that he could keep striking him across the back with sweeping strokes of the cane. The lad reached the fence and tried to thiefvault. He missed the bottom bar with his right hand and fell heavily on his head and shoulders on the far side, walnuts tumbling out of his shirt front. Iverson swung his bike in a tight circle and rode back to the tree.

He stopped under the tree and leaned against it astride his bike. For a while he stayed there breathing heavily. Then he rode a few yards from the tree, balanced himself with his good leg on the ground and the other still in its stirrup and looked up at the lad in the tree.

'Now Ronnie Widowson, tha might as well come down an' take thi beltin'.'

The lad settled himself into a fork in the branches and watched the younger boy hobble slowly away from the fence and back towards the village.

Over an hour passed and Iverson clumsily laid down his bike and sat beside it. The lad shouted suddenly from the tree.

'Bugger off you one-eyed, peg-leggid, old sod.'

Iverson sat for a while longer then remounted and rode out of the boy's sight along the far path. He stopped hidden by the estate wall and watched the tree through a break in the coping.

Slowly the afternoon passed into evening and the light softened and began to fade. The green of the field turned to grey. The boy waited until it was wholly dark before he slipped from the tree and walked quietly across the field towards home.

The four men were dinting the intake road to the face. A stretch of track had been taken up and the sleepers stacked by the roadside. The weight of the roof had flattened the ring girders till they were nearly square shaped and the men were digging the road down six inches to make a high enough passage for tubs. Three of the men were using light, sharp, miners' picks to tear up the floor and the fourth man shovelled the loose rock from the floor into a tub. When it was full he man-handled it back to the end of the track and brought up another empty tub.

The work-place moved slowly forwards. From time to time one of the men would unhook his lamp from a ring, bring it up to the front edge of the dint and re-hang it. Often the man would couple this with a long drink of water from his Dudley and stand for a minute or two, bent forwards, as tall as the low roof would allow, stretching his back and arms and staring at the growing length of narrow road, lowered and levelled, behind them. There was little talk as the hours passed.

Above the clang and scrape of shovel and pick there was the faint ringing of a bell from the main roadway. One of the men walked back to his jacket and took out an old Crown pocket-watch. 'Snaptime.'

The four men gathered up jackets, lamps, Dudleys and snaptins and moved back along the road to where the sleepers were stacked. They sat on the sleepers at either side of the road. As they began to eat the silence was broken by the liquid sound of a run of stone from the roof between them and the face. This was followed by the splash of single pieces of rock dropping from the roof and sides of the roadway.

'It's bittin' agen.'

One of the men took his lamp and walked down to the section of the roof that had fallen. He held his lamp to it, picked bits of loose rock from round the shallow cavity and walked back.

'What's up wi' it.'

'It's all this fuckin' shaly bind. Our kid could pull this bugger down.'

'They'll end up 'avin' to brick the lot to keep it up, just like they did on Sevens.'

There was silence for a while. The men ate slowly.

'Let's talk about cunt.'

'Y' can say what y'like. There's nowt nicer.'

'Tell 'em that tale about you an' that lass at Ambulance Brigade week at Blackpool, John.'

'Was she nice then, Jonathan.'

Jonathan Simpson carefully worked the buckled lid back on his snaptin and half-lay against the sleepers.

'Well, it were a few years back but I can remember 'er clear enough.'

'Let's hear it then.'

'It were near end of Blackpool week an' me and Walter Blanshard were knockin' round the Pleasure Gardens when we spotted these two. We chatted a bit then took 'em for their port and lemon. Walter palled up wi' the one a bit older, nice eager lookin' woman, well upholstered. I'm wi' the younger one. She'd be what, eighteen. Thin lass, very quiet. 'Er hair wor cut short in close curls. Bit of a dreamer by the look on 'er. Well, Walt was all'us a pusher and he soon says why don't we go back to our tent. Brigade were under canvas in a field up behind town. His woman agrees straight off but mine says no. Nobody had any doubts about what we were after, mark you. Anyroad, I reckoned as I was going to be a bit unfortunate but Walt kept on about goin' back to the tent and how cosy it was and my lass kept sayin' no. Then the older one says to excuse 'em a minute and she teks my lass off and we could see 'em arguin'. I don't know to this day what was said but when they came back it was all fixed up an' we buggered off up to the tent. It was just nicely gettin' dark when we crawled in and Walt's straight on top of his sleepin' bag with his woman and no messin'. My lass just sits on my beddin' for quite a while. We do a bit of kissin' and she's holdin' mi hands so I can do nowt else. Then all of a sudden she lies down. Straight off I'm down alongside 'er and feelin' for her breasts. She grabs mi hand again and holds it away. Well we lay like that for a bit then suddenly she lets go of mi hand and when I put it under her blouse she moves half-round like so I can 'ave a good feel. And it's funny you know, she looked thin as a rake but she was a reight lovely shape. Then I slid mi hand down to her knickers and she grabs it and pulls it out. I kep meanin' to ask her whether she wanted it or not but somehow we neither of us got round to sayin' owt. Well we lay there cuddlin' with 'er holdin' on to mi hand for quite some time. Young Walter had bin in and out by then and them two were just whisperin' together. Then, wi' no sort of warnin' the lass shoves mi hand straight down inside her knickers and leaves it there. It were like wet silk. So I play about a bit and she puts her hands on mi neck and face and she's kissin' me and strockin' me and then runnin' her nails up and down mi neck and Ah'm shakin' like old Nodder Jack. So I try to pull her knickers off an' it happens again, she jams her little arse tight to the beddin' and I can't budge 'em. Well I'd begun to twig by now that in a manner o' speakin' she were in charge and she knew her own know best, so I just kep lyin' up close and touchin' her. So we go on for a bit then she arches her back and I slide 'er knickers off. I slipped mi prick out an' got on top of her but she keeps her legs tight closed.'

'She din't know her own mind that lass.'

'Well, you say that but Ah'm not sure. Funny thing was that by then I'd stopped frettin'. I didn't try and push her legs open, I just lay still and she kissed me a bit. I felt I was lettin' her think about it.'

'What were to think about.'

'I'm buggered if I know, she seemed to find summat. I thought I might be too heavy for her and I tried hoddin' misen up a bit but she wouldn't 'ave it, she just kept me flat on top of 'er so she was bearin' all mi weight, an' she wasn't half my size. Anyroad she starts opening her legs reight slowly. I let miself sort of slip down in between 'em. Then I pushed mi prick into her cunt bit by bit, tekkin' mi time and she seemed to be holdin' her breath and she's sort of cuddlin' mi face with her hands as if I wor a babby.'

Simpson stopped speaking for a while and rubbed his hand slowly over his face.

'It was like comin' into a warm house on a cold day. She warn't very big inside and I could feel the top end of her cunt with my nob end but she were that smooth and she moved just a bit each time I went in. It felt like we bin goin' on for hours. I were fuckin' like a pig, fuckin' a bit an' thinkin' a bit. When she come she didn't writhe about or owt, she started to tremble, sort of a shiver that lasted quite a while and then she was reight still. I went on for a bit an' then I was near to comin' so I pulled out and turned with mi back to her. I took her hand, pulled it across me and put it on mi prick. Sure enough she pulls her hand away. I put it back again. This time she lets it just rest there a bit then she teks mi nob end ever so gently between her thumb and two fingers and she starts tossin' me off. She did it slowly as if she was thinkin' about it while she was doin' it. And she put her leg across me as if she were holding me down. It were funny. Walt still laughs about it. I must have been a good foot away from t' tent side but when I came you could hear the spunk hit the canvas four or five times.'

Simpson took a drink from his Dudley.

'Another funny thing about it. Next morning I had this letter from mi wife and there was a ten bob note with it that she'd saved, sayin' I was to 'ave a good time. But you know I felt rotten 'cos I knew she didn't mean it like that.'

'Y' mekkin' mi wish I'd joined Ambulance Brigade, John.'

One of the men ran his finger along the base of his lamp.

'I've got acid leakin' from this sod. Anybody got a bit of rag to tie it with.'

'I've a bit of coat lining I use as a snot rag.'

'Pass it o'er.'

There was silence for a while then one of the men took a watch from his jacket.

'They're overrunnin' on snaptime.'

'Sooner we start, sooner we finish.'

The four men picked up their gear and moved back to the dint.

There was a steady roar of talk in the long public bar. Sometimes sharper sounds came through the welter of noise – the clatter of boots on the uncarpeted, quarry-tile floor, the shout of someone calling across the room, the clicking of shuffled dominoes.

The cribbage players sat round a table by the wall farthest from the bar. Cards were played and totted and pegs moved in a swift unbroken pattern as they talked.

'For t' cards th'a pickin' up tha might as well not bother, Toddy.'

'It's bloody same when I back 'orses. I backed one on Sat'day at Pontefract. Ah reckon the bugger's still runnin'.'

'Who were up.'

'Smythe.'

'Ah thought he were reckoned to ride good horses.'

'Well this bugger'd got rheumatics alreight.'

The game stopped while one of the men went for more beer. He came back carrying the pints on a tray. His right sleeve and the front of his jacket were sodden.

'Look at that. Bloody bar's swimmin' in beer 'cos they haven't time to mop up and Ah leant right in it.'

'Tha can last rest o' t' neet suckin' on thi suit Aleck.'

The game began again.

A thin, whey-faced man sidled through the crowd and sat down on the bench, sideways to Sam Chard.

'Ah'm not wantin' to hold up thi cards Sam but what d'ye think this's worth.'

He handed Sam a gold half-hunter watch, old, with the ribbing on the winding knob worn down and the glass scarred, but with finely marked Roman numerals. Sam held the watch carefully.

'That were thi Dad's.'

'Aye.'

'What tha sellin' it for.'

'Tha knows bloody well what Ah'm sellin' it for, Sam. I've bin off work four months wi' mi back and now doctor says mi eldest lad has to be stopped workin'.'

'What's up wi' 'im.'

'Kellier's ummin' an aarin' but I reckon consumption. His sister went same way an' he's lookin' a lot like she did. He's got same flush.'

'It's a good watch.'

'Ah'll be sellin' a lot more than that afore this lot's finished.'

'What 'as bin offered.'

'Donny pawn shop says a quid and Billy Bell offered me two quid.'

'He wants jam on it, he does.'

'Billy bloody Bell.'

The small, wizened man sitting across from Sam Chard chimed in, raising his voice against the bar noise which had grown louder. 'He's a right fucker he is. I had egg from 'im t'other day. It were rank rotten, it stank. So I put it in a cup and told my littlest to tek it back to shop and ask Billy to swop it for a decent'n. Well t' lad goes into shop carryin' this egg and all t' customers start backin' off on account of the bloody smell and Billy goes mad. He starts callin' our kid up and down an' shoutin' at 'im to get out. Poor little bugger come 'om roarin' his eyes out. So I went down and I told Mester Bell, Ah says "Next time you shout at my lad like that Ah'll mek thee eat thi fuckin' egg, shell an'all." An' Ah will.'

'What's it worth, Sam.'

'If y' tek less than five you're Jewin' yourself.'

Concert night had just started and a small, prettily dressed man stood on tiptoe on the little stage and shouted in short, harsh phrases across the noise of the crowd.

'Now this boy – has worked hard – to get here – tonight so give the lad – a big hand.'

There was a brief clapping and a roll on the piano. A heavy-set, red-faced youth climbed on the stage and began to sing 'Mother Machree' in a soft, sweet, Irish tenor that failed to carry over the clamour.

The man leaned closer to Sam.

'He'll not offer more than two, he's in t' best end, I've just come through from talkin' to 'im.'

'Is this first time he's offered.'

'No. He offered a fortneet back and he's sent twice to ask if I've made up mi mind.'

Sam was silent for a while, playing his cards slowly, frowning.

'Would y' like me to come an' talk to 'im with you.'

'Ah'd be grateful, Sam.'

'Now think on. He's no friend o' mine and it might end up with you not sellin' it at all. An' you'll 'ave to stand by whatever I say.'

'You try it your own road Sam. Ah'm no good at all at this sort o' thing.'

'If it comes to nowt at all I'll ask round miself and see if I can find you somebody as'll buy it fairly.'

Sam played out the rest of the hand and finished his beer. The two men walked out of the public bar into the yard and round into the saloon bar. Bell was standing at the far end, his heavy belly pressed against the rail. The two men joined him. Talk was quiet and the row from the public bar faint.

'Nadden Billy, it's very kind of you t' buy us a drink.'

Bell scowled, squinting his eyes and fastening the lower buttons on his waistcoat.

'Who said I was buyin' you a drink.'

'Well, with us conductin' us business over Mester Perry's watch we'll need to oil t' proceedin's a bit.'

'What's it t' do with you.'

'Ah'm what you might call vitally concerned. Am Ah not, John.'

Perry nodded.

'Right then, shall we start wi' t' beer.'

'By fuckin' Christ Almighty.'

Bell turned away from the bar and stared at the big leaded window by the door. He turned to Chard.

'You make nowt but fuckin' trouble you.'

'Aye. Well bein' as we're with the nobs we'll have two best bitters.'

Bell stood a moment longer then bought the beers and a whisky for himself.

'All reight but the offer's still two pounds.'

'Aye, but seriously now.'

Bell's voice rose sharply and the scatter of shopkeepers and pit officials in the bar began to watch the three men.

'Fuckin' hell Sam Chard, what d'ye mean seriously. It were fuckin' serious afore you brought y' daft ways into it.'

'Ah don't think you quite appreciate the finer points of the situation, Mester Bell.'

'What y' talkin' about.'

'Ah well, tha sees it's like this. When Jack told me about his watch bein' on offer I made it mi business to tell it in Gath and publish it in Askelon like the Bible says. An' I got this bid. Five pounds. Now Ah've told Jack to grab at it but 'im bein' a big feller for fair dealin' he says you should have the chance to bid five quid as well an' if you do he'll let you have it, bein' as you made the first offer.'

'You're a fuckin' liar. There's no bugger offerin' five.'

Sam sipped his beer and looked round the room, nodding to one or two men at the tables.

'Who is it then.'

'It's a chap tha knows well, Billy, lives not a mile from where we're standin'. A chap as could buy Jack's watch an' thy grocer's shop out of 'is spare change.'

'Th'a mekkin' it up.'

'He made 'is bid at twenty past four today. I mind the time by Jack's watch 'cos he were holdin' it in his hand admirin' it.'

'Y're fuckin' romancin'. What's his name then.'

'Nay, be fucked to that. It's nowt to me if you won't bid against him. It means he gets the watch an' is pleased with me for showin' it to 'im. It's Jack's idea tha should 'ave another chance to buy it.'

'I don't believe you. What's his bloody name.'

'You'll know soon enough when y' see him wearin' the watch. He's got a fob as'll go grand with it too.'

'Are you party to this fuckin' tale, Jack Perry. How come you said nothin' about this earlier on.'

Perry stared at the floor and Sam put his hand on his shoulder.

'It's 'cos he were shamed to be dealin' behind you back, Mester Bell.'

'Let him speak for himself.'

'I stand by what Sam says.'

Sam took a long pull at his beer and smacked his lips.

'Now it's simple enough, Billy, there's no need to fall out about it. You just say you won't pay five and we'll be off to see my feller and not mither you.'

Bell looked round the bar and started to walk away. He stopped for a moment then came back to the two men.

'It's just your fuckin' daft way to get me to pay through the nose forrit.'

'You're entitled to 'ave it that road if that's how it strikes you, Billy. For mi own part I'd be happier if Jack lets it go to t'other chap, 'im bein' a friend of mine. Not, mark you, that we hob-nob a lot together with me bein' just a collier. Still, if I can do 'im a favour, I will. Not that he couldn't buy hisself a gold grandfather clock if he fancied.'

No one spoke for a while.

'I haven't five on me. I'll give you two now and rest later on.'

Perry started to speak but Sam Chard cut in.

'Be buggered to that Billy. There never was a time you weren't carryin' a deal more than five on you.'

'Will you let him bloody speak for himself.'

'I need the cash, Mester Bell.'

'By but that were a nice drop of beer, Billy, I wouldn't mind another while you're thinkin' on.'

Bell counted out five one-pound notes and thrust them at Perry who handed him the watch.

Perry bobbed his head and said 'Thank you, Mester Bell.'

'Ah well, I reckon my chap'll be reight disappointed.'

Sam patted Bell on the shoulder. Bell turned back to the bar and put the watch face up on it.

'You're a good man to do business with, Mester Bell.'

Sam and Perry walked out into the pub yard.

'Can I buy you a drink.'

'You geroff home with your money, Jack.'

Perry mumbled something that Sam could not hear and walked quickly across the road and down the hill. Sam stood a while, watching a few early miners clatter past on their way home from afternoon-shift and then went back into the din of the public bar.

As soon as they had finished the Yorkshire pudding Hilda Thomas served roast potatoes and Brussels on to the empty plates. Len Thomas carved the brisket of beef, keeping the outside meat for himself. When his wife and two sons were served he larded his own dinner with mustard and looked sharply at his older son.

'Don't you wrinkle your fuckin' nose up just because I'm usin' mustard.'

Hilda said 'Don't speak like that at Sunday dinner, Len' and the boy said 'Sorry Dad.'

They ate in silence for a while, Hilda Thomas looked directly at her husband.

'It's time we made up our minds about Dad.'

Her husband shook his head.

'I don't want to talk about 'im at dinner.'

'No, nor at breakfast nor supper nor any other time. But we have to. He's gettin' past the stage where he can take care of himself and it's up to us to take care of him.'

'I don't see that it's up to us at all.'

'Well who is it up to.'

'Well there's your sister Florrie and then there's Harold.'

'You know he could never get along with Florrie and my brother hasn't got the sense to come in out of the rain, much less take care of Dad. An' besides, he's not married.'

'I don't see what that's got to do with it.'

'It has everythin' to do with it.'

'Anyway you've never been all that fond of the old bugger.'

'Watch your language.'

'Well when I first knew you, you couldn't say enough bad about him.'

'He's still my father.'

'What about when he was drunk at your mother's funeral. You kept on about that for years.'

'That's all in the past.'

'Well he's still an awkward old sod and I don't want him in my house.'

'It's my house as well.'

'You know he'd be no end of trouble.'

'It'd be my trouble. I'll be the one that 'as to tend to him. You'll not.'

'He'd be better off in a home of some sort. Old soldiers' 'ome, summat like that.'

The older boy suddenly spoke.

'Hey Dad, do you know what he does for eatin'.'

'What.'

'Well you know when I was gettin' better from impetigo and you sent me to stay with 'im in that hut at Blackstone. Well he used to have this big iron pot on a stove in the middle of the 'ut all'us hot. An' when he thought on, he'd go an' shoot a rabbit and skin it an' purrit in. Or he'd get summat from t' garden or beg summat from the gypsies up at the camp. And then when he were hungry he'd just lob us out some of what were in t' pot. It like kept goin' all the time.'

'You see, love. He can tek care of himself well enough.'

'Don't talk soft. He nearly died last winter when he was ill. Nobody went near nor by.'

'Well what about the diddy coys he's such pals with. Can't they tek care of him.'

'You can't expect a lot of gypsies to look after him. Show some sense.'

'Anyroad we haven't got room forr'im.'

'We have. We can put another bed up in Dennis' room.'

The older boy looked up from his dinner and twisted his face.

'Aw Mam. He pisses 'is bed.'

'We'll get 'im a rubber sheet.'

'There's hardly room for me.'

'Don't argue.'

Len Thomas clattered his knife against his plate.

'We can't afford to keep 'im.'

'He's got his army pension. That'll more than pay for 'is food.'

Her husband muttered to himself and said 'I'll think about it. You all'us have to 'ave your own way. That's your trouble.'

Nothing was said for a few minutes then the younger of the boys touched his father's arm and said 'Dad, will you mek me a trolley.'

Len Thomas slowly mopped up his gravy with a piece of bread.

'You'd need a set o' pram wheels for that.'

'Rileys 'ave got some. They'll let us 'ave 'em.'

'I'll see what wood I've got. You're not to whittle on about it.'

Hilda Thomas cleared away the meat plates and brought a suet pudding to the table. The older boy said 'Mam, can I have some more Yorkshire and jam instead of spotted dick.' His mother nodded and he fetched it while she served the pudding and custard. She slapped the youngest boy's hand when he began tapping his spoon on his plate.

Len Thomas unbuttoned his waistcoat and said 'He'd be on about soldierin' in India all the time, enough to drive you off your rocker.'

'I'd see to it he didn't mither you.'

'What about the way he used to knock you about when you were kids. You said you'd never forgive 'im for that.'

'He couldn't help bein' a short-tempered man.'

Len Thomas snorted.

'Daughters and their fathers. You never know what's between 'em. I'm bloody glad I've got just sons.'

After a while he began again.

'He'd not tek kindly to livin' with anybody you know. He's been out on his own in the bloody wilds in that hut. He'd be as fratchety as 'ell. Honest love, I'm thinkin' of you. He'll be just like a child. I don't see why you should be burdened with 'im.'

'We've been over this time and time again, Leonard. He's my father and I want 'im with me.'

'Well I don't want 'im. An' that's for bloody sure.'

'I want him.'

No one spoke for a while and the children kept their eyes on their plates. Len Thomas pushed his plate away and said 'You'd best mek bloody certain he doesn't get under my feet.'

After a while the youngest boy said 'When will you mek mi trolley Dad.'

Len Thomas said loudly 'I don't know, I don't know.' He went over to the mantelpiece and searched for his pipe and tobacco. He turned to the boy. 'Anyroad. I'll 'ave to find a big bolt from somewhere to go through the crosspiece for steerin'.'

Hilda Thomas cleared away the pots.

The wind blew the snow from left to right past the windows of the Welfare Hall and pierced the cracks in the frame of the little side room, stirring up a sooty smell from the iron stove. The nine men in the economics class were bunched on the stove side of the room and the lecturer from the Workers' Educational Association stood stiffly by the table on which he had spread his notes. He was a small, pot-bellied man with a high voice. He ran his finger round the inside of his stark white celluloid collar and waved his other hand vaguely towards the men in front of him.

'I'll read the law out first in the formal way of putting it. We can take it to bits, as it were, after that.' He cleared his throat. 'If two coins are of equal legal exchange value, that of the lower intrinsic value will tend to drive the other out of use.' He paused, repeated the sentence and added 'The common way of putting that is to say that bad money drives out good.'

Clive Harris, from the back of the group said 'Can you give an example of that happenin'.'

The lecturer fingered his collar again and said 'Well for instance, take clipped money. In the times when silver coins actually contained valuable silver people used to shave the edge of a coin and melt the shaved bits down. It was a form of theft that was severely punished.' He took a shilling from his pocket and held it out. 'You'll notice our coins are milled around the edge and that was brought in to stop coin clipping. Now at the time when coins were often clipped it would be the case that unclipped coins would drop out of circulation and the shaved ones would be virtually the only ones that people used in common exchange.'

Sam Chard said 'People hung on to the good stuff.'

The lecturer nodded towards him.

'The reasons are complicated but in part, at least, it might have had to do with people tending to use, for saving purposes, the intrinsically more valuable form of the currency.'

Tom Barthrop shuffled his position on his chair and clasped his hands behind his head.

'Who was this Gresham chap that thought this up.'

The lecturer peered at his notes. 'Sir Thomas Gresham, born around 1519 and died in 1579. He was mainly noted as the founder of the Royal Exchange. That's the early form of what we would now perhaps call the Stock Exchange.'

Barthrop wrinkled his nose and said 'Be buggered to him then.'

The lecturer smiled. 'You have to judge him in the light of his times, Mister Barthrop.'

Barthrop said 'Tell us some more about him.'

'Well, he was born into a business family and was himself very successful commercially even while still very young.'

Norman Green said 'Clever young bugger with his ackers.'

The lecturer coughed and said 'His first very profitable venture started with the purchase of gunpowder at Antwerp.'

The oldest man there, John Steadman, shook his head and muttered 'Sounds like a war profiteer, armaments man.'

Clive Harris broke in before the lecturer could reply and said 'Let's go back to this law again. Is this what happened in Germany a few years back when you had to take a barrow load o' notes to buy a loaf o' bread. That were bad money reight enough.'

The lecturer rubbed his forehead. 'Only sort of. You see there the situation was like that of the South at the end of the American Civil War, total collapse of paper currency following a breakdown of the economy.'

Sam Chard leaned forward in his chair.

'In that sort of a set-up the rich'll do best out of it.'

'How do you make that out, Mister Chard. A worthless currency is a disaster for everybody. Everybody suffers.'

'Never. The rich don't really suffer. Look at it this way. If money's worth nowt you go back to barter, you're back to the value of goods. And who has got the goods. You can go a long time on the old family silver and suchlike but if you've got nowt to start with you're finished straight off.'

The lecturer spoke more loudly. 'I still contend that the present Depression is a disaster for everybody.'

Old Steadman cackled and shouted 'I'll believe that when they've got soup kitchens in t' Dorchester.'

Sam grinned at him. 'That's reight John, it's like the song says, the rich get richer and the poor get poorer.'

The lecturer shrugged his shoulders. 'Perhaps so, but what about Gresham's Law. Does everyone understand it.'

Willie Hankin said 'What good did it do for him to promulgate this law of his.'

'Well it was. It added to our knowledge. Economics is not an exact science, I admit. But Gresham was an early example. The aim is to make us less at the mercy of the play of market forces.'

Someone shouted 'What's that mean when it's at home' and the lecturer smiled and began again.

'In essence what Gresham did was to organize an equitable system for making loans and above all to inspire a spirit of honesty in all official dealings.'

Sam levered up the lid of the stove with a poker and said 'If I had what he had I could afford to be honest.'

Steadman shouted 'You can bet it'll be the Jews at the back of it' and several voices chimed in.

'You old blather, you all'us blame the Jews.'

'Well they're runnin' things.'

'Go on Old gaffer Owen runs Donny collieries an' he's been on thy back all thi life an' he comes from Sheffield.'

'An' what's at back of him.'

'Wust capitalist I ever knew were a Lancashire chap.'

'An' if the Labour lot ever get to be top dog they'll show you what bossin's about.'

The lecturer held up his hand for quiet and waited until Sam had put more coal in the stove before he began again.

'Very well. While we're talking about currency we'll consider gold and try and tie it in with the idea of the gold standard. You'll recall we discussed this a couple of weeks ago.'

Snow was falling thickly on the pit top, turning piles of timber, damaged tubs, gondolas, coal stocks, conveyor belting, lengths of track and bags of stone dust into strangely shaped humps. Freshly shovelled paths from gantry to lamp cabin to offices to screens were quickly lost under new snow. Miners coming off the day-shift walked hurriedly, head down, out of the gates. A steady blast of bitterly cold air tore down the intake shaft into the pit bottom. Lumps of ice, shaken loose from the shaft walls by the passing of the cages, cannoned from side to side as they plummeted into the sump below the cage blocks.

In the pit bottom hundreds of men coming off the district huddled against the walls, trying to shelter from the cutting gale that blew from the shaft entrance. The pit bottom onsetter and his men moved clumsily in heavy overcoats, gloves, balaclavas, scarves and lengths of sacking tied round their chests.

Each time the cage came down, men on both decks surged forward to get on it and the bottom deck onsetter struggled to pull some of them off shouting that it should be only fifteen men to a deck. The men shouted and cursed back at him and sometimes he was almost forced on the cage himself as he tried to bar their way.

In the end, although the cage was full and the gate closed he stood with his arms folded, refusing to signal it away. The freezing men roared and howled at him and his voice could be heard faintly above the din.

'You can fuckin' stay there. Coal Mines Act says fifteen to a deck. Ten of you buggers come off. Ah'm not 'avin it. You come off or you bloody stay there. I'm not touchin' that bell till I've got the right number.'

The men on the cage and waiting in the pit bottom shouted more loudly, odd words coming through the din.

'Gerrit movin' you old goat.'

'We'll fuckin' freeze to death.'

'Ring it off y' barmy bugger.'

'Let's gerrom.'

'Sod the bloody Coal Mines Act.'

'Push the snotty bastard in the sump.'

'It's t' cold to play silly buggers.'

The onsetter shouted but could not be heard above the storm of jeering.

Suddenly he walked to the shaft side phone and rang for the pit top. The men watched him but could not hear what he was saying. He put a hand over one ear and shouted, his mouth close to the bowl of the phone.

'Can you hear me Will.'

'What's up mate. What's holdin' you.'

''Ave you got anybody on your cage.'

'Ah'm nearly finished, there's a few haulage lads.'

'Well get the fuckers off.'

'What y'mean Percy.'

'I mean I want your cage empty for this run.'

'What's goin' on down there.'

'You clear your cage and whatever I signal, you pass it on to the winder.'

'It meks no fuckin' sense, Perce. What do you want this cage empty for.'

'Never you mind. You empty it, both decks. And don't argue wi' mi signal, just ring it on your bell.'

The pit top onsetter was still saying something when Percy Unwin put the phone down and turned to his bell push. As he raised his hand the noise in the pit bottom lessened and the men on the cage cheered mockingly.

The shouting died away altogether as Unwin went on rapping his bell long past the three–two signal for men riding. Somebody shouted 'What the fuckin' 'ell y' doin' Percy' as the repeater bell echoed the long signal. The cage lifted slowly away, rose a few feet, then stood still for a few moments, then rose a few feet more, then paused. Someone shouted 'the fucker's rung shaft examiners.' There was a faint shouting from the men in the cage that had disappeared up the shaft and the roar from the men in the pit bottom grew louder as they surged forward and surrounded the onsetter. Unwin's hands waved above the crowd that jostled him as he shouted back at them.

The day-shift undermanager came off the district and forced his way through the crowd at the shaft side. He had to climb up on the shaft gate and stand bawling above the crowd for two or three minutes before the men quietened. Then he spoke to Unwin.

'Right Perce. What's the trouble.'

Unwin's voice was hoarse from shouting and it cracked as he tried to speak loudly.

'Ah'm just tryin' to do mi job properly. Nowt more.'

The undermanager sat wearily on the top bar of the shaft gate and said 'who's stoppin' you.'

'They are. The Coal Mines Regulation Act of 1911 says this cage should 'ave no more than fifteen men on each deck. They keep pushin' on and pushin' on so Ah'm 'avin' to ring away with twenty odd men a deck. I can't 'ave that.'

The men started to howl again but quietened when the undermanager raised his arm and shouted 'give us a minute, let's get it sorted out.'

'I get your point Percy. Now what's this about shaft examiners.'

Unwin's voice was lower and he looked away from the undermanager. 'It'll teach 'em a lesson.'

The men began to shout again and as the undermanager waved them quiet he pointed to a fat man at the front of the crowd.

'What's happened Colly.'

'The mardy fucker's rung for a shaft inspection. It'll be like a soddin' ice box in that cage. By t' time they've tekken half an hour to get up they'll be froz to death. They'll have to chip the buggers out.'

The undermanager turned to Unwin.

'That right Percy.'

'They should've behaved reight in the first place.'

'Now we can't leave 'em hangin' about in the shaft with this cold, lad. You'd best ring for men ridin' and get 'em up to t' top.'

Unwin spat into the shaft sump.

'There's rules about changin' a signal when the cage is movin'.'

Somebody shouted 'You must 'ave bin born out of your mother's arsehole.'

The undermanager flexed his fingers and blew on them.

'You made your point, Onsetter, now I want them fellers tekken to t' top.'

'They'll get there. They'll just have time to think a bit.'

The men roared again and the undermanager shouted 'Fuckin' shut up.'

When the crowd hushed, he stood down from the shaft gate and put his hand on Unwin's shoulder.

'Now be reasonable Percy. Get your signal changed and I'll stay here and see you get no more than fifteen to a deck. I'll back you up. How about it.'

Unwin stared at the ground.

'They'll 'ave to come back down first and Ah want some taken off till there's just fifteen on each deck. Then Ah'll ring for men ridin'.'

Some of the men groaned and the undermanager turned away and said 'Jesus fuckin' Christ.' Then he turned back and said 'Ring the buggers back down.'

Unwin phoned the pit top to warn them of his change of signal, and after the windsman had been talked to, the signal was changed and the cage came back down. Ten men were hauled off and stood stiffly by the shaft side while the gates were shut and the cage sped away up the shaft.

Unwin stood with his back to the shaft gates, his arms folded.

Sam's landlady fussed over the table as he finished his tea, nagging him to eat more.

'I can boil you an egg.'

Sam shook his head.

'Would y' like another mug of tea.'

'I've not finished this one yet.'

'I've some blackberry jam. It's not shop jam.'

Sam pointed his finger at her and said 'Sit down Agnes.' She flounced to a chair by the fire, picked up her darning mushroom and needle and began mending a pair of heavy work socks.

Sam read the paper for a while then tucked his heels between the top two struts of the chair, folded his arms and rested his head on his knees. He was dozing when they heard the clatter of running footsteps pass down the side of the house and a loud knocking on the kitchen door.

He opened the door and the young woman stumbled into the kitchen and stood panting, her voice shrill and gabbling. There was a darkening bruise high on her cheekbone and Sam brushed her heavy black hair to one side and looked at it. She put her hand over her mouth, held her breath for a few moments and said 'He'll smash mi face in.' Agnes clicked her tongue and the young woman's voice rose to a squeak.

'He found the money I hid. He knows. Stop 'im Sam.'

'Alan.'

The woman nodded then shrieked and ran into the corner of the kitchen as Alan Spenny appeared in the little tunnel-shaped porch that fronted on to the kitchen door. Sam stepped intot he doorway and put his hand on the man's chest as he tried to come into the kitchen. The man shouted.

'I want Cissie.'

Sam stayed facing him and called to the woman.

'What do you want to do.'

The woman stayed in the corner of the kitchen and said 'No' several times.

'It seems she doesn't want to go with you Alan. Not just this minute.'

'I want Cissie.'

Sam shook his head. Spenny blinked his eyes and rubbed them.

'Cissie, come on out. I'm sorry I hit you.'

There was silence for a few moments. Spenny shouted 'You're comin' with me' and tried again to push his way into the kitchen. Sam held his arms and said loudly 'You don't come over the threshold of my house unless I ask you. And you're not to, not just now.' Spenny grunted with the effort of pushing against Sam and shouted 'She's my wife, she's my wife.' Sam half turned him, thrust him away and kicked the door closed with his foot.

Spenny shouted through the door.

'I won't hit you again Cissie. I won't. But you're not to go. I won't let you.'

He knocked, waited and began shouting again.

'Listen to me. I just want to talk to you. You know you can't run off. Don't be daft Cissie.'

He knocked again and spoke more quietly.

'You've got to come out of there sometime. You might as well come out now. Cissie. Listen to me. You can have the money to spend. Just to spend. I promise.'

After another silence he shouted 'Cissie' and they heard his footsteps going round the side of the house. He peered in at the kitchen window, shading his eyes. Nobody moved and after a while he went back into the street.

Sam felt along the mantelpiece till he found a packet of cigarettes. He lit one and stood puffing it with his back to the fire. Cissie Spenny came out from the corner of the kitchen and sat down by the table. Agnes went and sat in the chair by the pantry door with her hands clasped tightly in her lap. Cissie spoke with her head down, staring at the floor.

'He found the money. He knew I was going to leave him so he only gave me a bit at a time. Just a bit for shopping now and then. But I kept a bit back each time an' hid it. I had nearly eight pounds. Nearly enough. And he found it. And we had a row. That's why he hit me.'

Sam stretched and swung his arms loosely by his side.

'What do you want to do now.'

'He'll never talk to me about me leavin'. He just says I'll settle down in time. Or else he starts beggin' me.'

'Well.'

'I've got somewhere to go. He's an old man. He used to be a friend of mi father's. It's a long way away.'

Sam glanced towards Agnes and shook his head slightly. Cissie stopped talking, then said 'Anyway, if I had enough to get there an' get a job, I'd be all reight.'

'You'll have to have another go at talkin' to Alan.'

'I don't want to talk to him. I want to go. Now. I want to go an' catch the bus to Donny and catch the train. That's all I want to do.'

'You 'aven't got any of your things.'

'It doesn't matter.'

'What about money.'

'If you could lend me some I'd send it back to you. Honestly.'

Agnes coughed and Sam squatted on the fender and whistled softly between his teeth. They could hear shouting out in the street but the words were unclear.

'It seems a bit soft just to go off like that.'

'It's not that he's bad to me. He's not as bad as some. I just don't fancy livin' with him. It was him that kept on at me to marry him in the first place. He wouldn't shut up about it. It'll be all right he kept sayin', you'll see.'

'You mean just go out an' catch a bus and go off. Now.'

'Can I stay here.'

Agnes said 'No' sharply and Cissie Spenny looked towards her and said 'I'm sorry.'

'Alan'll not let you get on any bus.'

'You could make him let me.'

Sam sighed and muttered 'Bloody hell.' He rose, leaned on the sink edge and stared out of the kitchen window. Agnes wriggled on her chair and kept shaking her head.

After a while Sam went to his jacket which hung on a hook on the front door and took notes and change out of the pocket. He counted the four one-pound notes, put the change back into the pocket and turned towards Agnes.

'Will you lend me six quid, Agnes.'

Agnes clasped her hands tightly on her lap.

'She's his wife.'

'Will you lend it to me.'

'She's not twenty yet. They've only been married a year.'

'Agnes, love.'

Agnes looked towards Cissie and shook her head again.

'You're not entitled to come runnin' to Sam. It's not to do with 'im. If you want to be flighty you should leave him out of it.'

Cissie said 'You don't understand' and Agnes half-turned away and looked towards the fireplace.

'Don't talk to me. I was married twenty-three year. You married him. Now you want to play on people's sympathies. I know about bein' married. Just 'cos Sam's got a soft spot for you. You're like your mother. She was the same.'

Sam scratched his head and said 'What about it, Agnes.'

'She's his proper wife. I'm not lendin' her money.'

'I'm askin' you to lend it to me. Now will you lend me six pounds, Agnes.'

Agnes sniffed, tapped her foot on the tiled floor and went upstairs. She came back down and thrust six one-pound notes into Sam's hand but said nothing, seating herself again by the pantry door. Sam passed all the money to Cissie who mumbled 'Thank you.' He put his jacket on and said 'I'll have a gleg at what's goin' on.' He went through into the front room. Cissie started to say something to Agnes but stopped and followed Sam when he shouted for her. Holding the lace curtains to one side Sam said 'What do you reckon.' Cissie stared out of the front window at the two men standing in the road. Behind them a small crowd had collected by the opposite fence, watching the house. Cissie put her thumb in her mouth and sucked it.

'It's his mate, it's Benjy Holmes.'

'He's a daft bugger but he's big enough.'

Sam straightened the potted aspidistra that stood on the table top of the Bradbury treadle sewing-machine under the window.

'I'd best go have a talk to 'em.'

He stepped towards the door and Cissie ran round in front of him and kissed him.

'We should have got married, Sam Chard.'

'That would have been a rum do.'

'I never used to put any knickers on when I went with you.'

Sam said 'I recall that' and went out through the kitchen and up the path. He leaned on the front gate, looked at the two men and nodded. 'Alan.'

Alan Spenny pointed towards the house.

'Is she coming out.'

'I'm afraid she's set on leavin' you, Alan.'

'I'll talk to her about that. Is she comin' out.'

'She's bahn to have her own way in the end. You might just as well let 'er go. You can't keep her against her will.'

'I want no fuckin' advice from you, Sam Chard. Tell her to come out and talk to me.'

Sam lit a cigarette and looked up and down the street. A woman in the small crowd opposite shouted 'Can I 'ave an invite to tea, Mester Chard.'

Sam nodded towards Benjy Holmes.

'What's he doin' 'ere.'

'He's here to see fair play.'

Sam frowned and said 'what the fuckin' hell does that mean, fair play.'

'She's comin' home with me. We'll talk there.'

Sam puffed at his cigarette, blowing the smoke down his nose.

'We're goin' to get nowhere this way, Alan.'

Spenny said nothing and after standing at the gate for a further minute Sam went back into the house. The two women came out of the front room. Sam looked at the clock on the mantelpiece and took his own watch out of his jacket pocket.

'The half-past Donny bus'll be waitin' at the top now. Do you want to catch it.'

Cissie said 'Please' and Sam went into the pantry and came out with a half-shaped, oak pick-handle. Agnes made a little gasping sound and Sam smiled at Cissie.

'It's just to warn 'em off. I'll not hurt him.'

Cissie scowled and said 'I don't care if you do.'

Agnes put her hand on Sam's arm and he patted her and said 'Not to fret, Mother, it'll just be a shoutin' job.'

As they walked down the path to the gate Sam said 'Stay close to me and walk fast.' He did not pause but opened the gate and started for the main road with Spenny and Holmes moving alongside and the small crowd following. Spenny shouted 'What are you doing' but Sam did not look at him. He ran round in front of them and tried to grab his wife. She stepped behind Sam who flashed the pick-handle towards her husband. Spenny skipped backwards and the group moved on to the main road and turned into Hawthorn Avenue. Spenny shouted 'Cissie' several times. As they crossed a side road he made another grab for her. Sam jabbed the pick-handle into his belly. Spenny staggered back and stood bent over. He straightened up and ran after them. The crowd was shouting and Benjy Holmes kept trying to stand in front of Sam but ducked away each time as Sam swung the pick-handle in an arc just in front of his face. Cissie trotted awkwardly on her high-heels, trying to keep between Sam and the railings that edged the gardens.

The Yorkshire traction bus was standing at the top of the avenue and as they neared it Spenny shouted to Holmes to go and sit in it and stop Cissie getting on. Holmes ran ahead and climbed on the bus. He sat sideways in the front seat with his leg and arm across the entry. The conductor stared at him from across the aisle but made no move. Some of the passengers wound down their windows and began to shout at the crowd which had spread round the front of the bus. Sam walked a little way past the bus and stood with his back to the railings, Cissie next to him and Spenny a few yards away, facing them. A couple of lads in the crowd started to sing 'Who Were You With Last Night?'. Spenny rubbed his stomach and called out 'You're not going anywhere pet. You're going to have it out with me.'

Cissie stamped her foot and muttered at Sam 'Just because I'm his wife.'

Sam slid the pick-handle back and forth through his hands and looked away up the hill.

Cissie started to snivel and said 'What am I going to do, Sam.'

Sam bent his head towards her and kept his voice low. 'There'll be a Campbell Johns bus going past the other way, before this one leaves. When you see it on the hill, run across the corner and catch it by Naylor's gate. Get off at Five Lane Ends and walk up to Hampole station. You can catch the evenin' train to Donny from there.'

Cissie looked from her husband to Sam and nodded her head. In the minutes before the Campbell Johns bus came the three were silent, Spenny staring fixedly at his wife. As the blue bus came in sight lower down the hill Cissie ran across the road. Spenny started to run after her and Sam spun the pick-handle between his legs. He tumbled heavily forward and Sam scooped up the handle and stood in front of him, swinging it slowly from side to side. Spenny made no attempt to stand up but kept shouting 'Cissie' after his wife. She reached the stop in front of Naylor's farm gate just before the bus and it barely paused as she climbed on it. As it revved away over the top of the hill Spenny stopped shouting. Benjy Holmes came down from the Yorkshire traction bus and walked across and stood by them. Sam held the pick-handle down by his side and the crowd gathered in a half-circle round Spenny who was still sitting on the ground, his legs stretched out in front of him, his body bent over, hands on knees.

Sam said 'I'm sorry Alan but you can't make anybody do what they don't want to.'

Spenny spoke without looking up. 'Half the time you don't know what you're fuckin' doin' Sam. You know nowt about me an' Cissie. You don't know what'll happen to her.'

Sam walked off down Hawthorn Avenue and Benjy Holmes said 'Get up, Alan.' Spenny did not move and Holmes said 'Come on, there's a good lad, you'll have to get up.' Spenny stayed sitting in the road.

Someone in the crowd shouted 'You'll have to get Benjy to wash your shirts for you now, Spenny.'

The two boys marched down the hill, one behind the other, stamping their boots in step. Over and over again they chanted in time with their footsteps.

Colman's mustard
Colman's starch
Tell Missis Colman
To stick it up 'er arse.

As they reached the corner of Beech Road they raced across to the railings of the end house. They leaned against the railings shouting.

'Mickey.'

'Mickey Maxwell.'

'Mickey Mouse.'

'Are y' comin' pictures.'

'Mickey.'

A boy came running round from the back door of the house. He held a piece of bread and dripping in one hand, his other arm was half into the sleeve of his jacket as it flapped behind him. He mumbled. 'You're early.'

'We're goin' park on t' way.'

The three boys walked down the hill. Mickey Maxwell finished eating his bread and put his jacket on. He punched both the other boys on the arm and said 'Ah know summat you don't know.'

'What's that then.'

'Ah know the French alphabet.'

'Tha dusn't.'

'Ah do.'

'Well tell us it then.'

'You listenin'.'

The other two nodded and Mickey began reciting in a high sing-song voice.

'Ena meena macka racka rer ri domma nacka chicka packa lolla packa rom pom push.'

'That's never it.'

'It is, it's French alphabet.'

'How does tha know.'

'Mi brother told me it.'

'It's not French alphabet.'

'Does tha know t' French alphabet.'

'No.'

'Then 'ow does tha know that in't it.'

'It just dun't seem reight.'

'It is reight.'

'Tell us it again.'

Mickey repeated it.

'It sounds nowt like it.'

'Our Ted says it is.'

As they turned into Poplar Road a boy ran from near the Baptist chapel and caught up with them.

'Are you gooin' tupp'ny crush.'

'Aye.'

'Can I come with yer.'

'If you want. We're going' to t' park fost.'

'Alreight.'

As the boys walked towards the Welfare Recreation Park the tallest of them said 'Mi Dad's reight mad at Mester Thorne.'

'Who's 'e.'

'He lives next door to us. Mi Dad says he'll smash 'im to smithereens.'

'What's he mad at 'im for.'

'Well mi Dad lended 'im our two ferrets to go after rabbits. An' Mester Thorne put 'em down after a badger, an' t' badger killed 'em.'

'Can a badger kill ferrets then.'

'Easy.'

'I dun't like ferrets. Our kid 'ad one and it bit 'im through t'and an' it wouldn't let go of 'im.'

'Mi Dad says he'll 'ave to pay forr'em.'

'What do they cost.'

'Ah dun't know. A lot.'

As the boys came into the park they separated on to swings,

roundabouts, slide and monkey-climb. After a while the boy on the swings shouted 'Let's see who can jump farthest from t' swing.' One of the boys shouted 'Bags me foggy', another shouted 'Seggy' and the boy on the swing said 'Ah'm thirdy.' The boy who had claimed first stood up on the seat of a swing and began to work it backwards and forwards till he reached the height where his body was almost flat in line with the ground. Then, as the swing came up, he let go and hurtled outwards, landing feet first in the sand, tumbling forward and over. He stood up and marked his landing place with a line drawn in the sand. Each boy followed, jumping from the swing as it came forward. They squabbled about who had jumped the farthest. One of the boys shouted 'Let's go on t' rockin' horse' and they raced across the park to a long wooden box, mounted on metal rocking bars, with a running board on both sides. It had an iron horse's head at the front and the name Bonnie Bright Eyes was die-stamped on the neck. There were six iron saddles spaced along the box with a gripping bar fitted in front of each one. One of the boys shouted 'Bags me the murder seat' and he mounted the end saddle. The others took saddles and they began to jerk the box backwards and forwards in rhythm. The box swung higher and jerked violently each time it reversed. They howled and shouted till the boy in the end seat let himself go and was hurled out on to the sand. He rolled over and lay on his back shouting 'Ah'm dead, mi back's brok.' The boy at the front shouted 'We'll miss pictures' and they ran towards the far gate of the park. The boy on the ground jumped up and ran after them.

As they trotted along Mickey's shirt worked its way out of his trousers and flapped around his waist. One of the boys shouted 'Look, the little short-shirted avenger' and another shouted 'No, it's not, it's Gandhi.' They slowed down to a walk.

The boy who had joined them at the bottom of Poplar Road said 'Why don't we go to Addick pictures instead.'

'It's a rotten picture at Addick. Norman Holmes says so. He says it's supposed to be an aeroplane picture but it's all sloppy kissin'.'

'What's on at Carky.'

'It's about India. There's this fort an' all the natives are attackin' it. Ah saw comin' shorts. It's got this high fence an' this big bugger gets on top of it an' a bloke shoots 'im an' he goes topplin' off and smashes on t' ground.'

'What's serial.'

'Tom Mix. Ah saw last week's.'

'Where'd it end.'

'It finished at this bit where the coach wi' t' woman in it comes round a corner and goes ovver this cliff.'

'They're a cheat. Ah'll bet this week it dun't really go ovver t' cliff. It'll sort of come back on t' road agen.'

They started to run and went round the front of the picture house to where a high wall made a narrow alley to the back entrance. The alley was already crammed with children shouting and pushing so that the ones at the front were jammed against the doors. They joined the crowd and began pushing forward. A girl suddenly shouted 'I've dropped mi penny, I've dropped mi penny.' She crouched down to find it and her hands were trodden on as the children pushed forward. She grabbed the penny and stood up again crying and rubbing her arms.

The doors opened and the children surged against the four men who stood arms linked across the doorway. The men were forced back a foot or two then heaved forward to block the entrance. A smallish man reached over their shoulders and began taking two pence from each child. As he took the money from a child, the men would raise their arms a little and allow the child to slide underneath and into the cinema. Inside, the children ran up and down the aisles shouting and changing their seats as the cinema filled up.

'Eileeeen. Eileeeeen.'

Rose Whitaker stood by the garden fence, cupping her hands to her mouth to make her voice carry four doors down. Eileen Fox bobbed out of her back door.

'Copper's boilin'.'

Eileen shouted 'Be right over' and ran back into the house. She came out again clutching a bundle of dirty pit clothes and trotted out into the street and along to Rose's house. She hesitated at the open back door and peered in. Rose said 'Come in love' and pointed to the large under-fired copper that was concreted in beside the sink. Steam was rising from it and swirling out through the open kitchen window. Eileen spread out the clothes on the copper surround and took a large bar of yellow carbolic soap from her apron pocket.

'I am sorry to bother you, love. Our Jack keeps sayin' he'll get a piece of iron cut for the copper grate but he dithers. An' when I try to use it all the coal falls through into t' bottom.'

'Just you mek it your own.'

Eileen dipped the bar of carbolic into the water and began soaping the vests, underpants, neckerchief and shirt. Then she took a worn-down scrubbing brush from her apron and scrubbed the soap hard into the clothes. Rose fetched a half-completed shawl from the dresser at the back of the kitchen, sat down by the table and began to crochet.

Eileen wrinkled her nose at the smell of the clothes and half-turned towards Rose as she scrubbed.

'Is Marty any better.'

'Not really. He's still coughin' at night. I've told him as long as he works in water he'll be chesty.'

'Have they got water then.'

'There's ovver a foot of water in 'is stall, all the time. But he says so long as pit pays 'em extra water money forrit he's satisfied. I tell 'im your health's worth more than extra money but 'e teks no notice of me.'

'You're reight.'

Eileen dropped the vests, underpants and neckerchief into the copper and stirred and jabbed at them with a short dolly-stick for several minutes.

'I'll put the shirt in after, it makes such a mess o' the water. Come an' 'ave a look at it.'

Rose put her shawl down, crossed to the copper and ran her hand over the hardened front of the shirt.

'What does it.'

'He's some job where he has to carry a fat barrel round for greasin' things an' he hugs it to his chest. The fat's that thick it meks his shirt front stiff as a board. It leaves a terrible scum on the water when you wash it.'

Rose murmured in sympathy and went back to her crochet work. Eileen watched the clothes turning over slowly in the boiling water and poked them from time to time. She leaned back against the sink and took out a packet of cigarettes. She offered one to Rose who shook her head.

'Our Marty smokes enough for two.'

Eileen held the cigarette in front of her, lit it, then put it to her lips and puffed noisily, blowing the smoke carefully towards the open kitchen door.

'I'm afraid it's gotten to be a habit wi' me.'

She half-closed her eyes and coughed before she spoke.

'I hear Missis Norton's very upset about her Brian and Gracie Marsh.'

'Thinks nobody's good enough for 'im I expect.'

'Missis Adams says she saw them at it one night up by the bridle path.'

'Trust Polly Adams to keep her eye out.'

'They were standin' up but Gracie was leaned against a tree and he was doin' it to her.'

Rose pursed her lips.

'That'd be rough. Bein' pressed against a tree.'

'Missis Adams says they were well away.'

'Praps they thought Gracie wouldn't fall for it if they did it standin' up.'

Eileen tittered.

'I reckon you can get babbed just fancyin' a feller.'

Rose rubbed her eyes, sighed, took down her spectacles from the mantelpiece, put them on and started again on the shawl. Eileen fished the clothes out of the boiler with the dolly-stick and dropped them into the sink. She dropped the shirt into the boiler and turned again to Rose.

'Do you think he'll marry 'er.'

'He'll not have much choice. Gracie Marsh is a lot stronger character than 'im.'

'Missis Norton'll not like it.'

'Then she'll have to lump it.'

'Do you think it'll work. If they get wed. They say he's a bit workshy.'

'One man's much like another.'

'I don't know. I had a chance once. I've often wondered.'

Eileen pounded the shirt in the copper and then rinsed out the clothes in the sink. She twisted the water out of them, opened them out flat and draped them over the front ledge of the copper. Rose put her shawl back on the dresser and said 'D' ye fancy a cup of tea.'

'I do that.'

Rose fetched a plate with cake on it from the pantry and showed it to Eileen.

'It's only shop cake.'

'Ta.'

Rose sliced the large piece of Battenberg into two and put it out on plates. She swung the kettle over the fire on its stand, put tea from a pagoda-shaped caddy into the pot that stood in the hearth and then hesitated as she reached for the cups that hung from hooks above the pantry shelf.

'Shall we be a bit posh. Use mother's cups.'

Eileen nodded and Rose went into the front room and came back with two flowered bone-china cups and saucers. Eileen took a cup and held it up to the window with her fingers spread out behind it so that she could see them shadowed in the fine pot.

'Your mother had some fine things.'

'She knew quality.'

'You still miss her.'

'I suppose I all'us will. It's funny. The other day I saw that new bed of roses they've put in by the park gates and I thought to miself I must tell mother about this. And then I thought that there's no way I can tell 'er. And I got upset all over again.'

'It's a shame.'

'Would y' like to see the pot to these.'

She took Eileen through into the front room and showed her the dainty teapot in the china cabinet. Eileen admired it. The two women came back into the kitchen and Rose mashed the tea while Eileen rinsed out the shirt. They sat down at the table. Eileen smiled.

'It wouldn't do to serve our Jack with these. He'd still pour 'is tea into t' saucer to cool it.'

'I've broken Marty of that one.'

They stared at the scudding, piled white clouds that they could see through the kitchen doorway.

'Have you sorted out your little Jack's bother.'

Eileen pulled at her lip and shook her head.

'Not quite yet. Jack's goin' down to see bobby Pace at police house this aft'. He's goin' to ask 'im not to do anythin'. It was just little Jack and the Hughes boy lakin' in that cement yard by the picture house. They weren't pinchin' anythin'. Anyway there's nothin' to pinch there, just some bags of cement.'

'Pace'll let it go I should think.'

'Anyway, it was Billy Hughes' idea. He's always the leader and Jackie follers on.'

'I think he's a good little lad.'

'Jack just thumps 'im for everythin'. I tell him he should talk to the lad but he thinks a good thumpin'll settle matters. I've tried to talk to him but it's his father's job by rights.'

'He looks a lot like you.'

'I've got photos of him when 'e was a baby and photos of me as a baby. You can't tell the difference.'

Eileen pointed to the copper.

'I'll empty it and clean it out as soon as we've finished us tea.'

'No rush. Would y' like another cup.'

'Please.'

Rose picked up the pot from the hearth and filled the cups.

The bed had been moved downstairs to the living room and placed by the window. The white turnback of the sheets was tucked so tightly under the mattress edges that the man was pinned in the bed, his arms under the blankets and his head propped upright by a thick bolster. The papery skin of his face had a yellow sheen that sharply outlined the long bones of his jaw and cheek. His breath rasped loudly and from time to time he was racked by coughing. Sometimes, after a bad bout of coughing, he would close his eyes as he struggled to make his breathing even and murmur 'It's the bloody silicosis.' Sam sat on the edge of a low, hard, wooden chair by the side of the bed and waited till each seizure was over to begin talking again.

'They're closing Nines altogether. At the end of the month.'

'Why's that then.'

'It's a band of dirt in the coal. It's gotten wider and now it's not worth workin' the face, it's half dirt.'

'Too much dirt.'

'That's right.'

The man was silent for a while, then he wet his lips and said 'Shafton seam were often the same. More dirt than coal. They used to call it mucky Shafton.'

'Aye, I've heard 'em say that.'

Sam fiddled with his cap, opening and closing the stud that held the peak straight. The man caught his breath again and said 'Who's deputy on there.'

'Todd. Aubrey Todd.'

'He was never much. Even when it was easy goin'. Nor his father afore 'im.'

'I never knew his Dad.'

The man started to wheeze, then cough, then held his breath and the coughing stopped.

'Worked at a day-hole pit, Nostell somewhere. What they used to call a footrill.'

He licked his lips and his wife came across to the bed from her seat by the fire-place and said 'Do you want a drink, Barney.' He nodded and she held the glass from the bedside table to his lips. He took a small sip, then turned his head away. He winked at Sam.

'You know what they used to say about day-hole pits.'

'What was that then.'

'They used to say not a pit but a pity, pity the buggers was ever sunk.' The man tittered and began to cough again.

The woman turned to Sam. She was tall and towered over him as he sat on the low chair.

'Would you like another cup of tea, Mister Chard.'

'No thank you, Missis Sykes. I'll have to be goin' shortly. I'm on early turn.'

The woman seated herself by the fire. Sam looked back at Barney Sykes.

'They say band'll do well at competition this year.'

'I never cared for brass bands.'

The talk went on for a few more minutes then Sam rose to his feet and put his hand on the man's shoulder. 'I'll see you again then, Barney.'

'Do you have to go, Sam.'

'Aye, I was saying to your wife. I'm on early turn.'

The corners of the man's mouth turned downward into a crying face.

'You'll come again, Sam.'

'I will that, lad. Now you just rest yourself and see how you get on.'

As Sam moved to the door, the woman rose and said 'I'll see you out.' She followed him to the gate and they stood looking back at the house.

'He looks poorly, Missis Sykes.'

'Doctor says he'll not be with us more than a month or two at most.'

'I'm sorry he has to bear with the bad breathing and the coughing. It must be hard for you to put up with.'

'I've got used to it.' The woman smoothed her pinafore and touched Sam's arm. 'You will come again, won't you. He sets a lot of store by visits. And with what the doctor said.'

Sam opened the gate and smiled at the woman. 'I'll be sure to Missis Sykes. And I hope things'll be a bit peaceful for him.'

The woman nodded and watched till Sam turned the corner by the butter cross. She went back into the house.

The boy did not know Sam was watching him. He had his back to the railings and grunted each time he lifted a spade full of earth and grunted again as he dug back into the ground.

'Is it mekkin' you sweat, Jimmy.'

The boy turned and pulled a long face.

'Mi Dad says I have to dig all this lot before I can go out.'

Sam came in through the gate and took the spade out of the boy's hands.

'You're mekkin' it heavy for yourself, lad. Just watch for a minute.' He hung his jacket on the railings and began working swiftly along the line half-dug by the boy.

'You see, don't tek so much on your spade at one time. An' don't lift it right up in the air. That does nowt. You're just turnin' it ovver, that's all. And lean forrard on your spade a bit, let your weight do some of the diggin'. You've got to get a good swing goin', like a collier fillin' off his stint.'

'I can't go as fast as that.'

'No need. Just tek it steady.'

Sam started another line and dug it the full width of the garden. He handed the spade back to the boy.

'Give yourself a bit of a rest at t'end of each row. Then you've got that to look forrard to while you're diggin'.'

The boy began to dig.

'That's the stuff. Just lever back on your spade a bit and turn it ovver.'

The boy hastened his digging and began to gasp.

'Hoddup a minute. If you're breathin' hard you're goin' too fast. Pace yourself a bit.'

The boy slowed down and Sam watched him till he reached the edge of the path.

'Now, rest on your shovel a bit. Is your Dad in.'

'No. He's gone to Carky to see somebody.'

'Well, when he comes back, tell him I'll see him at Club toneet.'

'I'll tell 'im Mester Chard.'

Sam put his jacket on and opened the gate.

'Right Jimmy, back to your diggin'. We'll mek a gardener of you yet.'

The boy shook his head and walked back to the beginning of his row.

Sam saw her leaning against the gate as he came down the hill on the shop side. He started to cross the road, waited while a Yorkshire traction bus clumsily rounded the sharp corner of the railed public gardens and half-ran to where she was standing. He stopped close beside her, then stepped back a little way, his hands in his jacket pockets.

'Enjoyin' the sunshine, Cynthia.'

She nodded and smiled. She looked directly at him and he blinked several times.

'I've just been up to see Barney Sykes.'

'How is he.'

'He's goin' home fast.'

Sam looked back up the hill for a moment.

'It's a funny thing. I've only been there an hour but he kept coughing and wheezing till I could 'ave thumped him. Which is a bit hard when you think how badly he is. He just keeps on and on. How his wife stands it I don't know.'

Sam turned and propped his back against the railings so that he was standing sideways to the girl. He watched as the last of the few waiting people boarded the bus and it clanged into gear and came rattling past in a swirl of dust. A little boy came down the causeway, hopping and running on one roller-skate.

'Are you going to the Welfare dance on Sat'day.'

Cynthia stood on the bottom cross-tie of the gate and stretched herself, then stood down on the path again.

'I hadn't thought about it.'

'If you do go, who will you go with.'

'I usually go with Annie Jones and her sister.'

'I'll take you, if you like.'

'No thank you.'

'Why not.'

'You know why not.'

Sam took cigarette papers and tobacco tin from his inside

breast pocket and began to roll a cigarette with his fingers. He spilled some of the tobacco and then rolled it slowly in the machine which was fitted into the back of the tin. He snapped the tin shut, put it into his pocket and lit the cigarette. He blew a plume of smoke down his nose.

'When we meet at a dance, well sometimes, you're willing to dance with me. And other times you seem. Like at Fay Mill's weddin'. You were friendly. You spent more time with me than anybody. Well it seemed that way.'

The girl smiled at him and giggled. Sam spoke more loudly.

'I still don't see why. If you'll dance with me at the dance why won't you go with me. To the dance.'

'Because if I let you take me to the dance I become one of Sam Chard's women. And I don't reckon on that. Thank you very much.'

'It's not that. It's not like that at all. Be fair.'

'Fair's what suits you isn't it Sam.'

'I've always liked you. You know that.'

'You mean you fancy me. You'd like me to dance attendance on you like Sheila Gorman and Jean Williams. Always ready and willing when Sam puts his silk scarf on and whistles. And Arthur Cook's wife, if the gossip's anything to go by.'

Sam threw his cigarette down and rubbed it into shreds with his shoe. He muttered 'Bloody hell'. They were silent for a while, then Sam took a handful of wrapped sweets from his pocket and said 'Have a toffee'. Cynthia took one.

They watched Cynthia's father walk up the hill towards them, swinging his walking-stick in exact time with his stride. He stopped by the gate. Sam grinned.

'Afternoon Mister Henshaw. Nice weather we're havin'.'

'Afternoon.'

Cynthia opened the gate and her father walked through. He turned back towards them.

'Your mother will want a hand with the dinner Cynthia.'

'I'll be in shortly, father.'

Henshaw stood a moment longer, then strode down the path and round the back of the house. Sam clasped his hands behind his head and looked at the sky.

'And that's a good bit of the reason you fob me off. Charles Frederick Henshaw. Management checkweighman, you know. Responsible job. Quite an educated sort of a chap. Brought you up to be a bit special didn't he lass. Not to mess about with us common pitmen. Respectable and decent, a nice bit of linen on the table, none o' your oilcloth. And if we didn't dig the bloody coal out he'd 'ave nowt to check t' weight on. Would he now.'

The girl frowned.

'If I wanted to, I'd go with you Sam. I'm not ruled by my father.'

'Well I wonder. Still, you must admit, he doesn't reckon much on me.'

'It's just his way.'

'Aye, I suppose you can say that about anybody.'

Sam touched the girl lightly on the shoulder.

'You'll not come to t' dance with me then.'

'No.'

Sam started to walk down the hill, then turned and half shouted back.

'I'll bet I see you there though. And I'll have a dance with you. And I'll squeeze you a bit in the fishtail and lock. And you'll just about faint with delight when I do my twinkletoes bit.'

The girl laughed.

The fair took up half the village market-place. Hissing gas flares and coloured bulbs cast a dazzle of light over the fairground and threw a haze out into the darkness of the spring night. The swing-boats sailed upwards and downwards cutting across the riding waves of the big roundabout. People knotted and swirled around the coconut shies and sideshows. The noise was a deafening jumble of grinding dodgems and girls squealing each time they bumped, a big steam organ pumping out old music hall tunes, stallholders shouting at customers, the clapping of whizzing generator belts, the roaring chatter of the crowd and the scattered sharpness of mallet thump followed by clanging bell, nails being hammered into wooden blocks, balls thudding against backcloths, airguns popping, a laughing policeman-doll cackling, target plates shattering, toy trumpets blaring.

Dez saw her first as he was trying to throw an elastic covered rubber ball into a tilted bucket so that it did not bounce out. She was dark, with a pointed nose and chin and she wore a boy's overcoat that was too big for her. She held it round her with her hands in the large flap pockets. She was standing a few feet from him, wrinkling her face into comical looks as he tried to aim his throw. He missed the bucket altogether and she giggled. He picked up his snaptin and Dudley from the ground and walked off into the crowd.

He guessed she was following him when he was throwing darts at playing cards pinned to a board. As he missed with his third dart she shouted 'Cack Handed.' He picked up his belongings, stared at her and muttered 'What's it to do wi' thee' and walked away.

He was standing watching a stall-holder spinning great whirls of candy floss when she crept up behind him and hit him sharply on the leg with a rolled-up newspaper. He spun round. She had darted back a few feet and was half-crouched as if ready to run.

'What did tha do that for.'

''Cos I felt like it.'

'It 'urt.'

'It was supposed to.'

Dez rubbed his leg then shouted 'Bugger off' and hurried towards the centre of the fairground.

She chased after him, flicked the paper at the back of his head and started to laugh as he tried to grab her and dropped his snaptin. He picked it up and stood shaking his head.

'Stop it. Stop it.'

'I shan't if I don't want to.'

She ran towards him again and slapped him across the hand and dodged away.

He chased after her but she twisted and turned in between the stalls and twice Dez slipped to his knees on the cindered ground.

She ran out of the fair into the darkened top half of the market-place and just before she reached the grass by the bordering road he caught up with her, grabbed her arm and swung her round. She struggled for a moment, then stood still. They were both breathing heavily. She looked up at him and said 'What's tha going' to do wi' me.'

Dez let go of her arm.

'What d'y' mean.'

'Ah mean what are you goin' to do wi' me. Are you goin' to belt me.'

Dez slowed his breathing down and stepped back.

'I don't hit girls.'

'What do you do with 'em.'

'What d'y' mean.'

'You keep sayin' that. What do you do with girls.'

'I don't know what y' talkin' about.'

'You're a bit thick aren't you. Ah'm talkin' about what you do with girls.'

The lad half-shouted.

'Why did you 'it me. You'd no right to do that.'

'P'raps I fancy you.'

The girl held her arms out from her shoulders, did a slow, awkward dance turn and began to sing 'If You Were the Only Boy in the World' in a high voice. Soon she lost the words and began humming. Dez half-turned away.

'You're just playin' silly buggers.'

The girl stood still and put her hands in her pockets.

'I'll bet you don't do anythin' with girls.'

Dez hesitated and stumbled over his words.

'What's it to what's it matter what's it matter to thee for.'

'Are you frightened then.'

'No I'm not frightened.'

'Would you like to do somethin' with me.'

There was a long silence. Then one of a crowd of men passing shouted 'Heyup Dezzy, has tha won a coconut.' The others laughed. Dez looked away towards the horsefield next to the market place.

'Well. Do you want to do anythin' wi' me.'

'I might.'

'That's very nice of you, Dezzy Wheeler.'

'How d'y' know mi name.'

'I know a lot you don't know about.'

The lad fiddled with his snaptin and forced it into the pocket of his jacket, tearing the lining. The girl started to walk away. Dez shouted after her.

'Where y' goin'.'

The girl stopped and looked back over her shoulder.

'I might be goin' home.'

'What about what you said.'

'What did I say.'

'What you said.'

The girl turned, held back the collar of her overcoat and tucked her long hair inside it.

'Ah well, you only said you might.'

'I didn't just mean that.'

The girl looked at him closely, pulled her hair out of her collar, turned and began to cross the road.

'Are you comin' then.'

Dez still had not moved.

'Weer to.'

The girl carried on to the other side of the road and Dez ran after her and followed a few feet behind. She walked alongside the stone wall, topped by barbed wire, that edged the railway field and climbed the low gate by the Co-op warehouse. Dez climbed after her and kept behind her as she forced her way through the broken palings at the bottom of the yard and slipped into the field. She trod carefully in the darkness over the tussocky grass till she reached the old railway embankment. She spread her overcoat on the shallow bottom slope of the bank and whispered 'Give us your jacket.' She took the snaptin out, put it to one side with the Dudley, rolled the jacket into a pillow and lay down. Dez stood for a moment and then lay down awkwardly beside her, half on his side, propped on his elbow. She moved onto her side, pushed him on to his back, tucked her head against his and lay with her right arm and leg across him.

She sat upright for a moment and wormed her way out of her knickers and lay across him again. The noise of the fairground carried faintly across the field.

They lay still for several minutes then she put her left arm round his neck and kissed him. She moved her leg, opened the fly buttons of his trousers and began slowly rubbing his prick. Dez arched his body clumsily and she muttered 'just lie still.' Slowly his prick stiffened and she began brushing the tip with her fingers and stroking the stem. Dez started to say something but she kissed him again then spread her legs out and pulled him on her. He thrust forward clumsily but she held his hips. She said 'Let me show you.' She took his prick gently in her hand and as he started to thrust she said sharply 'No, you just lie still for a minute.' Dez lay stiffly, half-supported on his elbows. The girl held his prick tightly and slowly wriggled herself on to it. She made sighing sounds and when the lad said hoarsely 'I want it, I want it' she said 'Shush.' She took her hand away, put her arms round his neck and slid her legs, bent at the knees, behind his. 'Now,' she whispered, 'just a bit at a time.' At first he jerked in ungainly spasms and she had to keep pulling him forward to hold him in. Then he grabbed her shoulders and pulled her more tightly on to him and began to thrust steadily. She buried her face in his neck and he came quickly, his body shuddering as he suddenly stopped thrusting. She gave his hair sharp little tugs. He lay on her for a long time and then she pushed him off.

'You're gettin' heavy.'

She pulled her skirt down and folded his trouser flies. They lay looking up at the clouded night sky. She spoke suddenly.

'How old are you.'

'Fifteen.'

'How old do you think I am.'

He half-turned and looked at her closely.

'Sixteen.'

'No, I'm fourteen.'

'What's your name.'

'Betty. Betty Snaith.'

'Where do you live.'

'Broddy. By the Picture House.'

Dez sat up and looked round the field, then lay down again. They were silent for a while. The girl put her head on his chest and said 'Did you like it.'

'Yes.'

'A lot.'

'Yes.'

The girl giggled.

'I could tell you did.'

'What about you.'

The girl nodded her head several times against his chest. She sat up and put his hand on the top of her jumper.

'Feel in there.'

He fumbled his hand down her jumper and blouse, felt her small breasts, then took his hand out. The girl moved restlessly for a minute and said 'Have you ever seen between a girl's legs.'

'No. Only pictures once. Mi brother had some.'

'Do you want to have a look.'

'If you want.'

She pulled her skirt up and the lad leaned over and peered closely at her cunt.

'Feel it.'

He touched the small plume of soft hair and lay down again. The girl smoothed her skirt into place and rested her head on his chest. They were silent for a long time.

'I work at pit. With mi Dad and mi two brothers and mi sister's husband.'

'Do you like it.'

'It's all reight. What do you do. Have you left school.'

'I just help mi Mam. We've got a big family.'

She lifted her head and kissed him, then rested on his chest again. She muttered 'You should kiss me back.'

After a long time the girl opened his trousers and began to fondle his prick. The boy said very quickly 'I can't do it agen.' The girl went on feeling him and took the stem between her thumb and two forefingers and began jerking it up and down, slowly. She put her mouth against his ear and whispered to him.

'Do you do this to yousen.'

The boy turned his head and pushed it under hers. She went on jerking his prick slowly and when it stiffened she put her hand round it and squeezed each time she pulled and pushed it. She knelt across him and letting go of his prick lowered her cunt on to it. His prick slipped out and she put her hand down quickly and pushed it carefully back in, then made smaller movements. After a while she stopped, lifted her head and said 'Do you want to go on.' The boy said 'If you want' and she put her cheek next to his and went on pushing his prick up into herself. The boy's body went suddenly stiff and he arched his back. The girl pushed harder and more quickly and began to make little crying sounds. The boy grabbed her arse and pushed her strongly downward. For a moment they wrestled fiercely and she gouged her fingers into his chest. She tightened her thighs round him then went limp and lay loosely on top of him for a long time.

The noise from the fairground suddenly lessened as the steam organ stopped. The boy rolled her sideways and looked round him.

'What time is it.'

'Don't know. Ten p'raps.'

The boy lurched to his feet, buttoned his trousers and scrambled about for his jacket, snaptin and Dudley. The girl sat up and put her arms round her knees and hugged herself.

'What's all the rush for.'

'I'll be late for shift.'

'They'll manage wi'out thee.'

'You don't know mi bloody Dad.'

Dez started across the field then turned back to the girl.

'Will I see y'again.'

'If you want.'

Dez looked away towards the fairground and back at the girl. She said something he could not hear, then spoke clearly.

'Feast's still on tomorrer night.'

Dez said 'alreight' and ran off across the field. The girl shouted after him 'Goodnight Dezzy Wheeler.'

The boy raced to the wall, stumbling twice and stood looking at it. He turned and ran back along the wall to the warehouse yard, through the fence, over the gate and out into the road. Holding his side, he ran towards the pit, past a row of stone cottages. He turned into the lower pit yard by the screens. He was sprinting past the shuttered blacksmith's shop when he stopped suddenly, stood shuddering and gasping for air and was sick. He leaned forward, spewing away from his clothes and bent over for a minute, gagging. He groped his way to the wall and leaned against it cradling his head in his right arm. He was sweating heavily. After a minute he took out his handkerchief, wiped his mouth and went and sat down on a pile of sleepers. He sat for a quarter of an hour, breathing slowly and deeply.

He stood up and walked, unsteadily at first, across to the lamp cabin and offered his check. The lampman fetched a lamp and peered closely at him through the gate window.

'Tharra bit late Dezzy. Thi old man were askin' after thee at changeover.'

Dez muttered and took his lamp.

'He'll knock thi stocking tops off, lad.'

Dez trotted away to the gantry, up the steps and on to the shaft side. The onsetter finished locking a set of empty tubs into the cage, closed the gates and rang his bell for the windsman. He came across to the boy.

'What tha doin' at this time.'

'Ah'm late.'

'Th'a bloddy reight thy are. Well tha can't go down just yet, Ah'm windin' coal. Tha'll have to wait thi turn and go down wi' 'tricians on eleven o'clock nights.'

Dez went to the farthest corner of the shaft side and squatted down to wait. The left-hand cage came up and bumped on to its holding posts. The shaft side dinned with noise as the onsetter and his mates ran empty tubs down the slope to collide stunningly with the full ones on the cage and force them off. The gates were slammed to and the pit bottom repeater bell and the pit top signal bell rang clamorously to sign the cage away.

The three electricians arrived and stood out on the gantry smoking a last cigarette before coming in on the hour. Dez rode down with them, reported to the pit bottom deputy and sat behind the electricians on the paddy train that took them out to the district.

The boy stood in the darkness for a minute, watching the men working in the lighted area round the rock face of the heading they were driving. He crept quietly into the heading, laid his jacket, snaptin and Dudley on the pile with the others and started to pull a full tub back down towards the main plane. His father turned, saw him, threw down his pick and walked across to him. He looked at the boy for a moment then back-handed him across the face. The boy stumbled against the wall of the heading.

'What time do you call this.'

'I forgot the time, Dad.'

'I forgot the time, Dad,' the man's voice was a high mimicry of the boy's. Joe Wheeler raised his arm again and his son flinched away.

'Come 'ere you little sod.'

Dez came forward a step and his father's fist caught him in the mouth, tumbling him to the floor. He started to cry. The other three men had stopped work and were looking on. The oldest of them said 'Easy on him Dad.' Joe Wheeler turned to face him.

'Shut your fuckin' mouth.'

He turned back to the boy.

'On your feet.'

The boy stood up slowly and his father grasped his shirt by the neck, bunched it and twisted it, pulling the lad to him.

'Right, you twat. What's your fuckin' excuse.'

'I was at the feast Dad. I forgot the time. Honest.'

'Try sayin' that again, Dezzy.'

'I was at the feast Dad. An' they wouldn't let me down 'cos they were windin' coal.'

The father took the boy's hair in his left hand and pulled it, lifting his son off his feet. The boy screamed.

'You lyin' little sod. You've been fuckin' about with some girl. Tommy Smith saw you. He told me he'd seen you.'

He cuffed the boy and then let go of him. Dez dropped to his knees and clutched his head.

'Am I supposed to tram mi own fuckin' tubs then. Has it come to that. Answer me you little fucker.'

The boy mumbled 'No Dad.' The father pulled the boy back on to his feet and the lad stood shielding his face with his arms.

'Right. I'll attend to you in the morning. An' I'll make you sing. You're a fuckin' mess. Now get this bloody tub out and fetch an empty in. An' if I turn round once tonight and there's no fuckin' empty I'll kick your arse to t' pit bottom.'

The men turned back to the face of the heading and began swinging their picks, bringing down streams of rubble. Dez put his back against the full tub and, still sobbing, began pushing it along the track out of the heading.

After a while the older of Joe Wheeler's sons shouted over the noise of falling stone.

'Ah'm goin' to fetch another pick, this fucker's blunt.'

He walked away down the heading to where Dez was pushing the tub. As he passed him he ran his hand through the boy's hair and ruffled it.

'Tha do alright for thisen then, our young'n.'

The pit bottom was crowded with day-shift men leaving and afternoon-shift men arriving, when the news of Len Mappin's death came through. Swiftly the babble of talk rose to a roar, echoing round the high arched roof of the top deck. Men milled round, groups forming and reforming. The shaft side was jammed with a growing mass of miners as the cages brought more down from the pit top and others came in from the districts. The pit bottom onsetter shouted and pushed as he struggled to keep the space before the cage gates clear. The road doggy gave up trying to check his men as the crowd forced him so tightly against the wall that he could no longer keep his big men on books sheets open in front of him. The shaft side phones rang each time they were put down, as one pit top official after another tried to find out what was happening.

Men shoved their way into the pit bottom office shouting and the pit bottom clerk roared into the district phone.

'Hoddup a minute. I can't hear a bloody thing. Hoddon.' He yelled hoarsely at the men crowding through the doorway. 'Y'll have to back out an' get the fuckin' door shut. I can't hear a thing. Now come on, back your bloody sen out.'

For a while more men crowded into the office and the clerk shouted vainly. Then the tall, stooped, afternoon-shift undermanager struggled through the door and raised his voice above the babble. 'Right, every bugger bar officials out.' He pushed and shouted and slowly enough of the bystanders were forced back into the pit bottom to get the door shut. The clerk went back to his phone and there was a long silence in the office while he listened.

'Right, I'll ring you back.'

The undermanager leaned against the door, ignoring the knocking and shouts from outside. 'Well, Sydney, what's to do.'

'Run o' tubs near the top of East Scower and the rope broke. They went back down an' the jack catches didn't hold 'em. Tommy Pritchard's lad tried to get some lockers in but one spun out an' broke his wrist. Everybody got clear bar Len Mappin. He were a bit slow startin' to run. First he run up the drift for the nearest refuge hole. Then he seemed to change his mind and started to run down again. Hodson swears he still had plenty of time but he fell ovver an' he seemed to be in a bit of a daze. He was scrabblin' for his lamp when the tubs jumped the track and caught him.'

'Have they got him out.'

'Aye. Hodson says his back and his neck are broke.'

The undermanager tapped his stick on the floor.

'Mappin were always a bit of a gormless bugger.'

He straightened himself and put his hand on the door latch.

'You lot tell the men what's happened.'

He opened the door and the noise dinned into the office. The officials pushed their way out and the undermanager shut the door after them.

'Right, Sydney. You ring the manager and tell him to send somebody fast to tell the widow so she hears it properly and not bi rumour and he's to let the mines inspector know. Tell him I've gone down to t' Scower and he can join me there. Then get hold of one of the safety men and send him down after me. An' tell Hodson I'm on mi way an' apart from shiftin' Mappin, things are to be left just as they are till I've seen 'em. I want to talk to ivryone as were there. 'Ave they got an ambulance man to young Pritchard.'

'Harry Settle's come up from Sixes.'

The undermanager lingered in the doorway and the clerk waited, hand on phone.

'It'll be a fuckin' compensation case this, wi' t' rope breakin,' so get me a fitter to come an' look at it.'

The undermanager left the office and the clerk phoned the pit top.

There were only half a dozen men on the cage that brought Sam Chard down. Most of the remaining afternoon-shift men were staying on the pit top. The men in the pit bottom were quieter now, standing in line at the shaft side. Sam stopped at the head of the line and spoke to the first few men.

'You lot goin' back up then.'

'You've heard about Len Mappin.'

'Aye.'

'It's a mark of respect.'

'What's a mark of respect.'

'Tha knows fuckin' well Sam. We're lakin' this shift as a mark of respect to Len Mappin.'

'Ah'll tell you what, Brother Vance, let's all work this shift and give pay for it to Annie Mappin. I reckon she'd find that right respectful.'

Several of the men spoke at once.

'When a man's killed we don't work the shift.'

'It's a mark of respect.'

'Show a bit o' decency.'

'Tha knows it's custom.'

Sam waited till the men quietened.

'Then it's a fuckin' daft custom. We can mek do wi' two minutes' silence instead.'

He walked a few yards down the line of men then stopped and turned to face them.

'All reight. Anybody workin' wi' me and givin' the shift's money to Mappin's family. We can reckon it's his benefit match if you want.'

'They 'aven't even brought his bloody body out yet and you're wantin' to start work.'

'That's reight Jimmy Rose, an' by the time I'm halfway through the shift Ah can tell thee where tha'll be showin' thi bloody respect. Tha'll be in t' Half Moon suppin' thisen silly an' tellin' everybody about thi respect for Lenny Mappin.'

Sam walked away on to the main plane and a dozen men left the line and followed him.

The small, Evensong congregation, mostly elderly women and a few children, was scattered in the pews round the centre aisle of the church. An old man with a dirty straggle of beard and a stained raincoat held tight with a leather belt sat at the rear, a worn army knapsack by his side. Everyone sat stiffly, staring towards the big wheel window above the altar. Its stained glass showed pastoral and crucifixion scenes in deep reds and blues and greens and purples. The altar was crowded with vases of white chrysanthemums, hedging in an ornamented brass cross. The pitted stone pillars rose to the dark timbered roof of weathered oak. Dust danced in the evening light that streamed through the pointed windows.

The church was quiet until the parson, choir and vergers filed into the transept and the heavy organ filled the building with a rich sound. The members of the little procession took their places and the congregation shuffled to its feet for the first hymn. Their singing was thin and was carried along by the choir.

The congregation knelt and the parson led them mumbling through their first prayer.

'Almighty and most merciful Father; we have erred, and strayed from thy ways like lost sheep. We have followed too much the devices and desires of our own hearts. We have offended against thy holy laws. We have left undone those things which we ought to have done; and we have done those things which we ought not to have done; and there is no health in us. But thou O Lord, have mercy upon us, miserable offenders. Spare thou them, O God, which confess their faults. Restore thou them that are penitent; according to thy promises declared unto mankind in Christ Jesu our Lord. And grant, O most merciful Father, for his sake; that we may hereafter live a godly, righteous, and sober life. To the glory of thy holy Name. Amen.'

Prayers and hymns alternated and the chief verger read the lessons from Proverbs and the Gospel according to Mark.

The parson crossed to the high stone pulpit. He was a tall, stooped man with a grey, wrinkled face. He walked with a limp and his hands shook. He held tightly to the rail as he climbed the spiral staircase to the lectern. He coughed harshly and squinted at his Bible. He spoke slowly, his voice sometimes near a shout and sometimes muttering so that he was not clearly heard. He gave the text 'Let not the sun go down upon your anger.'

'Science tells us that sleep is not a kind of emptiness, not just a blotting out. When we sleep much is happening within us. So, it may be, it may be that if we go to our rest with our anger still within us then it is sealed into us and we awake with it. So we must resolve our anger before we sleep.'

He seemed to lose his thread and was silent for a while, then he spoke loudly again.

'Bad temper is arrogance. It is arrogance. When we choose to rebuke others, we lose our temper with them, what are we doing. Are we not making them little and ourselves big. Are we not imagining ourselves to be of much greater importance than those with whom we are cross. We are saying, you are nothing but an irritation to me who is so important. So, bad temper is a kind of arrogance of the spirit.'

His voice dropped and only the phrase 'arrogance of the spirit' could be heard. Suddenly he repeated his text loudly.

'So you see that the sun going down refers to sleep and it means that our quarrel must be made up before we sleep.'

He talked on of the making up of quarrels and said three times that pride was the deadliest of the seven deadly sins. His voice sank lower and he stopped speaking. Suddenly his voice rose.

'We must not put another person out of our mind. To put a person out of your mind is an act of great arrogance. It is cruel. You may think what you will of someone but you must not put them out of your mind. We live in the minds of others. Remember this. We live in the minds of others.'

He paused and then went on to make announcements about forthcoming meetings of the Sunday School committee and the Mother's Union.

He climbed down from his pulpit.

During the final hymn one of the vergers took the collection in a cloth bag suspended from a wooden rod. People put their closed hands into the bag before letting go of their coins. The verger approached the old man sitting at the back of the church but he kept his hands in the pockets of his raincoat and stared at the floor. Ther verger waited for a moment then walked back down the aisle.

The congregation stood until the parson had walked to the door of the church. As they came out he shook hands with each one, nodding but saying little. The last out was the old man with the strapped raincoat. He did not shake hands but stood directly before the parson and said 'Have you anything for me.'

The parson blinked and said 'You need something.'

'The Sally Army always gives you something. I'm on the road.'

The chief verger came across to them and said 'Do you need me at all, Parson.'

The Parson said 'No, it's quite alright.' He turned to the old man. 'Would you like some food.'

The old man nodded and the parson said 'Come with me' and

led the way through the graveyard. He half-turned to the man as they walked.

'Did you like the service.'

'I'm not religious.'

'I see. Still, sometimes the church is a comfort even if you are not religious.'

They went through the lych gate and along the path towards the rectory. The parson stopped suddenly and said 'Why are you not religious.'

'I've got nothing to be religious about.'

'The church should be a home for the homeless.'

The man waved his arms and said 'Don't preach at me.'

The parson walked on a few steps but the man stood still. The parson turned round and said 'I'm sorry. Preaching is a habit with me.'

The man shouted 'You want to talk religion. I'll ask you a question.'

'Surely.'

'Alright then. Tell me this. Adam and Eve had two sons Cain and Abel. Right.'

'Yes.'

'And Cain killed Abel and he went away and he took unto himself a wife. Right.'

'So the Bible tells us.'

'Right then. Where did he get his wife from. There's only Adam and Eve and they only have two sons. So where did he get his wife from. Tell me that.'

The parson smiled and said 'I don't think you can read the Bible in quite that way.'

The man spat and shouted 'You see. That's religion. Never give a straight answer.' He turned and started to walk away.

The parson limped after him and called out 'Please. Come and have supper with me. We can talk.' The man walked more quickly and the parson stopped and stared after him, as he went down the path away from the church.

In the three shifts the closed face had been stripped of nearly all its gear. The two men and the lad were dismantling the last of the heavy iron roller pans that had carried the conveyor belt. Norman Green and Joe Galashiels unbolted each pan in turn and pulled it loose from the line, while the lad dragged them up to the intake road and manhandled them on to the loader end conveyor belt. As each pan was settled on the belt he waved his lamp and the loader end lad moved the belt up a little to make room for the next.

Galashiels swore steadily and kept sucking his fist where his spanner had slipped on a rusted bolt and skimmed his knuckles. By halfway through the shift the pans were all stacked on the intake belt and they rode them down to the loader end and lifted them into empty tubs. The run of eight tubs was coupled up and lashed on to the overhead rope. Green pulled the bare signalling wires together and rang two. The rope tightened and pulled the tubs away. They walked alongside the run to the end of the intake road, unlashed it, pushed it over the points and round the turn and lashed it to the main plane rope. The rope started on signal and they walked slowly alongside the tubs up the plane.

They had gone about a mile when the rope stopped, started and stopped again eight or nine times, then stopped for good. They stood leaning on the tubs for about ten minutes. Galashiels walked a little way up the plane and crouched down to peer along it. Green shouted after him.

'Walk up to the hauler Joe. See what's holdin' the buggers up.'

Galashiels walked away and Green and the lad squatted down at the side of the track. Green offered the lad a chew of tobacco and the lad said 'No thanks, Mister Green.'

'You're right to refuse, lad. It's a filthy habit. Still, it does keep the spit flowin'.'

The lad collected together five stones, cleared the dust away from in front of him and began to play snobs. He played swiftly as far as pigeonholes then spreading out the fingers of his left hand with the tips on the ground he put four of the stones down in the spaces between his fingers and finger and thumb. He tossed the other stone up with his right hand and while it was in the air touched one of the stones into the space under his hand and caught the falling stone as it came down. He repeated the task until all four of the stones had been flicked out of sight under his arched hand. Taking his left hand away he looked to see if the stones were together. Three were but one had been flicked too strongly and was lying about five inches from the rest. He threw the one stone into the air and tried to scoop up the four and catch the falling stone. He swept up only three. Green said 'What comes next.'

'Jinks and no jinks.'

'I can 'ardly remember it. Let's have a try.'

The lad handed him the five stones and he scattered four of them on the ground.

'Now let's see. I'll try no jinks. I have to pick up in ones, then twos, then three and one, then four and I mustn't let this stone jink against 'em when I catch it.'

'That's reight.'

Green tossed up the stone he was holding, picked up one of the stones from the floor between his first finger and thumb and caught the falling stone silently in his palm. He said 'Now then' and went on with the task. When he picked up three stones together the lad said 'I heard it click' as Green caught the tossed stone. Green nodded and said 'You try it then.' The lad's stones jinked on four and he threw them to the floor. 'It's no good. I'm out o' practice.'

Galashiels walked back down the plane and squatted beside them.

'You wouldn't fuckin' believe it.'

'What's up Joe.'

'It's old Scully runnin' the engine an' you know what a daft sod he is. Well he got fuckin' fretted over his signals and kept stoppin' and startin' and one of the rippers from the headin' got a bit radgy and comes down and cusses him out. Just a bit of fuckin' and blindin' an' old Scully starts cryin'. He's like a big soft lass. Anyroad, he's in a sulk now and won't run the fuckin' engine.'

Green sighed.

'What they goin' to do.'

'They've sent for the paddy man to run it.'

'What's the time.'

'I don't know.'

'We'll be fuckin' lucky if we get this lot out by shift end. I'll go an' check time.'

Green walked back down the plane to the phone and wound two rings for the pit bottom. 'Nadden, Sydney.'

'Heyup.'

'What's the time lad.'

'Time you bought yourself a fuckin' watch. Ten past seven.'

'What's it doin' on top.'

'Rainin'.'

'Thank you Sydney.'

Green walked back and sat down by the other two.

'It's after seven.'

They sat without speaking till a wireman passed them going up the plane and they said 'Evenin'.' When the man was well away from them Galashiels said 'that's a soft bugger I wouldn't change places with.'

'Who, Ernie Rice.'

'Aye.'

The lad said 'Why wouldn't you change places with 'im Mister Galashiels.'

'Because of his wife, lad.'

'What about her.'

Galashiels looked at Green and said 'Shall I tell him.'

'Please yourself.'

'You see Jack, when it comes to fuckin', Gracie Rice is like a Sally Army soup kitchen, you all line up. Hey Norm, did I tell you I saw her at Sun Inn a few week back.'

'I don't recall you sayin' owt.'

'Well you know Ernie does a bit of pianner playin' there, odd nights. Well he's tinklin' away an' this bloody quarry foreman comes in, from Fields, I can't remember his name. Big chap. Anyroad, he's reight lovey dovey with Gracie and then he buys Ernie a pint and teks Gracie out round back. I nipped out t' lav a bit later an' he's down with 'er on that bit of grass at side of dog track. She's on top humpin' him like mad. An' she's no bigger than fourpennorth o' copper. An' Ernie's inside playin' his pianner, soft as a barmtub.'

'My guess is Ernie knew what he was tekkin' on when he married her. Gracie never kept it a secret how keen she was.'

'Ah sod a man who'll marry a lass that other blokes have been at.'

'You reckon we should all marry virgins then, Joey.'

'I bloody do. When I get wed I shall want to be first an' last.'

'It's a funny thing, I've never been able to work that one out.'

'What y' mean, work it out.'

'Well let me put it this way. You must have dipped it into a fair number of lasses in your time.'

'What if I 'ave.'

'And I've slipped the ferret now an' then miself and most fellers I know seem to get a bit extra from time to time.'

'What the hell you drivin' at, Norm.'

'Well it's like they teach you at school about addin' and subtractin'.'

'What you on about.'

'I just keep wonderin' where all these virgins are comin' from that we're supposed to be goin' to marry.'

'Are you tellin' me a bloke should marry somebody else's leavin's.'

'It's like I said. If we're all, so to speak, busy deflowerin', then where do we find the flowers when the time comes.'

'You think you're a clever fucker don't you Norm Green.'

'Not especially. But I was always a dab 'and at arithmetic.'

'Well I think nowt of a bloke that'll marry a pro.'

'Now come on Joe, you've never heard of Gracie tekkin' owt forrit. She's too fond of it for that.'

Galashiels turned to the lad.

'Tek no gorm on 'im Jacko, he'll 'ave you marryin' any old ooer.'

The lad looked from Galashiels to Green and back.

Green rose, stretched and sat on the side of a tub.

'If we're late gettin' this lot up we'll leave 'em in the yard and shift 'em to t' fittin' shop tomorrer.'

The sound of shouting came faintly from up the plane. Galashiels grunted.

'That'll be Scully at it again.'

The boy yawned and said 'Will we be changin' shifts to days next Mister Green.'

'We might. Why.'

'I'd like to go to the pictures. It's a gangster picture.'

'You'll not 'ave to miss that lad. If we're still on afters you'll have to play a shift.'

Galashiels stood up, winced, put a hand to his back and said 'Every picture tells a story.'

A while later they heard more shouting from up the plane, then the rope started up and the tubs moved away. They walked alongside them to the pit bottom.

Sam came home from the pit at seven in the morning, had his bath and breakfast and slept till midday.

His landlady watched him put on a new, soft-collared, white, summer shirt and his best flannels and sports jacket.

'You're titivatin' yourself up very smart for a Monday afternoon, Sam.'

Sam brilliantined his hair and carefully combed in a parting. 'Well, it meks a nice sight for the village, Agnes. Seein' me togged up beautiful.'

'Fancy yourself then.'

'Now come on, love, you know if it weren't for mi face I'd be a right good lookin' chap.'

'Expectin' to bump into somebody.'

'A nice sunny day like this, you never know.'

He turned from the mirror and stood to attention in front of the old woman.

'Will I do.'

'I've had flashier fellers in mi time but you'll do.'

Sam kissed the old woman and stood for a moment at the back door.

'Right. Don't set tea for me. I might scrounge some bait on mi travels.'

He went out into the street and turned the corner onto the hill. Whistling 'Lily of Laguna' he walked up the hill, past the butter cross and down to the dyke bridge. He watched a man beheading and gutting eels on the top of the stone wall that ran alongside the dyke and up to the bridge. Ducking through the fence he squatted beside him.

'Nadden, Tommy, they bitin' alright.'

'Not bad, I put the lines under the bridge last neet.'

Sam watched the entrails, newly cut from the eels, squirm and wriggle.

'Never could fancy 'em miself, though mi Mam was partial.'

'They mek a supper.'

Tommy Bettney closed the gutted eels into an old paint tin and began to clean his jack-knife with a piece of rag.

'Hast heard about Frank Dean's lad.'

'The one they call Nellie.'

'Aye.'

'What about 'im.'

'I heard as I were passin' pit on mi way up.'

Bettney gave Sam a cigarette and lit one himself.

'About eight o'clock he's bringin' his pony into pit bottom stables. He puts a nosebag on him burrit seems there was a mouse in the meal. Anyroad, the pony goes mad with the bag tied on 'im and this mouse runnin' about inside and when Nellie tries to hold him to get bag off, he lashes out and catches the lad right on t' knee-cap.'

'Is it bad.'

'Smashed it. They reckon he'll have one leg and a swinger from now on.'

'Poor bugger.'

Bettney stood up and tucked the tin under his arm.

'Ah'm off back 'om, Sam.'

'Goodday then Tommy.'

Bettney nodded, slipped through the fence and walked up the hill.

Sam sat on the wall, legs dangling over the stream and finished his cigarette, flicking the stub into the darkness under the bridge. He looked upstream and saw the boy fishing. He was wading barefoot in the stream, his hands gripping the ends of his handkerchief, pulling it into the shape of a closed scoop. As he moved along, facing the bank, he dredged it through the reeds, then gazed into it to see if he had caught anything. Sam dusted his trousers and walked up the bank and knelt by the boy's jam jar. It was full of tiddlers, sticklebacks, stoneys and barbels. The boy came up the bank, letting the water stream through his handkerchief. He emptied another tiddler into the jar.

'Th'a not at school then, Robert.'

'Ah'm poorly, Mester Chard.'

'You've got too many in there, lad.'

The boy held the jar up to the sun.

'They're all reight.'

'Never. How would you like it, livin' that many in a room. Havin' half your family standin' on your 'ead.'

'Ah don't want to put 'em back.'

'Have you got any more string.'

The boy pulled a tangled piece of twine from his pocket.

'Right. Now up where the fence crosses the dyke there's a bit of a rubbish dump. Go an' see if you can find a couple more jars.'

The boy looked silently at Sam for a moment.

'Will you watch mi jar for me.'

Sam nodded and the boy went off. Sam shouted after him 'Mind your feet.' The boy came back a while later, with two jam jars.

'Wash 'em out.'

The boy waded into the stream and cleaned out the jars, scrubbing his hand round the insides, scratching the labels off and filling and emptying them half a dozen times. He brought them filled to the bank. Sam bit the string in two and fitted carrying loops to the new jars. With Sam holding his hands as a funnel they divided the fish between the three jars. Then they sat watching them glint in the sunlight as they swam round and round.

Sam pulled an old Empire pocket-watch from his jacket and checked the time. He said good morning to the boy and began to walk back to the road. The lad ran after him.

'Have you got any fag cards Mester Chard.'

Sam took his cigarette packet out and looked at the card.

'Famous Footballers. Number twenty-nine.'

The boy smiled.

'Can I have it.'

Sam gave it to him and the boy ran back to his jars. Sam slipped through the fence, keeping his jacket clear of the broken railings and walked towards the Great North Road. At Five Lane Ends he stood across from the old quarry until he saw the small blue Campbell Johns bus come slowly along the North Road. He moved to the bus stop. The conductor was sitting in the first seat as Sam climbed on and he paid his fare and walked to the back to sit down beside Cynthia Henshaw. They smiled at each other but said nothing for a while as the bus motored slowly towards Ackworth.

'What hast brought to eat.'

Cynthia tipped the carrier bag on her lap towards him.

'Ham and beetroot sandwiches, cheese and pickle sandwiches, chitterlings, cold roast potatoes, malt loaf, parkin, two custards, tea for me and beer for you. I had to smuggle the beer.'

'You'd think we were goin' for a week.'

'Got to keep your strength up, you're a growin' lad.'

Sam took his cigarettes out and offered her one. She shook her head.

'Go on, be a devil.'

She pondered for a moment then said 'I'll try a puff of yours.'

Sam lit the cigarette and gave it to her. She held it gingerly, her thumb and two fingers right at the bottom, and sucked slowly on it. She coughed loudly and gave it back to him.

'I don't know what you see in it.'

'Well it's just an old Woody. For you it should be Turkish with a gold end.'

The bus driver stopped at Mile Lane and waited while the conductor took a parcel across to a farm.

'What did you tell your Mam.'

'She thinks I've gone on a picnic with Elsie Harrison.'

'And what does Elsie Harrison think.'

'She thinks I don't want mi mother to know where I am.'

'So I'm a dark secret then. Not fit to be seen in company.'

'Sam, we agreed there was no point in getting my father stirred up. It's all right for you. You don't have to live with him. I do. There's enough rows without adding any.'

Sam was silent for a minute, then he gave a huge mock sigh.

'It's a terrible thing to be a black sheep.'

Cynthia tittered and jabbed him with her elbow.

'That will be enough of that, Sam Chard.'

They talked about the Roman Rig and Robin Hood's Well and the bluebell wood they could see through the windows of the bus, until they reached the Barnsdale stop.

Sam handed her down from the high step and as the bus pulled away they crossed the road and climbed the stile into a narrow strip of bordering trees. They walked on through the pasture land, thick with cowslips, that led to the farm and Sam stopped by the milking sheds and offered a cigarette to the goat tethered there. The goat ate it and Cynthia giggled and slapped him.

'Y' daft thing. It'll upset it.'

'Never. Goats can eat owt.'

Half a mile beyond the farm they came to a line of small crags which they climbed slowly. At one point Sam lifted Cynthia down from an outcrop of rock and stood with his hands on her waist. She looked at him solemnly.

'I'm safely down, Sam. You don't have to hold on to me.'

Sam grinned.

'I don't have to.'

He kissed her. She kissed him back, slipped out of his hands and walked on. They skirted a briar patch and entered Smeaton Woods. The fern was high and near the centre of the wood they trampled a circle of it flat and sat down. Cynthia spread the food from the carrier round them and they ate the picnic. They talked about the taste of the food and the strike at Upton colliery and

Cynthia named the birds that were singing. Sam told the story of how, years before, the police constable, Andy Pace, had caught old Ted Barraclough in bed with Missis Pace and had chased the old man, who had no trousers on, the full length of Poplar Road and into the Baptist chapel. Cynthia shared the last of Sam's beer and complained that it tasted cankered like sucking a penny.

They packed the remains of the picnic into the carrier bag and Cynthia lay full length, facing the sun, with her eyes closed. Sam lay beside her, resting on his elbow, looking at her. He kissed her several times and she crooked her arm around his neck. He rested his hand on her breast and kissed her eyelids. She lay very still and he put his hand under her frock and tried to take off her knickers. She quickly pushed his hand away and sat up.

'I didn't come here for that.'

Sam lay on his back and put his hands behind his head.

'You're a liar.'

Cynthia looked round her at the trees and at the crumbling old estate wall that ran near the edge of the wood. She tucked her arms round her knees and rested her chin on them. After a while she said 'I'll take them off myself' and she stood up and walked away a few yards. She came back in a moment and tucked her knickers into the carrier bag. She lay down again by Sam.

Sam felt in his trouser pocket and pulled out a sheath in a cardboard packet. Cynthia turned her face away from him and said loudly 'I don't want that.'

'You'll be takin' a risk.'

'I don't care, I don't want it.'

'Come on Cyn, be sensible.'

'If I were sensible you wouldn't have got me up here.'

She turned over on to her stomach. Sam ran his fingers through his hair and looked at the sky.

'It's for your own good, love.'

'If you say any more about it I'm going home. I won't have a rubber good. Not the first time. Another time perhaps. Not the first time.'

Sam sat for a minute, then put the sheath back into his pocket. He undid his trousers, turned Cynthia on to her back and kissed her.

She said tartly 'What am I supposed to do.'

Sam shrugged his shoulders and said 'What do you want to do.'

Cynthia lay still for a minute then opened her legs.

Sam got between her legs and lowered himself on her. He began to push his prick slowly into her. She lay very stiffly and made low hissing sounds. She gripped the muscles of his arms tightly. He pushed more deeply and suddenly she opened her legs more widely and lay slackly underneath him. He rubbed his face against hers and moved slowly in and out of her for a few minutes. Then, still fucking her, he supported himself on his arms and looked down at her. She smiled, grabbed hold of his hair and pulled his head down beside her. After a while she bent her legs at the knees, hit him with her clenched fist and began arching her back over and over again, forcing him to thrust more quickly and deeply. She murmured 'You bugger Sam' then butted his head and gave a soft squeal as she came.

After a stillness Sam rolled over on to his back and she rolled with him. She unbuttoned his shirt and rubbed her face against his chest. She said 'I can hear your heart beating fast.'

'I'm not bloody surprised.' He looked over her shoulder, down at her back and thighs. 'You're bleeding a bit.'

'I know. It's alright. I do my own washing. Mi mother won't know.'

Sam stroked her head, then suddenly tittered.

'You'd better remember to take your knickers out of the carrier. You'd have a job explaining that to your Mam.'

Cynthia laughed and hiccuped then lay down again with her head on his chest.

They dozed in the afternoon sun for a long time.

Cynthia said 'Elsie Harrison says some men can do it twice.'

Sam laughed and Cynthia sat up and pushed him sharply.

'What are you laughing at.'

Sam's laughter died to a giggle.

'Miself, love, honestly.'

'That's all right then.'

She lay down again and said 'Well.'

Sam moved close to her and said 'You might try givin' me a bit of encouragement.' Cynthia made a startled sound, then started tugging at his cock fiercely.

'Steady love, you wouldn't want it to come away in your hand.'

She fondled it more gently and it stiffened. Sam pulled her down on him and said 'Let's try it this way.' He went into her and she tried to move in time with him but her movements were jerky and after a while she sat up astride him and shook her head.

'I like it better the other way.'

They rolled over and Sam lay on her and probed into her. At first they moved uncertainly, then quickened. He let his full weight rest on her and held her breasts. She gouged her fingers into his arse and arched to pull him hard against her. A heavy blush of sweat broke from her as she came a minute before him. While he came she kissed him many times, pulling his head to her. They lay holding each other tightly, shuddering. For a long time they did not move.

As they moved apart she said 'I'd better put my knickers back on before I forget.' Sam buttoned himself and sat smoking while she carefully smoothed her frock and wiped away smears of blood from the hem of her frock and from her legs with a spit-soaked handkerchief. She sat with her legs tucked under her and combed her hair. She said 'There's two sandwiches left, shall we finish them up.'

Sam nodded and stood up.

'Give us the flask. There's a beck by the wood. I'll fetch us some water.'

He fetched the water and they finished the sandwiches. She packed the carrier and stood up.

'We'd better be getting back, Sam.'

Sam squatted a moment longer.

'Are you alright, Cyn.'

'I'm fine, love.'

They walked out of the wood and down the crags holding hands. Sam gave the goat another cigarette and they sat on the wall by the bus stop. Cynthia started to sing 'Linden Lea' very softly and Sam asked her to sing up. She sang it clearly.

'That's nice. That's what comes of all that choir practice.'

'Thank you kindly.'

'Of course, they always warned me about going out with girls from the choir. Very fast, choir girls, they said.'

'And what did they say about colliers from Beech Road.'

'Innocent as lambs. Widely known.'

Cynthia smiled broadly and said 'Tell you something funny.'

Sam nodded.

'My mother used to tell me it was a sacrifice that women had to make for men. Which goes to show.'

'What does it go to show.'

'You want me to say I liked it, don't you.'

'Well did you like it.'

She kissed him and tweaked his nose.

'I'll leave you to guess. When's this bus comin'.'

On the bus Sam put his arm round her and she rested her head on his shoulder. They sat silently till it reached Five Lane Ends.

They stood for a while after the bus had gone. There was a duskiness in the early evening air and they watched the birds wheeling round a tractor driver who was harrowing the field next to the road.

'I'd better go on my own from here, Sam.'

'Aye, lass.'

Sam shuffled his feet.

'I'm not workin' Friday night. Do you fancy Donny pictures.'

'I'd love to.'

'Shall we meet in town then.'

'Whereabouts.'

'Do you like beehives.'

'What are you talking about, Sam.'

'Well they've got a grand beehive at Donny museum, with a glass front so you can see 'em all graftin' away. If you could come a bit early we could meet there at, say, five o'clock.'

'All right.'

'Five o'clock at the museum on Friday then.'

'I'll be sure to be there.'

She kissed him quickly and began to walk away towards the village. Sam shouted after her.

'Goodnight, Cyn.'

She called back goodnight.

He watched her till she was out of sight and then turned into the road by the quarry, taking the long way to the village, round by Burghwallis.

Nodder Jack walked slowly down the hill, his head dropping forward and jerking back in time with his footsteps. On the warm summer day he wore no jacket, his black waistcoat flapped unbuttoned about him and the neck of his striped shirt was open with a collar stud hanging loosely from it. He stopped, turned on the kerb and stood for a moment, his clogged feet groping for the pavement edge. He crossed the road just above Naylor's farm. A group of children ran out of the farm gate and skipped along in front of him, shouting at him.

'Heyup Nodder Jack, are y' noddin' at me.'

'What y' noddin' at Jack.'

'Are y' daft, Nodder Jack. See, 'es nodding' 'is head. He agrees wi' me. Y'r daft then Nodder Jack.'

'Are y' lookin' for sixpence on t' floor Jack.'

'What y' noddin' at then, Nodder Jack.'

Sometimes Nodder would flail his arms at them, mumbling 'Young buggers, young buggers.'

They left him as he turned into the Working Men's Club.

He bought half a pint of mild at the long bar and carried it to a table, holding it carefully. He drank in little sips, holding his head down to the rim and gripping the glass tightly in both hands.

The small windows by the door were leaded and the nearly empty room was criss-crossed by deep shadow and bright sunlight. The click of dominoes came from a table near the far end of the bar. The four men played silently until one of them looked up, saw Nodder and waved a salute.

'A funny thing, there's Nodder's head shakin' like that and I've yet to see him spill a drop o' beer.'

'Ah like watchin' Percy Bishop tryin' to shave 'im. He has to catch 'im on t' recoil an' whip a bit off each time.'

'You were there when he started noddin', weren't you Les.' Les Buckley stared at the dominoes in the palm of his hand and knocked to pass.

'Aye. That were funny an'all. Can't 'ave bin more than thirty yards from t' pit bottom and half the bloody roof come in. Nodder was standin' about waitin' to tram some tubs and he were right under it. All small stuff. It were like he were standin' under a waterfall. He just vanishes under this bloody great pile o' muck. It left a hole in the roof you could put a church into. Anyway, we're all runnin' about shoutin' and Sugden teks charge, he were pit bottom deputy then.'

'Staffordshire chap warn't he.'

'That's 'im. Not long after he took a shop in Donny, up by Waterdale.'

'He's still theer. Little sweets and tobacco shop. Does ıeight well I should think, that close to t' bus station.'

'Anyway, Suggy climbs up onto this fuckin' great heap and starts tellin' us all to dig 'ere and clear away there an'all of a sudden the muck right under his feet starts heavin' up an' he's nearly thrown off balance. An' it were Nodder, face down. Suggy were standin' on top of him. Anyway, we fished 'im out and his nose an' mouth were all crammed up wi' muck. We cleaned him up a bit but most of us thought he were dead, there was no sign o' breathin'. Suggy won't 'ave it he's dead and he starts givin' him aıtificial respiration. He were at it a long time and then Nodder starts breathin' again and shekkin' his head an' it's bin shekkin' ever since.'

'Din't they give 'im a job sweepin' up pit bottom after that.'

'Aye, but e' were not a lot o' use at it an' he retired on his compensation.'

'His daughter teks care of him, dun't she.'

'Jenny.'

'I thought she were goin' t' marry Scott's lad.'

'She were. They were courtin' for years but she packed him in to tek care of Nodder.'

The game blocked on sixes at both ends and the men counted up their spots.

'Thy turn Les.'

Buckley leaned across and placed the glasses on the bar, rapped for the barman and ordered the next round of beer. When it was drawn he stood up and fetched it to the table. He started to pay the barman and stopped for a moment.

'Pull us a pint o' mild.'

He carried it across to Nodder Jack and put it by him.

'Wrap yourself round that lad.'

Nodder muttered his thanks and Buckley went back to his table. The dominoes had been pudding shuffled and the men drew for the next game.

There was no talkin in the classroom but it was filled with small sounds, the scratch of pen nibs, the creaking of forms, the scuffing of feet, the heavy mouth breathing of children. It was an art lesson and each child leaned over a sheet of squared graph paper. On the board was a pattern and each child copied this pattern on to the graph paper by inking in some of the squares. They repeated the pattern over and over again until the graph paper was filled. Most children made blots with the coarse powdered ink and then filled in more squares round the blot to cover it or they miscopied the pattern and the design grew more and more irregular as their paper was filled.

Miss Bennett sat behind her desk on the raised platform at the front of the classroom. She was a big woman with heavy, hanging breasts and a yellowing, puffy face. Her hair was pulled tight to her head in a bun and she wore a thick, brown, tweed jacket and skirt. Sometimes she would come from behind her desk and walk slowly up and down between the five rows of desks, cuffing any child whose paper was messy or who she saw was staring out of the window.

When she heard the tapping on the classroom door she leaned forward to look round the end of the blackboard. The tapping went on and finally she stood up and left the classroom, closing the door behind her. She faced the dark-haired young woman who had stepped farther back into the corridor when Miss Bennett opened the door. The teacher stared at her and said 'Yes.' The young woman put her hands into the pockets of her raincoat and held it close to her.

'I've come about George Carver.'

'Well.'

Miss Bennett looked back through the glass panes in the door, into the classroom, then faced the young woman again.

'I'm Peggy Carver.'

'What about him.'

'I want to know why you hit him.'

Miss Bennett buttoned her jacket.

'What is it to do with you.'

'I'm his sister.'

'If you want to say something you make an appointment with the headmaster.'

'Why did you hit him so hard.'

Miss Bennett looked back into the classroom again and said 'There's a lesson going on.'

'You cut him at the back of his ear. He says you hit him with a ruler.'

'I punish him often. He's lazy and he's insolent.'

'He's got swollen glands. He shouldn't be hit like that.'

Miss Bennett turned and put her hand on the knob of the classroom door. Peggy Carver spoke more quickly.

'I haven't finished yet. There was no need to hit 'im like that. He's only a child.'

Miss Bennett turned round again.

'I refuse to talk to you.'

'Well you're goin' to. The other teachers just cane him on his hand or smack his behind. They don't cut 'im like you did.'

'I will not be accused.'

'You must be a bad teacher to do that.'

'Don't you talk to me about bad teachers. You know nothing about teaching. You are ignorant.'

'And you're vicious.'

Miss Bennett's hands began to tremble. She took a step nearer the young woman.

'You get out of this building. Now.'

'He's got swollen glands. We've been to the doctor with them.'

'Get out.'

'You could 'ave hurt him badly.'

'If you don't leave immediately I shall fetch the headmaster.'

'You're just a bully. He's only eight.'

'Don't you talk to me. Don't you talk to me. You are to leave. Go on.'

The teacher tried to say more but was breathless. She turned and went back into the classroom and leaned with her back against the door, her whole body shaking. The whispering of the children stopped immediately. She walked slowly back to her desk and sat down. She held her hands in front of her, resting on the desk, tightly clasped.

Peggy Carver stood outside the door for a while, then walked back down the corridor, turned past the cloakroom and went out into the school yard. She kicked at a stone and walked quickly round the corner towards the girls' end of the school and the gate. Halfway to the gate she stopped and ran both her hands through her hair. She stood for several minutes, turned and ran back again to Miss Bennett's classroom. She banged the door open, walked across to the desk and hit the teacher sharply across the face. Miss Bennett tried to grab hold of her hand but she stepped backwards and shouted 'Bully.' The teacher stumbled from behind the desk and tried to slap the younger woman who dodged to one side and hit her in the breast. Miss Bennett screeched and the children began shouting and standing up at their desks. Miss Bennett blundered after Peggy Carver trying to take hold of her. Peggy Carver skipped away slapping her hands down. An elderly man ran into the classroom and began shouting 'Quiet, be quiet' at the children. Miss Bennett missed her footing on the platform and fell heavily between the desks. She lay there sobbing and Peggy Carver ran out of the classroom. The elderly man kept shouting 'quiet, be quiet, this minute, all of you.'

'Mester Chard.'

The lad's voice was pitched high and he waited a while between each call.

'Mester Chard.'

Sam woke up and looked round the room. In the clear moonlight he could see the square chest of drawers, the brightly coloured painting of a cottage on the wall, his pit clothes over the back of a chair, his good suit hanging from the door hook. He sat slowly upright.

'Mester Chard.'

He swung his feet out onto the cold lino and sat for a moment. He walked across the bedroom, pushed up the lower window and leaned out.

'Nadden.'

'Mester Chard. Mester Davis sent me. The plane deputy. He says y'r to come. The fire's worse on Old Sevens. I've been to your gang and you're all to meet him at Sevens return and he says y'r all to come straight away. I've told Mester Camm an' Mester Walters an' Mester Peter Tate an' Mester Reg Tate. Mester Davis says as he'll—'

'Hoddup a minute.'

The lad was silent for a moment.

'Mester Chard, Mester Davis said it was a lot worse and I was to tell your men to meet him an' he—'

'Hoddup.'

The lad's voice had risen almost to a squeak. Sam leaned further out of the window, his arms resting on the sill.

'It's Arnie Widowson's boy, isn't it.'

'Yes, Mester Chard.'

'Did Davis say anything about fire money.'

'No, Mester Chard. He just said to fetch you.'

'Was Patricks there, the undermanager.'

'He was at first but he went off. I think he went to t' West district. Mester Davis fetched me from the pipe fitters to tell me to fetch you.'

A dog in the next yard began yapping. The lad shuffled his feet and stared up at the window.

'Dost know George Absalom's house. Union secerterry.'

'No, Mester Chard.'

'There's a street of back-to-backs facing Addick railway station, it's called Jupiter Street. Well, he lives at the next to t'end house, at the far end, on the side facing the station. You know where I mean.'

'At the end by the mill, Mester Chard.'

'Reight. Now go to his house and tell him to meet me at pit gates. Say there's a gobfire and I want to talk to him about fire money. Now run all the way.'

The lad put his cap on and then took it off again.

'Mester Davis only said I was to fetch you and Mester Camm an' Mester Walters and the two Mester Tates, Mester Chard.'

'Aye, well tha'll do this little errand for me. Now you know where to go.'

'Last but one facing Addick railway station at mill end.'

'And run all the way.'

The lad walked to the corner of the house and stood there.

'Off you go then. Tell 'im I'll see him at pit gates.'

The lad turned by the fence that ran alongside the house and Sam heard the gate swing to and the rattle of clogs going away down the hill.

George Absalom trotted through the allotments behind his house and clattered over the wooden mill bridge. He kept to his pace across the fields behind the Reform Club and only slowed to a walk when the moon clouded over as he crossed the lower end of the pit tip. He ran once more between the wages office and the lamp cabin and reached the pit gates at the same time as Sam Chard. He was breathing hoarsely and spat noisily into the gutter.

'Hast a fag, Sam. Ah left mine on t' mantelshelf.'

'Just the one.'

Sam took a match and a single cigarette from the top pocket of his pit jacket and split it between them. Absalom sucked deeply on the half-cigarette and spat again.

'What's this about fire money then.'

'Old Sevens' fire's hottin' up. They want my gang to close down the return road and block the air off. I could tell Davis we'll not tackle it unless they agree to your fire money rates, for this job and any more after this.'

Absalom said nothing for a while, walking jerkily to and fro across the open pit gates.

'Davis can't agree to that, he's only main plane man.'

'No. But Patricks can and he's down pit now.'

Absalom rubbed his face harshly with both hands and tapped Sam on the chest.

'He'd never fuckin' wear it.'

'He's not got a lot o' choice. If the gobfire keeps going he'll 'ave to close the whole soddin' district down and that'll still not be the finish of it.'

'He'll get somebody else.'

'There's nobbut a few bank holiday maintenance men down the pit. And if he sends for Cherry's men or some other gang you can turn 'em back at the gate. Tell 'em it's in dispute.'

Absalom did a little shuffle and clasped his hands behind his head.

'Christmas fuckin' awake. I've had that many set to's with Patricks and that big soft manager about fire rates.'

'You want to try it then.'

'If Patricks does agree he'll mark you for it, Sam. He'll knacker you next chance he gets. He's a bad bugger.' He jigged into another little dance and stared at the shop that stood by itself, across from the pit gates. 'Fuckin' hell. I wish I had some gafs. I could knock old bloody Talbot up and get some. Did you know Talbot used to be a burglar.' He hoisted himself on to the wall and sat swinging his legs. 'All reight then. I'll turn anybody back if they send out. An' you tell Patricks we want Staveley rates. That'll stop arguin' about what he's agreein' to.'

Sam had started across the pit yard when Absalom called after him.

'I were thinkin' you were goin' into the lion's den, Sam, but it's more like them chaps as went into the fiery furnace, in't it, Shadrach an' 'is mates.'

'You can tell you're a Baptist, George, Anyroad, I don't suppose them fuckers got fire money either.'

He drew his lamp and found his men waiting by the shaft side. The onsetter reached for his bell to signal men riding but Sam stopped him and took the men back out on to the gantry.

'I've had a talk with the union secerterry. I want to tell Patricks we'll not tek this one on unless fire money is agreed to, for good.'

Herbert Walters sighed and seated himself on the gantry rail, swinging his Dudley by its rope.

'Sod it Sam. You must like trouble.'

The onsetter came out on to the gantry and stared at them.

'Ah've got Davis on t' phone, shittin' his pants. He says what's keepin' y' and what tools d'y' want.'

'Tell him we're comin' an' I want picks, two Sylvesters, ring spanners, pipin' and spare full Dudleys. An' I want extra brattice cloths across the intake.'

The onsetter walked back to his phone.

'It'd want a proper meeting wi' union and manager to agree fire money.'

'If Patricks agrees it's on, it'll be on.'

'What if they get another gang to do it.'

'Absalom's sitting by the gate to stop anybody taking us place.'

'What if Patricks'll not sit still for it. What d'y' do then Sam, let the fuckin' pit burn up.'

'It'll not come to that.'

'It fuckin' hell as like. Mines inspector'll close it for a start if that fire's not out sharpish.'

The talk wrangled on with the men walking restlessly up and down the gantry, their shadows looming hugely on the yard below.

'Let's find out where we stand. Jack.'

Sam looked at Jack Camn, who was carefully shredding chewing tobacco into the palm of his hand.

'Ah'm with you. Bi reights we should 'ave fire money. An' Patricks can fuck 'isself, as far as I'm concerned.'

Sam turned towards Peter and Reg Tate. Peter nodded and Reg hesitated and then muttered 'All reight.'

Herbert Walters was half-turned away from the group.

'You've not left us a lot of fuckin' choice, Sam, fixin' it up with Absalom first.'

'Well, till he agreed there was no point in raisin' it.'

'You could 'ave done it t'other bloody way round.'

'Ah'm sorry about that.'

'You're not fuckin' sorry. You just thought you'd be clever.'

Sam went over and stood closer to him.

'Well it's a tricky thing.'

'I joined this gang to graft and mek a bit o' brass, not play fuckin' politics.'

Nothing was said for a while.

'I'm sayin' nowt. You're the one with the gift o' the gab. You can do all the talkin'. You've got enough mouth.'

Sam led the way back to the shaft side.

The paddy train rattled and bounced along the intake airway. The men sat one to each of the low benches, arms on knees, heads bowed, swaying to the curve of the road. The old man who conducted the train sat on the first bench, flashing his light along the sides and roof of the tunnel, watching for falls of rock or jutting props, his rheumy eyes half-closed against the swirls of dust. He breathed heavily, jaws hanging slackly, dribbles of spit running from the corner of his mouth. As the air doors at the road end came in sight he took the T-shaped, metal bar from between his feet and slid it along the overhead signalling wires. The repeat bell rang clearly and the paddy train came slowly to a halt. Sam leaned forward and tapped the old man on the shoulder.

'Tommy, you go back to't' pit bottom and wait, you might have to pick somebody up.'

The old man climbed stiffly from his bench and walked to the other end of the train. The men stood by the air doors and watched his lamp swing about as he climbed on to the front seat. They heard the clearly spaced double ring. The rope that pulled the paddy tightened, surged, went slack again for a moment and then pulled the train smoothly away.

Sam lifted the rubber flap in the middle of the first airdoor and Walters heaved the door open. They worked their way through the second and third doors and came out on to the return airway.

Suddenly the air seemed to be burning and their skins prickled with the heat. Camn uncorked his Dudley and took a long swallow.

'We should 'ave brought us taters and we could have roasted 'em in their jackets.'

They found Davis a hundred yards further into the pit, sitting on a pile of stone dust bags, just short of where Old Sevens return branched off. He stood up as they reached him. Sam nodded to him.

'Tha's got a bonnie one 'ere, James.'

Davis waved his arms about. His shirt was unbuttoned and flapping out of his trousers and his voice wheezed.

'I've put more fuckin' sand on that face than they've got on Blackpool beach an' it's still hotter than the hob of hell.' He walked to the corner of the return and pointed to a pile of tools. 'I've got what you asked for and there's some cardox shells in case you want to fire a shot or two.'

'I'll not bother wi' that.'

Like the rest of the men Sam had uncorked his Dudley and was taking small sips of water.

Davis spoke hoarsely. 'If you can get that far in there's an old lip of Conky Smith's, near the face, with a lot of weight on it. You should be able to fetch it down without too much trouble. Once you've got the road blocked off, leave it alone. We'll go round and tackle it from the intake end. I'll stay by the phone in case you want owt.'

Davis looked round the five men.

'Are y' right.'

Sam took another sip of water.

'Bar agreein' fire money we are.'

Davis was silent for a while.

'What the fuck are you talkin' about, Sam.'

'Ah'm talkin' about agreein' Staveley rates for workin' where there's fire.'

'How the hell. What about Staveley rates.'

'It's all down on paper. Absalom's put it forrard often enough.'

'Fuckin' arseholes. We can't stand here negotiatin' bloody rates. Ah've got a gob goin' like bloody bonfire night and you want to talk about bloody rates.'

'That's the general idea.'

'Don't be daft, Sam. It's not the bloody time.'

'Seems a reight grand time to me.'

Davis took his shirt off and wiped his face with it.

'Sam lad, I'm not the fuckin' management. I can't agree owt.'

'No but Patricks can.'

'He's not 'ere.'

'Aye, but he is down pit. West district, last I heard.'

Davis walked over to the stone dust bags and sat down. His face was dry and shining in the heat and his voice cracked as he talked, half to himself.

'It's a grand job this is. If the fuckin' bosses are not bootin' your arse, the bloody colliers are. I shoulda been a fuckin' shop-keeper like mi faither. Staveley soddin' rates. Just feel this soddin' heat.'

He muttered on till Sam broke in.

'Are you goin' to fetch Patricks then.'

Davis rose to his feet and came and thrust his face close to Sam's.

'Sam, be a bit decent. Do this job now and I'll go with you to see Patricks in the morning. I'm in your favour an' I'll tell him so. It's a promise. Come on lad. I'm bein' straight with you.'

'I can't do that, James. You'd best get Patricks here.'

Davis went and sat on the stone bags again.

'You're right fuckers you are. I've a good mind to go and close the bloody road off by miself. Show you fuckin' lot. I've been in this soddin' place a week. I'm dried up. I should think it's burnt half mi insides out bi now. I can't breathe without the bugger 'urtin'.'

He sat a while longer then stood up and walked to the phone. The five men spaced themselves along the walls and sat down, legs sprawled out into the roadway. The sweat was pumping steadily away from them. They could hear the sound of Davis' voice but not what he was saying. He was several minutes at the phone and then came back and perched himself silently on the bags of stone dust.

They heard the distant thump of the air-door and saw the lamp bobbing down the roadway as Patricks walked towards them. He was a tall, well-built man, square chested and heavy shouldered. He moved and spoke slowly. Reaching upwards with both arms he was tall enough to grip the arched ring above him and lean his weight on it. Already he was breathing more heavily in the simmering air of the return.

'Chard.'

'Mester Patricks.'

'We'll talk about fire money later. For now I want that gobfire sealed off.'

'It has to be settled now, Mester Patricks.'

Patricks looked at each of the men in turn.

'Are the rest of you in on this.'

Jack Camn nodded his head several times and said 'That's right, that's right.'

The others said nothing.

'Right. Well you can go back up pit, check your lamps and fuck off home. I've sent out for Cherry's gang. They'll be down shortly to see to this.'

'Not very likely, Mester Patricks. George Absalom's waiting by the gate and he'll turn 'em back. It's a union matter.'

Patricks was silent for a while, then he turned towards Davis.

'I'll borrow your Dudley, James.'

Davis hurriedly uncorked it and passed it to him. Patricks took a long swallow.

'You fancy your chances at blackmail then, Sam Chard.'

Sam moved restlessly from sitting to squatting on his heels.

'What rates are you asking for.'

'Staveley.'

'Mester Absalom's old sweet song.' He passed the Dudley back to Davis and pinched his nose with his thumb and forefinger. 'Very well then, it's agreed. But I'll bear in mind tonight's little effort. Now if you've completed your parlimentary business Mester Chard, I'd be obliged if you'd attend to a bit o' pitwork.'

The men climbed awkwardly to their feet and Patricks walked away up the plane. Sam turned to Davis who had not moved.

'How long's Conky's lip been stood.'

'More than a month, I've had him and his mate on trackin'.'

'An' it's up near the face.'

'Very close. It's the third rip in.'

The men shared the tools between them and walked into the return road towards the face. Davis leaned back against the wall and closed his eyes.

As they moved nearer the face the air became hotter. They had dried out of liquid and only when a man drank from his Dudley would a flush of sweat follow a little later. By the time they were halfway to the face they were breathing in short, harsh gasps and looking towards Sam to see if he intended to go further in. Jack Camn dropped his tools and put his arm across his mouth. His eyes were screwed up as if he were going to cry and he turned and started back down the roadway. Sam turned him round, put his tools back in his hands and pushed him gently forward.

'Nearly to it lad.'

They moved slowly, leaning forward like men in a high wind. By the time they reached the lower section of roof which Smith and his mate had been ripping, the roadway had become furnace-like. Peter Tate dropped to his knees swearing in a breathy whisper, 'Bugger and sod, bugger and sod' over and over. Sam pulled him upright and led him and his brother under the lip. His voice was a croaking shout.

'Get the Sylvester on to this first ring and hook it to the track.' He set Walters and Jack Camn to hooking up a Sylvester to the other leg of the steel ring that supported the roof. 'I'll undo the fishplates.'

They groped feverishly about and stopped from time to time to drink water or pour it on head and chest. Sam climbed up on the scaffolding set at the lip and began to undo the bolts that held the two halves of the ring together. The weight had flattened the top of the ring and canted the fishplate, jamming the bolts. He fitted a length of hollow metal pipe to the handle of the ring spanner to make a lever. One by one he wrenched the bolts loose. When he came down again the Sylvesters had been hooked on and he set Camm and Peter Tate to work the lever arms back and forth. With Walters and Reg Tate he began pulling the middle scaffolding planks out from under the lip and dropping them to the roadway. The ratchets of the Sylvesters clicked quickly at first, then more slowly as the chains began to pull hard on the supporting arch.

There was a creaking of side timbers as the feet of the arch were pulled slowly backward and the centre joint dragged free. Small falls of roof began as the lip lost its support. Sam waited for a bout of coughing to end and then spoke to Walters.

'Herbert, we'll stand one on either side of the scaffolding and work it with the pick. As soon as it starts coming down steady we'll get back.'

Walters nodded and stood staring dazedly at the ground for a moment before he searched for a pick and climbed on the planking at the side of the lip. Reg Tate was under the lip, crouched over, trying to unfasten the Sylvester chain from the leg of the ring. Sam pulled him away.

'Leave the fucker. We can't stand it a lot longer.'

Camm and the Tate brothers retreated down the roadway and watched the two men swinging their picks at the centre of the lip. The roar of falling rock grew louder and the two men were soon shrouded in thick clouds of choking dust. The roar grew to a thunder as more of the roof caved in and the two men came blundering back down the roadway, lamps swinging wildly from their belts.

The thunder of the collapsing lip stopped as the roadway was wholly blocked and there was only the chatter of small stones sliding down the face of the fall.

In spite of the dust that seethed along the tunnel it was suddenly cooler.

A high stone wall ran down the north slope of the hill, shielding the small estate from the road. It was pierced by a wide, rising gate, opening on to a gravelled drive which led through a patchwork of spruce and beech to a Georgian house, fronted by a square, trimmed lawn. The house was made lopsided by a large conservatory, stable and garage that had been built on one end. A crowd of mothers and their children, with a few husbands, stood stiffly on the drive, at the edge of the lawn, looking towards the house.

Inside the house Captain Dorman-Davis walked restlessly up and down the wide corridor that curved from the front door round to the lounge. He examined the portraits lining the walls and carefully straightened one from time to time. They were mostly oil paintings of men in military uniform. His wife smiled at him as she came down the staircase and hurried towards the kitchen at the back of the house. He put out his arm and stopped her.

'We should have taken this up,' he said, pointing to the thick Brussels carpet that ran nearly the full width of the corridor, 'they'll trample on it.'

His wife patted his arm.

'No dear, I plan to let them in through the French windows.'

'Oh. I thought they could see the portraits.'

'We can bring them in this way if you like dear.'

Captain Dorman-Davis looked at the portraits, tugged at his moustache, clasped his hands behind his back and looked at the carpet.

'P'raps not. Let 'em straight into the lounge.'

His wife hurried to the kitchen where her daughter, the cook and the maid had just finished laying out crockery and food. She examined the rows of teacups, sugar bowls, milk jugs, plates of triangular ham sandwiches with the crusts cut off, assorted buns and fruit cake. She checked the heavy iron kettles standing on the gas stove and the large brown teapots on the side table. She clasped her hands and turned to the two older women.

'There, what a fine sight. It all looks very good. Now then. Doris, you and Missis Dodd can go into the lounge now and listen to the concert. Please sit near the door so you can slip back and make the tea when I give you the signal.'

The two women bobbed, murmured 'Thank'y' mum' and left the kitchen. Missis Dorman-Davis faced her daughter who was sitting on a Welsh dresser swinging her legs.

'And you'll help serve the tea, won't you Elizabeth.'

'I suppose so. I don't see why we have to do this at all.'

Missis Dorman-Davis stared at the tea plates for a moment then fetched a pile of paper serviettes from the pantry and began laying them out, one to each plate.

'It's our contribution to the life of the village, dear.'

'Oh, Mummy. They're miners not our local peasants. Anyway, it's just as boring for them as it is for us.'

'Nonsence, dear. People love hearing their children play the piano. It makes them very proud. And Mister Elliott always gets his pupils up to such a high standard.'

'Most of them can't play for toffee.'

Captain Dorman-Davis came into the kitchen and said 'Any chance of a cupper before the off.' His wife shook her head.

'Not enough time dear.'

Elizabeth ran her fingers through her thick blonde hair and pouted.

'Daddy, don't you think this is all jolly silly.'

Her father shrugged his shoulders.

'You must ask your mother about that dear. It's her jamboree.'

'It's the men I feel most sorry for. They always look so terribly uncomfortable.'

'Funny thing about miners. In the war, fine soldiers. Marvelleous for trenching, sapping, all that sort of thing. Then the damn government took 'em away from us. Said they were needed for the mines. As if we didn't need 'em.'

'Why don't the high and mighty Holdsworths do this sort of thing. At least they own the bloomin' pits. Awfully swell Jiminy Holdsworth doesn't have to play serving tea. Too busy flying his blessed aeroplane.'

Her mother took one last look round and murmured 'I'm sure you'll really enjoy it dear.'

She went towards the lounge, followed by her husband and daughter. At the door to the lounge Captain Dorman-Davis held her arm and said 'Did you get all the bric-a-brac moved out.'

His wife said 'Yes dear, just a little left for ornament and that's all behind the piano.'

Her husband muttered 'I'm never sure all this does the piano any good either' and they went through into the lounge.

Missis Dorman-Davis took a long look at the large, sunlit lounge. The polished, rosewood grand piano stood near the door and the high ceilinged room was filled with upholstered armchairs, bentwoods, hall benches and folding garden chairs, laid out in rows. She nodded to the maid and cook who were sitting by the door and went across to the French windows. Through them she could see the crowd standing at the house end of the drive. She unlocked and opened the French windows and waved her arms. The crowd moved slowly across the patch of lawn and filed into the lounge. They moved carefully, hardly speaking and it took them a long time to be seated. Missis Dorman-Davis greeted the music teacher and took him across to the front of the room talking rapidly. Captain Dorman-Davis took a postcard from his pocket, put on a pair of steel rimmed spectacles and stared intently at it. When everyone had settled down he looked towards his wife. She nodded and he began to speak loudly, rushing jerkily through each sentence and pausing lengthily between sentences.

'Ladies and Gentlemen, it gives me and Missis Dorman-Davis and our daughter great pleasure to welcome all of you to our house this afternoon. This, as you all know, is the occasion of our twice yearly, musical soirée. That is to say, it would be if it were evening. However, afternoon, or any time, is a good time for fine music. All of the music will, as usual, be played by the pupils of Mister Elliott and we can rest assured that the pieces have been specially prepared, and doubtless endlessly practised, for our delight on this occasion. There will be an interval in which, as always, tea will be served. And I am sure that we are all grateful for the efforts of my wife and daughter and their staff in this regard. Let me say that, on these occasions, I am always absolutely bowled over, so to speak, by the talent which abounds, in our village. Let me say finally, that you are all of you most welcome, as guests in our house and I trust you will enjoy the occasion. So now I call upon Mister Elliott to introduce to you his first young pupil, who is to go, over the top, as it were.' Captain Dorman-Davis sat down and there was a long period of clapping.

People coughed and wriggled while Elliott led forward a boy and seated him on the piano stool. The boy was wearing new green velvet shorts and a white blouse. His hair was heavily brilliantined into ledges. The music teacher leaned over and whispered to him.

'Now you know you can play it well. You've done it often enough. But you know if you get the first chord wrong you do it badly. So set your fingers over the keys ready. Alright.'

The boy nodded and splayed his fingers over the keys. Elliott stood up and put his hand on the boy's shoulder. He spoke slowly.

'Ladies and gentlemen. Our first item in this afternoon's concert will be played by Desmond Cooper who is nine years old and has been studying the piano for three years. He has chosen to play 'The Gavotte' from Mignon by the nineteenth-century French composer Ambroise Thomas.'

Elliot pulled a chair close to the boy at the piano and sat down. The boy mis-hit the opening chord and then stumbled through the following bars, striking the notes more fiercely as he went on, so that the sound became harsher and more jangled. Elliott grabbed the boy's arms and held them tightly for a few seconds, then let go. The room was quite still. The boy wiped his hands on his trousers and shuffled himself on the stool. He licked his lips, put his fingers loosely on the keys of the first chord and stared at the plaster moulded cherubs that decorated the wall lamp opposite him. He struck the chord truly and flowed quickly into the piece. The ringing tones of the grand piano filled the room.

The back tub of a full run of six had sided off the bank. The two men tried a straight lift back.

'Nadden. Up y' bugger. Let's have 'im.'

Their lift stopped just short of the bank ledge.

'Y' sod. Who's sittin' on this bugger beside me.'

'Hoddup, we'll 'ave to tip some coal out.'

'We'd best get a shovel then. There's one down at engine room.'

'We look fuckin' well arguin' wi' this bugger in us arms. Tip it o'er.'

They propped one pair of wheels against the bank and tipped the tub. Coal splashed on the lower track. They easily swung the half empty tub back on the upper track and coupled it to its run. One of the men said 'I'll get the shovel' and walked off up the drift.

The other man stretched himself, yawned, sat on the bank ledge and took a piece of Lady twist from his waistcoat pocket. He slipped it under his bottom lip and began sucking it. The hauler was stopped on his signal and the only sound was a faint shouting of somebody at the far end of the drift.

The mice ran into the pool of light from the man's lamp and then began scuttering back and forth. The crippled mouse they were hunting stayed close to the drift wall, its damaged leg crooked against its body, moving in odd jumps. Time and again one of the mice ran forward from the pack and bit the cripple whose dust grey coat was shining with blood.

The man spat a stream of tobacco juice into the pack and they scattered into the darkness.

The man leaned back against the tub and half-dozed.

Soon there was a faint clatter of clogs as his mate crossed a plated section of track and the rounded white glow of his lamp floated into sight round the drift bend.

'Give hod.'

The man handed over the shovel he had brought and stood to one side while the spilled coal was swung high and back into the tub.

'Right, shall I ring the bugger off.'

The man with the shovel took a watch from his waistcoat pocket, opened the covering case and looked closely at the face.

'Not worth it. Nigh on snaptime.'

'We'll tek the shovel back and have snap by t'engine.'

In the gathering darkness Cynthia found it harder to keep her footing as she scrambled up the side of the pit tip. Sam held her hand and hauled her along so fiercely that she stumbled across the ridges of hardened slag, gasping and spluttering. She pulled her hand free and stopped, leaning over, hands on thighs. Her long hair hung forward over her face and she shook with coughing, trying to catch her breath. Sam squatted and looked down at her. She called out to him.

'Damn, damn.'

Sam laughed.

'Such language. You mek me blush Cynthia Henshaw.'

'It's stupid. What are we climbing up here for.'

'Why, young lady. When I heard you'd lived in this village all your life and niver climbed pit tip.'

'What's so special about it. It's just a dirty great pile of muck.'

'Never. Think on it. In winter, wi' snow on it, it's finer than the Swiss Alps. It's best playground ever invented for kids. When we're on strike we mine it for free coal. An' from top you'll see a view like a picture postcard.'

'I'm surprised you haven't had holiday chalets built up here an' rented 'em out.'

'Now there's a clever idea. Come on lass.'

He held out his hand. She took it and they climbed slowly. As they neared the top they could hear the wind blowing softly and the creaking and squeaking of the steel rope as it travelled along the pylons. At the top he put his arms round her waist and steadied her where the sides of the tip had built up, leaving a hollow trench in between. He lowered Cynthia into a trench and climbed in after her. He led her along to a point where the raised side had broken away and slipped off his overcoat. Sitting on it they looked down on the village. She patted his coat and said 'Just like Sir Walter Raleigh.'

'Who.'

'You've heard of him.'

'Course I have. His mother used to do our washin'. That was afore he invented the bicycle.'

She tittered and Sam said 'What do you think of it.'

In the darkness the street lamps made looping necklaces of light around the village.

'It is pretty.'

'Best view there is of the place.'

She pointed to the red neon sign away to the south.

'Empire picture house. And what's that glow over there.'

'That's the gas flare they burn off at Asky pit.'

'What are the dark patches at the top of the village.'

'It's them houses near Laurel Terrace. The ones that are built in squares with a green in the middle.'

'Where's my house.'

'You see the nearest row of lamps. Well just behind there's a curved row.'

'Yes.'

'Count four from the right 'and end and Henshaw Mansions is just behind it.'

'And your house.'

'That short row running straight up from us. Me and the widow Jones is halfway along.'

She was silent for a while and he put his arm round her and they kissed. She put her face against his and then leaned back against the side of the hollow. Sam whistled a few bars of 'Me and My Shadow.'

'When I was a lad and the street lamps were on gas I used to come up here and I could follow just where the lighter 'ad got to as he put each lamp on in turn.'

Cynthia shivered and pressed against him. 'It's funny, from up here at night it all looks clean and pretty.' She put her hand in his and spoke quietly so that Sam leaned towards her. 'When I was little my father bought me a painting from Donny for my bed-room. It was quite a big one and it showed a land with waterfalls and clumps of trees and in between there were marble buildings with columns and towers, always on the top of a hill. And I used to lie for hours in bed looking at it. I used to think that that was where I would go to live.'

'Where was it.'

'I don't know. I don't think it was anywhere.'

'A made up place.'

'Mmm. I was quite dippy about it.'

'Barnsley Town Hall with nobs on.'

She laughed and punched him on the chest.

'You're tryin' to spoil it for me.'

'No love, you'd fit nicely into a place like that.'

'But you're happy where you are.'

'It's fair enough. I've always fancied tekkin' some fairy lights down t' pit. Beautify the place a bit.'

She kissed him and said 'What are you going to do Sam. In the long run.'

Sam grinned.

'Go there and back to see how far it is.'

'Seriously.'

'Go to t' back o' Brough's in an orange box.'

'Sam.'

'Alreight. I'll become a big union man and then go into parliament. How about that.'

'That would be fine if you were serious. You could do it.'

'Steady on love.'

'No, I won't steady on. You tell me why it has to be a joke.'

'Gentle Jesus.'

Sam sighed and picked up a stone and tossed it out of the hollow. It rattled away down the side of the tip.

'For that sort o' thing pet, you have to be solemn. It's like keepin' your face straight when you fart in company so nobody thinks it's you. You've got. You've got to think you're God's gift to the workers. Now can you seriously see me gabbin' on about put your faith in me.'

'You certainly think you're God's gift.'

'I think you're lovely.'

'O Sam. You make me cross.'

'Ah'm sorry.'

'You look it.'

'No, I am, honest.'

'Well at least. At least why don't you think about settin' up on your own instead of working for somebody else all your life.'

'You're right. I'll start up a pit of mi own in our back garden.'

'Sam. Think about it.'

'I will. I will think about it. Hard. Word of honour.'

'Come on, let's go down.'

Sam took her hand and said 'Just a minute. I want to show you something.'

'What.'

'You see the lights coming down from the top of the hill. Well if you count six down you come to Jonah Reed's house.'

'Well.'

'Well, it just so happens that his old Mam and Dad are away at Cleethorpes for the week an' Jonah's gone to Donny with the Grange darts team. An' it just so happens he left the house key wi' me to take care of for him.'

'And you think I'm going to go to Jonah Reed's with you and let you work your will on me.'

'Well, it's rightly called William but you can call it Will for short.'

Cynthia cuffed him and they kissed and started off down the side of the tip.

One of the two men carried an electrician's lamp and he shone the beam round the edges of the huge, cast iron, box-shaped casing of the hauler motor. It was snugged down in a pit near the drum that had once carried the steel haulage ropes. The other man spat down on it.

'Why can they not strip the fucker where it is and bring it out in bits.'

'The sod was put in near flush to the sides. They can't get in to it. They're reckonin' on us hoisting it up wi' block an' tackle, restin' girders across the sump and lowerin' the motor on to em'. Then the fitters can get to it and tek it to bits.'

'Who've we got.'

'We've Horace and Davy Thomas and Coxy. He's gone off to fetch the tackle.'

The two men sat on the edge of the hole, where the fencing had been stripped out and talked. A few minutes later Horace Thomas came through the air doors on to the main plane and squatted beside them.

'Where's Davy then.'

'Ah reckon you can count 'im out for this shift, Herbert.'

'For why.'

'Busy like.'

'What's tha mean, busy.'

Horace laughed and said 'By Christ.'

'Ah want to know why I've not got mi full gang.'

'Well, it were like this. You know we moved lodgin's last week.'

Herbert Bailey nodded.

'We moved to Markham Avenue, to Mrs Marshall's, a widder woman. Dost know 'er.'

'Bi sight.'

'She's a sprightly woman, about fifty. Husband was killed at Duncil explosion. Anyroad, I was up first and ready an' waitin' for Davy to get hissen dressed. He's standin' by t' fire warmin' his trousers afore he puts 'em on.'

Horace laughed.

'You see the widder lady comes downstairs and teks a long look at Davy. He's standin' there with his balls hangin' down warmin' his trousers. An' she says "They're hangin' a bit slack Davy. I'll tighten 'em up for you if you like." Well that did it. Ah'm here and Davy's back there havin' his bollocks tightened up for 'im.'

Bailey stood up and put his hands on his hips. 'By the powers, he's tommin' an' we've got this bugger to shift.' Then he grinned and said 'Still, we've only the three tackles so that still leaves us a bloke spare to see what's goin' on.'

'Why not four tackles, one each side.'

'We can't get one on to t' back side, it's too close to the wall.'

'It's not come up square then.'

'If we put the two side chains well to the back it should hang reight.'

'Can we get the hooks under the casing.'

'Aye. It's standing on timbers so there'll be enough play under it.'

The three men talked until Cox came down the plane, carrying three blocks and draped with chains.

'You look like the bloody mayor, festooned with them chains, Coxy.'

Cox dropped the blocks and let the chains slide from his shoulders. Bailey said 'Support girders are down by t' slit turn so we'll bring them up first and get 'em placed ready to slide under.' All four men made two trips to the turn and back to fetch the eight foot girders. They lined them up pointing in towards the pit. Bailey jumped down on to the casing and shone his lamp on the roofing girders.

'Now then. Horace ovver 'ere, Dick this side and Coxy at front. Set your blocks on the roof girders and your hooks under the casin'.'

The chains were half-tightened and moved from side to side until Bailey was satisfied they would pull evenly. He climbed back up on to the roadway and the other three men perched themselves on the sides of the shaft formed by the pit, one arm out to the pulley chains. Bailey crouched and shone his lamp on the casing and said 'Pull steady.' The men pulled on the chains and for a while the casing did not move. The chains tightened and stretched and the roofing girders creaked on their wooden lids as the weight came on them. Then one side of the casing tilted slightly.

'Hodup a minute. Horace you pull on your own. Just a bit. Easy.' Horace Thomas pulled on his chain and his side of the casing came up even. 'Hoddup. Now all three of you. Just a bit at a time.'

Inch by inch the 150-horsepower motor rose. Often Bailey stopped them and had one man pull on his own to bring it level.

Twice they stopped and climbed back into the road and stretched their limbs leaving the motor hanging from the chains.

The huge iron box had been lifted nearly five feet and was close to the level of the roadway when the girder carrying Dick Ward's tackle slipped slightly in its socket in the back wall. There was a clatter of stone falling from the roof on to the metal casing. All three men stopped pulling and Ward said 'Pass thi light up here Herbert.' He took the lamp and shone the beam on the girder, leaning across but staying close to the outer edge of the pit. He looked at it for nearly a minute then said 'Let's get back on the road. This fucker will pull right out in a bit.' They stood well back on the road for several minutes watching the motor hanging on its chains. Suddenly the girder tore loose from its socket in the wall, the casing tilted, then slipped from the hooks and crashed down into the hole, cracking the floor timbers and raising a cloud of dust. The chains jangled madly to and fro and the loose girder lay crosswise with one end resting down into the pit.

Bailey walked across to the hole and shone his lamp into it. He turned and stood looking at the three men.

'Ah fuck the sod. Let's 'ave a bit o' snap. Then we'll start agen.'

The men fetched their jackets, snaptins and Dudleys and climbed up into the driver's space above the old engine and began to eat. Horace Thomas pointed back down to the engine and said 'What silly fucker put it down in a hole like that in the first place.'

'Martin Bainbridge. The old head fitter. Donkey's years ago. I helped dig the fuckin' hole.'

'What were he thinkin' of.'

'Fuck knows. Wanted it tucked out o' t' way, I suppose. It were all'us a bloody pest to the maintenance men, 'avin it hedged in like that.'

'Silly bugger.'

Ward opened one of his sandwiches and spat.

'Bloody jam. Ah keep tellin' our May jam's no good for t' pit. Too bloody sweet.'

'Hang on a bit. Bainbridge. Din't he 'ave a brother 'as went off his head. Jesus Bob.'

Bailey nodded. 'That's reight. Jesus Bob Bainbridge. I were in t' pit the day he blew up his fuckin' face belt motor.'

'What wor that about then.'

'He were always a bit touched. They used to call 'im Jesus Bob 'cos if owt went wrong he'd sit down in t' road and keep sayin' fuckin' Jesus wept, ovver an' ovver again.'

'What did he blow up the motor for.'

'Well, you could see why he got riled. He were deputy on Fours and he had this motor pullin' his face belt that were always brekkin' down. Useless old thing it was. Well every time it breks down Jesus Bob sends for a fitter but while the belt's stood his colliers will never stop shovellin'. So bi the time they'd got the motor fixed, bloody belt'd be laden wi' coal and the motor couldn't get started on pullin' it. Too much dead weight. So Jesus Bob used to 'ave to crawl up and down the face shoutin' at his blokes to shovel it all off the belt so he could get it started.

'It used to tek him hours to get goin' again and this must 'ave 'appened any number of times. Anyroad, this time, when it happens, old Jesus Bob doesn't send for t' fitter. The motor packs in an' he just walks off the face. No fucker could reckon out what he were doin'. He comes back a bit later wi' a Cardox shell. Rams the bugger into the motor, wires it up to his battery box, steps back and fires it. It yanks the bloody middle out o' the motor and there's Jesus Bob walkin' up and down, pleased as Punch, shoutin' "that's fixed it, never 'ave no more trouble with that, I've fixed it." An' he had. So they sacked him an' a while later they took him to t'asylum.'

Cox swilled his mouth out with water and then took a pebble from his waistcoat pocket and began to suck it.

'Mark you. It weren't first daft thing he'd done. I've see him that full o' temper he's tried to bite through a two-inch steel rope.'

'You're kiddin'.'

'Ah'm not. Down on his bloody knees howlin' and bitin' at the rope. Another time. All of a sudden. He drops his trousers and shouts somebody fuck my arse.'

'Anybody tek him up on it.'

'No. There were nearly a fuckin' strike ovver that.'

Bailey put one sandwich back in his tin and said 'Let's go an' look at it.'

The men followed him down on to the roadway and gathered

round the hole, looking down at the hauler motor. Bailey stepped down on to the casing and gazed at the space between it and the right-hand-side wall. He climbed out again.

'Dick, you and Horace get that girder up straight an' just rested in its old slot. Me an' Coxy'll fetch a couple of baulks o' timber and we'll see if we can prop the girder up so it'll tek the weight.'

Ward and Thomas climbed down on to the casing and the other two walked up the roadway.

The two youths and the girl dawdled down Ings Lane, a big Alsatian pup leaping round them and two small boys trailing thirty yards behind. The girl turned and looked back.

'What are they follering us for. Tell em' to leave off.'

The older youth shouted 'Bugger off, you two' and the boys stood still for a while, then began following again. The girl stopped by the gate that opened on to the allotments and swung on it. She said 'Let's go an' look at Aslam's pigs.' The older youth pulled at her arm.

'Come on, Winnie, let's gerron with it.'

'Gerron with what, Shack Boyce.'

'Tha knows what.'

'I don't know owt o' t' sort.'

'Well Ah've got summat special in mind.'

'Like what.'

'I'll tell you when we get down to t' tip.'

The other youth giggled. 'It's reight special, Winnie.'

Winnie Roberts frowned.

'Why does he 'ave to come with us. Ah'm not lettin' him do anythin' Shack.'

'I promise you Geoff's not doin' owt.'

Geoff Cook laughed and slapped his thigh and did a little dance, kicking up the gravel of the lane.

'Then what's he actin' daft for.'

''Cos he is daft. Come on Win, let's go on to t' tip.'

The girl rode the gate wide open and walked on through the allotments.

'I'm going to look at Aslam's pigs.'

The youths followed her. They leaned over the sty fence and watched a litter of Essex saddlebacks rooting about in the shit and the straw. The sow lay asleep.

'He gives 'em a bit of coal to eat, sometimes.'

'Do they eat it.'

'O aye. It's supposed to be good for 'em.'

Boyce looked round then went into the allotment nearest to the sty and pulled up a handful of parsnips. He came back and threw them into the sty and they watched the pigs tumbling over each other's backs as they scrambled for them. They left the allotments by the bottom gate and walked down to the tip-side bank of the dike. As they started up the slope of the tip the girl stopped and faced Boyce.

'He's not goin' to watch.'

'It dun't matter if he watches.'

'It does to me. I don't like it. He watched last time. It's not reight.'

Boyce turned his back on the girl and winked at Cook.

'You wait 'ere then. With the dog. Keep tight 'old of the dog.' He turned to the girl and said 'Come on then, I want to talk to you about summat.' They climbed a little further up the slope and into a sort of tunnel that had been driven into the tip to mine for coal left in the slag. Inside there was sacking and old bits of timber and a wheelless tub on its side. The two small boys stood on the dyke bridge and then edged nearer to the bottom of the tip.

In the drift Shack said 'Tek your knickers off then' and the girl slipped them off and started to lie down on the sacking. Shack took her arm and said 'Just a minute, sit on here.' He pointed to the tub.

The girl sat on it and said 'What for.'

'I want to ask you somethin'.'

'What.'

'You know you said you'd let me do it to you any way I liked.'

Winnie licked her lips and looked at the ground.

'Well.'

'Did you mean it.'

'What do you want.'

'Did you mean it.'

'You have to tell me what you want first.'

'No I don't. Will you promise to do anything I want.'

'I don't know what you mean.'

'Promise.'

Winnie scowled and gave a small breathy laugh.

'You've done it every way there is. Back and front.'

'Promise.'

'Tell me what it is. Whisper it to me.'

She leaned forward and Shack whispered into her ear.

'I want you to do it with the dog.'

For a few seconds the girl sat quite still, then she tried to run past the youth and out of the drift. Shack grabbed her arm and they whirled around as she tried to break loose. Shack shouted 'Geoff, Geoff, gerrup 'ere.' She punched at him with her free arm and her words tumbled out breathlessly.

'I won't, I won't, I won't do it. You filthy bugger. You're rotten. You're filthy. I won't. I won't let you. You mustn't. You mustn't.'

Geoff Cook ran into the drift dragging the dog by its collar and caught hold of the girl behind, his arm across her chest. Shack was shouting at him and at the girl.

'Keep 'old of her. You said I could do owt. You said that. Get 'er ovver to t' tub. I won't 'urt you. Just for a bit. Pull her across the tub.'

They stumbled as the dog tangled itself in their legs. Shack lifted the girl by the ankles and they carried her to the tub and stretched her across it. She bucked and kicked and started to scream and Shack shouted 'Put your 'and ovver her mouth.' Geoff said 'Tek the bloody dog then.' As Shack got hold of the dog's collar Cook slipped his left arm under Winnie's elbows and pinned her half lying across the tub. He covered her mouth with his right hand. She bit his hand and he grasped then squeezed her jaw and cheeks so that she could only make strangled, gurgling sounds. Shack pulled her right ankle outwards, knelt against it with his left knee and pulled her left ankle outwards and pinned it with his right knee. He stayed still for a while, his head bowed, catching his breath and patting the dog. He looked up at Geoff.

''Ave you got her alright.'

'I thought you said she'd most likely be willin'.'

Shack pulled back her skirt and put the middle finger of his left hand gently into her cunt, running it upwards and downwards a few times.

'Is she right.'

'She's juicy enough.'

Shack picked the dog up in his arms and said 'Right then, let the dog see the rabbit.' Winnie began to heave and Geoff leaned his weight forward to hold her still. Shack lowered the dog onto its hind legs, placing them between the girl's. He pulled its front paws forward till it was laying across the girl's chest and held it there by its collar. He slid his right hand under the dog's belly and took hold of its prick, pushing the dog forward with his own body. Winnie moaned and tried to twist to one side. Geoff held her more tightly and said 'Is it doin' owt.' Shack did not answer for a while and then said 'it's not stiff, it won't go in.'

'Toss it off a bit then.'

Shack slowly rubbed the dog's prick and then placed the tip against Winnie's cunt and leaned against the dog to force it in. After a while he leaned back.

'I can get the tip in but nothin' happens. The bloody dog doesn't do owt.'

He let go of the collar and the dog licked the girl's neck.

'Let me try it then.'

'It's a waste of bloody time.'

Shack stood up and the dog slid off Winnie and went and sat down by the opening to the drift. He leaned back against the wall of the drift.

'What we goin' to do then.'

'Lerrer go.'

'Let me feel her a bit first.'

'Just let her go.'

Geoff took his right hand from the girl's mouth and put his finger into her cunt and thrust it roughly in and out. Then he let go of her and stood back.

Winnie sat up and pulled her skirt down and rubbed her arms. She stood up and started to cry. She picked up her knickers and put them on and went and stood outside the opening to the drift. She screamed at Boyce.

'Just you wait Shack Boyce. I'll tell mi father and he'll kill you. You're filthy. You dirty bugger. He'll kill you. He will, he'll kill you.'

Shack grinned at her.

'You don't even dare tell 'im you've been with me or he'll kill you.'

'You pig. You rotten sod. I'm not ever goin' out with you again. You needn't think I am.'

'Please yourself.'

The girl turned and ran down the tip and back up the lane, watched by the two small boys who had come part way up the tip side. Shack and Geoff came out of the drift.

'Tha knows what wor wrong Geoff.'

'What.'

'Bloody dog's too young. It didn't know what to bloody do.'

'It's all reight when you toss it off.'

Shack picked up a piece of slate and threw it at the dog. The dog yelped and ran along the tip side, then sat and waited.

'Will she tell her Dad.'

'She'll not tell anybody.'

'I'll bet she'll not 'ave owt to do with you anymore.'

'Don't you be so sure.'

'What we goin' to do.'

'Let's go along top o' t' tip and down to Carky.'

'Orreight.'

They started to walk up the tip side. Shack stopped and said 'Hey Geoff, you know what we should'a' done.'

'What.'

'We should'a' tried it wi' one of Aslam's pigs.'

Geoff Cook laughed and punched him in the chest and the two

youths started to run to the top of the tip with the Alsatian pup racing round them in wide circles.

One of the two small boys pointed after them and said 'What were they doin' with her.'

'Just fuckin' her.'

'Then why was she mekkin' so much row.'

'I dunno.'

'When we've spied on 'em before she din't mek a row.'

'Well.'

'Let's go bod nestin'.'

They walked down the tip and searched along the hedge that bordered the dike. In a few minutes the smaller of the two found a nest with eggs.

'It's a throstle's.'

'It never is. They're not right colour.'

'They are then.'

'Are you goin' to tek 'em.'

'Just one for blowin'.'

The boy took one egg, plucked a thorn from the hedge and carefully pierced the ends of the egg, a smaller hole at the slimmer end and a larger hole at the base. He blew gently through the smaller hole till the egg was empty, wrapped it in his handkerchief and put it down the front of his shirt. Slowly they worked their way further along the hedge.

The pit yard was crowded with men gossiping in the pale spring sunshine. The pay-line was short but each time it dwindled to one or two, a group of men broke from the crowd and moved to the pay-window. As each miner gave his name and put down his lamp check the old man standing behind the pay-clerk nodded his recognition and the clerk flipped the pages of his pay-book, ticked the entry and counted out the wage. Most of the men put their pay in their pocket and drifted back into the crowd. Sometimes a man would hurry over to the small group of women waiting by the gate and hand over his money to his wife. Now and then a man would dispute the sum he was paid, claiming that not enough overtime or water money had been added or that too much lost tool money had been taken off. If they argued for long they were shifted to the end window to talk to the head clerk.

A few men at the far end of the yard stood in a circle, playing pitch and toss for their odd halfpennies. Just outside the gate an old man played the spoons while the lad with him blew loudly on a mouth organ. Sometimes a miner, leaving the pit yard, would drop a copper into his cap and the old man would break into a stiff clog dance.

The clerk handed Sam Chard his pay and then took a card and a typed note from the back of the book and pushed them across the counter. Sam pocketed his money and then read the note. He stared at the clerk and said 'What's this.'

The clerk spoke quietly. 'It's a dismissal notice.'

'I know that. Why.'

'It's nothin' to do with me. They just put a note against the pay entry and I give the notice out with the money.'

'Then I'll have a word with some fucker it is to do with.'

'You'll have to go to the end window and talk to Mister Scott.'

'Bring 'im down here.'

'He deals with enquiries at the end window.'

'Bring the fat fucker down 'ere or I'll fish you out of your little winder.'

The clerk went away. Sam handed the dismissal notice to the man standing behind him and it was passed down the line. By the time the head clerk came to the window a crowd had gathered round Sam and men were moving from all over the yard towards the pay-office.

The head clerk stooped to peer through the window. Talk in the crowd died down as Sam spoke.

'What's the idea, George.'

'There's no idea about it. You're sacked.'

'Why am I sacked.'

'Tha knows full well we've been layin' two and three men a week off for months. Company policy. We've more men than work.'

'Don't talk fuckin' daft. Tha knows the rule is last in first out. I've bin at this pit seventeen year. Sin' I left school. You'd 'ave to sack 'alf the pit afore you come to me.'

The head clerk fidgeted with the pay-book.

'It's Patricks in't it. Patricks said I was to be sacked.'

'It's a company decision.'

'Company be buggered Fattie Scott. It's Patricks as wants me nobbled.'

'I'm not at liberty to disclose who says what. 'Appen it was felt the pit would be better off without you.'

'Y' mealy mouthed fucker. You'd lick Patricks' arsehole if he told you to.'

The men nearest Sam began shouting and the head clerk backed away from the window. He bent down to look through the small window-frame and shouted back. 'You can say what you like Chardy. That bit of paper says you've no right even to be in this pit yard.'

Sam thrust his arm through the open window but could not reach Scott. He turned and walked across to the management offices followed by a still growing crowd of men. He stopped at the bottom of the wide wooden steps that led up to the offices and shouted. 'Patricks. Get your fuckin' sen out here. Patricks. You hear me.' Some of the men standing round him began to shout for Patricks. The noise grew louder by the minute. Patricks came out of the office and stood at the top of the steps, looking down at the crowd. He was still in his pit clothes but he had part washed and held a small sacking towel with which he dabbed his face.

'What the fuckin' hell you lot caterwaulin' about.'

At first Sam's voice could not be heard through the clamour, then the noise quietened.

'You're victimizin' me, Patricks.'

'What you on about.'

'Givin' me the sack.'

'O you've been sacked 'ave you.'

'You know fuckin' well I have. And it's thy handiwork. You vindictive fucker.'

'You must think you're summat special, Chard, that I should be that bothered.'

'You fuckin' marked me down ovver that fire money. That's what's back of it.'

'O aye, Ah seem to remember you bein' a bit high and mighty over that. Well now's your chance to try tellin' some other pit how to manage its business.'

'What about when the union hears you're not stickin' to last in first out. Fire money was their business too. It'll cost you summat settlin' your own scores through t' pit.'

'You'd better bugger off before you frighten me to death.'

Sam jumped to nearly halfway up the steps. He tried to spit at Patricks but the spittle ran down his chin.

'You wall-eyed fat-gutted bastard. If you 'adn't got company backin' you'd be nowt. Why don't you come round to t' lamp cabin yard and settle it wi' me there.'

'Don't talk so fuckin' soft.'

'You shitbag. You're too fuckin' frit to stand up to me on your own.'

The men at the foot of the steps began shouting at the two men.

'Pur 'is een Sam.'

'Come on you bugger, tek 'im on.'

'Marquis o' Queensberry and a pick 'andle apiece.'

'Get squared off then.'

'Knock his block off.'

'Go for the big sod, Sam.'

'Now what about it Mester Patricks.'

Patricks started to walk back into the office and then turned and roared above the noise.

'What you think this is then. A fuckin' schoolyard. Two kids goin' to tek their coits off. Y' soft buggers.'

Sam grinned at him.

'Y' don't fancy owt but writin' little notes. Don't feel like standin' up for yourself. Come on, 'ave a little dance wi' me.'

'You earned your sack Sam Chard. Now stop actin' like a daft kid and clear off out the yard.'

'I'll wear that fat gut down for you a bit. Come on flower, you and me out by t' lamp cabin. What about it.'

'Ah've got better things to do than prance about wi' thee. Bugger off.'

Some of the men started a chant of 'Mardy kid, mardy kid' and Patricks spat at them.

Sam pointed to him and shouted 'He dast not tek 'is under-manager's hat off. Look at the windy sod.'

Patricks started to turn away, then he whirled towards Sam and roared at him.

'Right you stupid bugger. I'll mek a good boy of you. I'll be across in five minutes.'

He walked back into the office, slamming the door. The crowd cheered and shouted and half-carried Sam across the yard to the space behind the lamp cabin, slapping his back and calling out to each other that Patricks was for it now.

Sam pushed his way through the still gathering crowd asking 'Where's Blacky Todd, 'as anyone see Blacky.' He found him leaning against the lamp cabin wall, a tall old man, shining bald, wide chested, his nose a shapeless lump on his face, his voice thick as if he had a cold.

'What you reckon Blacky.'

'Ah reckon you 'aven't got the sense you were born with.'

'Do you not think I can tek him on.'

'Ah reckon it's a matter of whether he kills thee or just cripples thee.'

'You used to be a booth fighter, tell me how I should tackle him.'

'Tha should start runnin' now and not stop till th'a t'other side of Hampole.'

'Bloody 'ell. You're a reight encouragin' bugger.'

'Show some sense Sam. He's got two stone i' weight and three inches in reach on you. An' he's hard as a teak prop. I once seen him lift an' fishplate a fourteen foot ring on 'is own.'

'All reight. But he's not King Kong. What's best way for me to go at 'im.'

Todd wore his belt buckle behind his back and he fiddled with it and drew it in another notch. He asked one of the men listening to them for some tobacco and tucked a small piece into his mouth, settling it against his lower gum and sucking it.

'If tha 'its him flat on tha'll only brek thi hands. Tha'd best do like the old bare-knuckle fighters used to do. Slash at him wi' your knuckle ends and try and cut 'im, ovver 'is eyes if you can get to 'em.' He looked at the sky for a few moments. 'Try an' stay away from him and keep choppin' 'im about. Patricks allus fancied 'imself a bit of a good lookin' feller an' if you mark 'im a bit it might mek him mad enough not to get set reight.'

'I'll try that.'

'An' keep dancin' about, it's only department you might better 'im in.'

'Thanks Blacky.'

Todd grinned at him and patted his head.

'You're a silly fucker, Sam.'

The noise grew as Patricks walked across the pit yard. He elbowed his way through the crowd and stood a few feet from Sam, hands on hips. Sam took off his jacket, unlaced and took off his boots and handed them to Todd. The crowd drew back to form a circle round the two men.

Sam turned sideways to the heavier man and dropped into a crouch, left arm leading. Patricks stood square to him, fists cocked at shoulder height. He said 'Right, let's see if there's owt to thee besides thy fuckin' big mouth.'

Sam came forward lightly, almost on tiptoe, he moved back a little then suddenly came forward again and slashed Patricks across the lips with an outward sweep of his left fist. Patricks' lip split and he turned his head sideways and spat blood into the crowd as it surged round him. Sam moved forward again, dropped into a lower crouch and caught Patricks with his left, grazing his cheek. Patricks stepped towards him and Sam weaved away then found himself hindered by the ring of men. They started to move back to give him room as Patricks hit him right-handed, on the chest. Sam rode the blow backwards and circled to his right. Patricks followed him round, shuffling forward and bringing his hands closer together in front of him. Sam jumped to his left and clawed Patricks' neck. As Patricks clutched for him he dropped to belly height and smacked his right fist upwards into Patricks' face then slid away, leaning on the men behind him for support as he came upright again. Patricks charged him and he stepped sideways and slapped his left fist across Patricks' head as the heavier man tried to turn from his forward run.

Patricks moved back into the centre of the circle and wiped the blood from his mouth and nose with his arm. He stood for a few moments watching Sam circle him then moved forward, still facing square. Sam caught him left-handed in the face as he came on. Patricks still came forward, stooped, and hit Sam heavily in the ribs with his left hand, then tried to pull him close. Sam grunted, elbowed him in the throat and slid under his left arm and back into the middle of the circle.

The crowd yelled and heaved round the two men, making themselves part of the fight.

Patricks came forward all the time now, swinging his fists in clumsy sweeping blows, hitting Sam on shoulder and forearm as Sam weaved and ducked and backed away. As Sam crouched forward Patricks hit him with a chopping blow on the top of the head. Sam fell over and Patricks dropped on him. For a while the two men wrestled on the ground, butting and gouging. Sam broke free and stumbled to his feet. As Patricks came upright Sam swung his right fist into his belly and Patricks doubled over, his arms flailing. Sam stepped back, blood streaming from a tear in his cheek and hammered at Patricks' face. The crowd bellowed and roared, almost on top of the two men. Patricks caught hold of Sam's arm and swung him away so that the two of them fell and rolled on to their knees, a yard apart. Both men were lathered in sweat and their chests heaved madly as they struggled to breathe.

Patricks clambered slowly to his feet, stepped awkwardly forward and grasped Sam round the chest, pulling him upright and crushing him. He half-pushed, half-carried him backwards until he had him pinned against the wall of the lamp cabin, his arms locked round Sam's back in a bear hug. Sam's eyes bulged and he made high pitched rasping sounds as he tried to get his left hand under Patricks' chin. The bigger man kept his chin tucked down, buried in Sam's chest. Sam's right hand groped slowly downwards and slid crabwise between Patricks' straddled legs. He grasped Patricks' balls and squeezed them hard. Patricks squealed, dropped his arms and lurched away to stand bow-legged, his right hand gently cupping his balls. Sam put his hands on his knees and half-knelt, his head bowed, his body jerking as he retched.

The crowd cheered and hooted, then its whirling slowed to a shuffle and the shouting lessened.

Patricks slowly straightened himself, stepped forward and pulled Sam upright by the hair with his left hand. He smashed his right fist into Sam's belly, stepped back and hit him hard in the face. Sam tumbled sideways, rolled over and stumbled back on his feet. He put his arms out as Patricks came towards him but they were knocked to one side and as he half-turned Patricks hit him under the left armpit. Sam's feet skidded but before he could fall Patricks caught his right arm and pulled him back to the lamp cabin wall. Patricks held his arm tightly and hit him three times in the body and once in the face, pausing between each blow. He let go of him and Sam slid down the wall into a sitting position.

The crowd had gone quiet and still. Patricks leaned towards Sam, hands on his thighs and slowly steadied his breathing.

'Dost want any more, fatgob.'

Sam's eyes were closed and the clotted blood round his nose bubbled as he breathed deeply.

'Can tha get up.'

Sam opened his eyes and stared at Patricks.

'Ah can but Ah'm fuckin' not goin' to.'

Patricks stood upright, turned and walked slowly and clumsily through the crowd that moved aside to give him room. He went across the pit yard and into the management offices.

Most of the crowd drifted away in a mutter of talk. A few tried to gather round Sam but Blacky Todd thrust them back and, clutching Sam's boots and jacket, he hauled him on his feet and dragged him through the side door of the lamp cabin. He slammed the door behind him and lifted Sam so that he could sit on a low bench, his back against the wall. He fetched a clean rag from the lampman's office and wetting it with water from his Dudley he carefully wiped the blood from Sam's face, neck and chest.

'Your face is not as bad as Ah thought.'

Sam leaned forward a little and slowly moved himself about. 'You'd better send for one o' t'ambulance fellers, Blacky. He's busted some fuckin' ribs.' His voice was muffled by his swollen lips.

Todd went across to the head lampman and asked him to phone through to the ambulance hut. As he came back Sam was feeling inside his mouth, with his forefinger.

'He's broken a tooth off.'

'Ah'm not surprised.'

Sam was silent for a while, his eyes closed. Then he looked at Todd again.

'Dost realize, Blacky. Ah'm out of work.'

'Aye well. Tha can worry about that tommerer.'

'First time Ah've ever bin out of work.'

'Tell thee what. If tha can mek it to t' club toneet, I'll buy thi beer and tell thee about time I fought Sinker Priest and he brok mi jaw twice in the one do.'

Sam closed his eyes and said 'That'll be grand.'

The only sound on the hill was the hissing of the rain. It poured down roof tiles and splashed over guttering. Eaves, window ledges and paths streamed and raindrops hitting the road burst into a bright tent of spray. The culvert at the bottom of the hill overfilled and spread a pond across the field. Waves formed against the wall ends of the dike bridge.

The two small boys worked their way up the hill picking up spent matches. They were wearing sodden overcoats, squelching wellingtons and souwesters. At the top of the hill they stood side by side at the edge of the kerb, watching the torrent of water spilling down the gutter.

The older boy half-shouted above the noise of the rain.

'Are we set then.'

'We race 'em as far as Adam's shop.'

'First one into t' gratehole just there.'

'An' if it gets stuck you count ten.'

'That's reight. But you've got to count ten reight. Not rush it. Like one, two, three, an' that. And then you can just touch it to gerrit loose.'

'An' ten if it goes down a gratehole.'

'You've got to stand on t' gratehole as it comes up and you can reach out and move it to t' far side. But if it goes down, you count to ten and then stick a new one in on t' far side of grate.'

'Worrif both matchsticks get stuck together.'

'We'll stop and start 'em off again level.'

'Worrif I start with a bad one an' Ah want to change it for a new one.'

'You can but you've got to count ten before you purra new one in. Just like if it were stuck.'

'An' there's ha'penny on it.'

'Aye.'

'Worrif it's a draw.'

'It can't be a draw, all that way down.'

'Worrif it is.'

'Then we don't give each other nowt.'

The older boy sorted through his matchsticks and held one up.

'I'll back this one.'

The younger boy chose one and said 'I'll have this'n.'

'I'll brek the burnt bit off mine so we can tell which is which.'

'Which do you want to be. Causy side or road side.'

'Causy side.'

The younger boy stepped out into the road and placed himself exactly level with the older boy. They crouched down, holding the matchsticks just above the water coursing down the gutter.

'Are tha ready.'

'Reight.'

'On your mark. Ready, set, go.'

Both boys dropped their matchsticks into the water. The matchsticks raced away down the gutter, dipping and turning. The boys walked alongside shouting as the matchsticks spun in and out of the current, slowing or speeding up. The younger boy's matchstick stuck against a stone. He counted to ten, freed it and followed it down the hill.

In the late evening the billiard hall was in near darkness save for a splash of light over each table which threw the cloths into a blaze of green. Ledges of cigarette smoke lay above the tables and each player was shadowed until he bent forward under the cowling of the bulbs and came into a yellow glare. The murmur of talk was broken by sporadic laughter or shouting and the clear sound was the endless, echoing click of billiard balls.

Duggy Price lifted the triangular frame gently away from the reds and spotted the pink ball. Sam placed the cue ball on the right-hand side of the D and looked along the line of his cue. He struck the ball lightly and it rolled past the base of the triangle and touched the cush with enough side on it to come back and rest against the pack. Duggy shook his head, leaned over, made a high bridge with his left hand and clipped a red so that the cue ball came off three cushes and back down the table. Sam started to sight his shot as Eric Dyson worked his way to the end table and peered under the light.

'Evenin' Sam.'

'Evenin' Eric.'

Dyson nodded at Price.

'Could I have a word with you, Sam.'

Sam clipped the one loosened red into the top right-hand pocket.

'I don't want to spoil your game, Sam. You could join me later on in the Half Moon. I'll wait for you there.'

Sam moved to the cue ball which was close to the left-hand middle pocket and crouched to see if the pink could go into the top right. He pouted his lips and lined up on the blue.

'Alright then, Sam. In the Half Moon. In the snug.'

'Don't fancy the pub tonight Eric.'

Sam potted the blue in the middle pocket with just enough top on the cue ball to bring it off the cush close to the reds. Dyson moved round the table and sat down on the wall bench by the cue rack.

'Well look. I'll just watch while you finish your game, then we can tek a walk and have a chat.'

'You just talk away, lad. It'll not interfere with mi game.'

Sam gave the cue ball a very slight prod and it rolled to rest against the pack. Price came round and scowled down at it while Sam moved his score marker to six.

'Bloody hell Sam. You're not leavin' me owt to play with.'

'Dab hand like you ought to be able to mek summat out of it, Duggy.'

Price chalked his cue slowly. Sam perched on the bench, next to Dyson.

'Nadden Eric, you were sayin'.'

'I've just come from the meetin Sam. I'd like a chance to explain it to you. In private.'

'You speakin' official then, Eric.'

'Aye. In my capacity as Union Chairman.'

'That's grand.'

Price had forced the cue ball back to the bottom of the table behind the yellow. Sam rose and leaned over to study the snooker.

'Is it summat that'll 'ave to be secret from Duggy for ever then.'

'Well no. It'll be reported to the Sunday meetin'.'

'So he might as well hear it now.'

Sam came off two cushes and safely struck the reds but broke up the pack. Price stepped quickly forward to take a red that was resting on the lip of the top left pocket.

'It's just a matter of wantin' to hear your opinion, Sam. Talkin' it out.'

''Ave you taken your decision then.'

'Aye.'

'Then what the fuckin' hell does my opinion matter.'

Price tried for the black but cut it too fine. He marked his one on the scoreboard.

'We want you to understand how things are, Sam.'

'Well tell us then.'

Sam put a red down in the bottom right pocket and the cue ball came back up the table. Dyson stood up and walked to and fro on the wall side of the table.

'Bloody hell, Sam. You've to understand our position. We've every sympathy for what's happened. There wasn't a man at that meeting didn't think you've been unjustly sacked. Nobody. And they know why.'

Sam doubled the pink off the cush into the middle pocket.

'We must 'ave talked it out nigh on two hours. Everybody were agreed it's rank victimization. A clear-cut case. We all know Patricks' reputation. We were not in any doubt.'

Sam chalked his cue and tried a long shot. The ball rattled in the jaws of the pocket for a moment but jumped out. Sam scored his seven.

'But you've got to tek the overall position into account. We're sadly low on funds and we've got a lot of hangin' in the balance just now. We've got a new home coal agreement just nearly settled. And there's a compo case we can likely get without a court business. It's just come at a bad time.'

Price potted an easy red then rolled the ball behind the brown leaving a snooker. Sam looked at it closely. He took the high rest.

'You know we've been twice to t' management Sam and if there'd been any way to get 'em to budge we would 'ave done it. You know that.'

Sam took th; ball off the side cush and touched a red just below the centre spot. Dyson started to speak again but Sam cut in.

'What did George Absalom say.'

'He backed you up strongly.'

'What did he say.'

'Well he said we shouldn't leave things be. He were opposed to the decision. But you must understand Sam. A strike at this time could do untold harm. It's not that we don't see the injustice. It's simply—'

'What did he say.'

'I've told you.'

'What did he say.'

Price had potted a red and was lining upon a yellow for the bottom right pocket. Dyson half-turned away and fiddled with one of the cues in the rack. Sam chalked his cue.

'What did he say.'

'He said that if we'd stand for this we'd stand bottles breaking over our 'eads.'

Price missed his shot and Sam moved to the table.

'Good for little George.'

The game went on in silence for a while and Sam made a break of twenty-three. He marked his score and turned to Dyson.

'They tell me it wasn't just the union 'mittee at this meetin'.'

Dyson rubbed his nose and stared at the table.

'Well it was an important decision.'

'You'd got the Labour men there.'

'Just the Party Chairman and Secretary.'

'An' what worrit to do wi' them.'

'They were only advisin'.'

'An' what did they advise.'

'Well they took the overall view that this wasn't a good time for a head-on clash.'

'By but it's reight popular, this overall view.'

'Hammond was agreed you were bein' made a political scapegoat of. By the management—'

'But there's nowt to be done.'

'He's goin' to see your case is made public through the Party.'

'But no strike.'

'Not in view of the situation, no.'

'He's bothered you might use up too many union dibs and leave nowt for Labour Party funds then.'

'That's not a fair thing to say, Sam.'

Price tapped his cue on the table edge and said 'Thy go Sam.'

Sam went to the table and slammed a red into the top pocket putting bottom on the cue ball so that it was stunned and stopped in line for the black. He walked round to the side of the table.

'You know what you can do with the Labour Party, Eric.'

Dyson flapped his hands vaguely.

'You can fuck the Labour Party.'

Dyson half-turned away.

'There's nowt more to be said Sam.'

Sam hit the black gently and it rolled into the top left pocket. As Dyson started to walk away Sam shouted after him. 'You know what Eric. If you'd decided to come out on strike ovver me I was goin' to tell you not to bother. You wouldn't have won.' Dyson had stopped, then he started again, walking towards the door. Sam shouted after him. 'Chance would 'ave bin a fine thing.'

Sam stared at the table for a while after Dyson had left before screwing a red into the top right pocket, rolling it along the cush. He missed the black, cutting it too fine. Price potted a red with a table-length shot.

'What's this about fuck the Labour Party, Sam. You goin' Conservative.'

'Am I fuck as like.'

'Well we've got to get the bloody mines nationalized 'aven't we.'

'What for. We'd just be changin' bloody bosses.'

'How do you reckon that.'

'How many pits does Donny Amalgamated own.'

'Eight, nine.'

'Aye. And a bloody long strike or a ca'canny and they're shittin' their pants. They've only so much bloody brass in the kitty. They can be shaken. We've done it a time or two.'

'Meanin' what.'

'When the bloody government runs all the pits, how do you reckon we're goin' to worry them bastards. It'd 'ave to be a national strike every time.'

Price tried a long shot with the cue ball resting on the cush, muffed it and went in off. He scored the penalty points to Sam.

'What's the idea then.'

'We run the bloody pits usselves. Like the Welsh miners wanted to in 1913.'

'That's no good. You've got to 'ave a boss of some sort.'

'Why.'

'Well, to give the bloody orders.'

'If you believe that you deserve a fuckin' boss.'

'Well Ah'll all'us have one whether I deserve it or not.'

Sam potted a red with a plant shot, shaved the brown into the centre pocket and cleared the last reds and the colours up to blue. Price sighed and chalked his cue.

'Fuckin' hell Sam. How much did we 'ave on this game.'

'A tanner.'

'Are you sure it wasn't thrippence.'

'Ah'm fuckin' sure.'

The pub had been closed a while but noisy groups of men were still scattered round the wide, macadamed space between the pub front and the road. Spots of rain drifted in the night breeze.

Clarry Moore stood swaying in the middle of a knot of men, shouting across the argument.

'Not a British fighter worth the name since Bob Fitzsimmons. Not a fuckin' one. We've not 'ad one. Not worth namin'.'

'What about Jimmy Wilde then, like greased lightnin'. Built like a kid an' hit like a hammer.'

'That bloody Yank beat him.'

'He were a bloody old man then, countin' him as a boxer.'

'He wor no bigger than our kid.'

'The Cornish blacksmith. Last one we had to match the Yanks.'

'Dempsey would have fuckin' murdered him.'

Moore put his arm round the shoulder of the man and tapped his chest.

'You can't say that. They were never fuckin' matched.'

'He were not in t' same street. Anyroad, they couldn't be bloody matched. One were afore t'other.'

Each man's argument overlapped his neighbour and voices became louder.

'What about Battlin' Siki, he spoiled that Frenchie's looks for 'im.'

'He went and fucked himself to death with women. They all do. Look at Larry Greb.'

'It warn't Larry. Harry. Harry Greb.'

'He fucked himself stupid. An' drinkin'.'

'They say he was a religious feller.'

'Fuckin' funny way o' showin' it.'

Moore pushed one of the men fiercely away.

'He wasn't just a fuckin' mauler you know. He invented the solar plexus punch. That's where all the nerves come together. He showed 'em how to do that.'

'Worrabout this feller Farr then.'

'He's a fuckin' Taffy. They're no good for owt but dancin' around.'

'Don't be bloody daft. Do you say that about Petersen then.'

'Any Yank, Tunney, any of 'em. They could take the bloody lot on together with one hand tied behind his back. Nowt easier.'

'What you fuckin' know about it anyway. My faither seen 'em all. An' he said we 'ad real fighters. Not fuckin' freaks.'

Moore waved his arms wildly about him and walked away from the group.

'You know fuckin' nowt. He were older than you when he took it. Become champion. And he were a gentleman. He were a fuckin' science fighter. Fitzsimmons was. The best. Best there was.' He tripped on the causeway edge and fell to his knees, lurched upright and walked on down the hill. The other men argued more quietly for a few minutes. Then the group broke up.

Moore weaved unsteadily from kerb to road, muttering to himself till he came level with a collier in his pit dirt, hurrying up the hill. He clutched him and patted his arm.

'Sithee, Charlie, are tha well.' The man tried to pull himself free. 'Hoddup a minute. Hoddup a minute. Ah want to tell y' summat. Sithee.'

'Nay lad, Ah'm bahn 'om.'

'Listen a minute. Hoddup just a second. Tha'll know what Ah mean. Tha'll know reight enough.' The man tried again to jerk his arm loose but Moore leaned against him. 'You 'ave a good shift then. Are y' mekkin it pay.'

'We're doin' grand Clarry. Now I must get off to mi supper, there's a good lad.'

'Right then. You go an' 'ave your supper. You're entitled to it. You've worked hard. 'Ave your bit o' supper and get yoursen to bed. That's best thing for you. In't it.' He let go of the man who trotted away up the hill.

Moore started to cross the road, then came back and leaned against the lighted window of a shop. He stared hard at a row of coloured glass, animal figures, cupping his hands to his eyes. The floor of the window was covered with a patchwork of table mats showing hunting scenes. Moore knelt down and looked at them, shuffling slowly along on his knees to the shop doorway. Someone shouted to him from across the street and he waved his arm. He pulled himself upright by the corner post of the window and then walked unsteadily across into the narrow unlit street facing the shop and went halfway down it, brushing his hand against the railings in front of the houses. He fumbled with the latch of his gate and swore at it. He made his way round to the back of the house and into the kitchen.

The gas lamp glowed yellow where the mantel was cracked. Gladys Moore sat by the fire. She was a woman of thirty, with thin, stick-like limbs and a pale, drawn face. She did not look up. Her husband leaned with his back against the door.

'Nadden love. Still cronkin' by the fire.'

He sat down heavily at the kitchen table and struggled awkwardly to take off his jacket. He tried to hang it over the back of the chair but it fell to the floor and he left it there.

'Weer's mi supper then.'

'There's some mashed potato I can fry up for you an' some bacon.'

'Aye, but why in't it ready.'

'I didn't know what time you'd be home. Pubs closed an hour ago as it is.'

'Got nowt to do wi' it. You're not fuckin' bothered, that's trouble.'

Gladys Moore crossed to the gas ring by the copper boiler, lit it and began to fry mashed potato and strips of bacon in a heavy blackened pan. Clarry watched her for a while.

'Don't I like tea with it then.'

Gladys filled the tall kettle that stood on the hob and bedded it down on the fire.

'Where's paper.'

The woman took it from the sideboard and placed it in front of him. He spread the pages across the table and began to read, turning the sheets restlessly, putting his head close down to them and blinking as he peered at the print.

She stood holding the plate, waiting while he slowly folded the paper. She put his supper in front of him, took a knife and fork from the table drawer and poured his tea.

'You not 'avin any then.'

'No.'

She sat down by the fire. Clarry ate noisily.

'Where's Brian then. Little Lord Muck.'

'You know where he is.'

'Ah said where fuckin' is he.'

'He's in bed.'

'Didn't wait up to say goodnight to his dad then.'

'He did all his homework and went to bed.'

'Not bothered about seein' me.'

'What for. You only shout at him.'

'I do bloody well to shout at him. He thinks he's the bloody prize sin' he got 'is scholarship. Toffy-nosed bugger. Well Ah'm goin' to straighten him out a bit.'

'Why don't you leave him alone. He's got to get on with his schoolwork.'

'You've made that much fuckin' fuss of 'im. He's like a big soft lass.'

The woman rose and went to the back door, locked and bolted it and started towards the stairs.

'What about it then.'

The woman turned and stood with her hands folded in front of her.

'What about what.'

'You know fuckin' well what. Do I get owt tonight or don't I.'

'I don't feel like it.'

The chair scraped harshly back as Clarry stumbled to his feet.

'You fuckin' felt like it when you used to oppen your legs for Sid Naylor. Any bloody time he fancied.'

The skin tightened across the woman's face.

'Shut your filthy mouth.'

Clarry's voice rose to a shout. 'Don't tell me to shut up, you bitch. Ah'm not your fuckin' bairn.' He lunged across the room towards her, his arm raised. 'You don't like the fuckin' truth do you.'

His wife flinched but did not move.

'I'll not be bloody told. I keep this place. It's my house. I fuckin' earn it. One way an' another. You should know that.' His voice trailed away and he sat down by the fire. Gladys Moore went upstairs.

Clarry sat for a while, head lolling forward. He stood up and poured himself a mug of tea and stood sipping it, looking vaguely round the room. He searched along the mantelpiece behind the framed photographs and ornaments and old letters till he found a small clay pipe. He fetched his pouch from his jacket pocket, filled the pipe, lit it and sat down, staring at the silverfish that scuttled about inside the fender. He nodded into sleep then woke as the pipe bowl burned his fingers. He put his mug, plate, knife and fork into the sink and banked up the fire with slack from a bucket in the fender. He crouched and poked holes in the slack, under the bottom bar of the fire. He checked that the door was locked and very slowly pulled the chain of the gas lamp till it dimmed into darkness. He groped his way up the stairs, bumping the walls as he turned on the landing. He said 'Gladys' as he came into the bedroom but there was no answer. He took off his shoes, socks and trousers and laid them in a pile across the end of the bed. He grunted as he knelt down by the edge of the bed and pissed noisily into the chamber pot. The bed creaked as he pulled himself in. His face half-buried in the bolster he muttered 'Sorry I shouted.'

He turned clumsily several times before he fell asleep. His wife lay awake for a long time, staring at the wall.

The cutter canted over as it struck hard coal, teeth broke away and the driving belt jammed. Hughes leaned across and snatched at the switch. The motor whined and stopped.

Cranshaw dropped the following cable he was dragging and went over from kneeling to lying on his hip. He swung his boot at the machine.

'Hell's flames afire. I could cut coal with mi cock better than this fuckin' thing.'

Hughes sat back against the coal face and closed his eyes.

'Tha welcome to try Joseph.'

Cranshaw took his lamp from a prop and shone the light over the cutter arm.

'It's stuck in proper. We shall need to chop all this top coal away afore we can towse it out.'

'Leave the fucker for a minute. It's goin' mad headed as jammed it in the first place.'

Hughes fingered the pockets of his waistcoat and found a small piece of twist tobacco. He bit off half and passed the rest to Cranshaw. Cranshaw hooked his lamp back on to the prop, unbuckled his knee-pads and chafed his knees.

'What time is it.'

'About an hour to day-shift I reckon.'

'We shall have Mussolini down on us, only half-cut.'

'He can please his fuckin' sen.'

The men sat in silence for a while.

'What's up wi' your knees then.'

'Feels like rheumatics.' Cranshaw crawled round to the front of the cutter and pulled on the chain. 'We better slack this bugger off a bit. It's stretched like elastic.'

'Let it bide. We'll start agen in a bit.'

Cranshaw moved back behind the cutter and lay down.

'What's this about your lad joinin' up, Joe.'

'Aye, end of this month. He's fed up of bein' on and off work. He never fancied pits a lot, anyroad.'

'You reckon he'll fancy army bullshit.'

'Well, he'll not be told owt.'

'What's your missis think.'

'She's not bothered a lot about him. She's all for t' young'n.'

'It'll be the smart uniform and travel to foreign parts he's thinkin' on and not 'avvin to—' Hughes stopped speaking as he heard the sound of shouting from farther up the face.

The lad staggered from side to side as he came towards them at a stooping run, first on the conveyor belt and then on the spillage between the belt and the face. He was still shouting when he reached the two men but the words were a jumble and he stood shaking, waving his lamp wildly about him. Hughes slid over the cutter and grabbed the lad's arms.

'Now gently, Bobbie. What is it, lad.'

The lad stopped shouting, tried to catch his breath and began to cry.

'Come on Bobbie, tell us.'

The lad said 'Mister Hughes, Mister Hughes' several times. Hughes held him tightly.

'It's Mister Seneschal, he's buried. Mister Seneschal.'

'Where Bobbie.'

'In the gob, by the castin' end.'

The lad shuddered and suddenly quietened.

'He were fixin' a chock and I were bringin' lids up to him. An' the chock just crashed down and there was like a bang and the roof fell on him.'

'Could you see him.'

'Yes I could. His head and chest's clear but he doesn't move. An' I daren't go near him, Mister Hughes. I was frightened.'

Hughes let go of the boy's arms and wiped his hand across his mouth.

'What shall I do Mister Hughes.'

Hughes shook his head to and fro then spoke slowly and loudly.

'There's a good lad. Now you go to the phone at the loader end and tell the pit bottom we want a doctor an' an ambulance an' they're to send the paddy train to this end. You understand.'

The boy nodded his head fiercely.

'A doctor and an ambulance and they're to send the paddy train to this end. What do I do then Mister Hughes.'

'You stay at the loader end for messages. Now away you go.'

The boy turned and hurried back, crouching, along the face. His lamp disappeared from sight as he ran into the intake airway. Hughes turned to Cranshaw but looked at the floor as he spoke.

'There's some trackers on Nines, Joe. You'd best go and fetch 'em. Bring 'em back along the return, it'll be quicker. I'll go up and see what's to do.'

Cranshaw followed him as far as the intake airway then turned off. Hughes carried on up the face, holding his lamp well out in front of him and leaning forward at the waist, taking long fast strides. He stopped as he neared the far end and peered through the pall of dust that was only slowly settling from the fall.

After a while he saw Vincent Seneschal. He was lying well back in the gob, as if on a sofa. His head was propped up by the remains of the chock and part of his chest was clear of the loose dirt that covered the rest of his arms and body. His eyes were closed and he was still. Hughes went down on his knees and stared at the roof. The whole of the gob up to where Seneschal lay had come down, breaking clean away from the forward part of the roof which still seemed solid from the face outwards. Hughes inched his way towards the fall, craning his neck and holding his lamp high. He stopped several times and listened but there was no sound of further weight. The face was silent except for the spaced splash of small stones dropping from a point beyond the fall. He eased himself up to the buried man and slid his hand under his shirt. He could feel Seneschal's heart beating very slowly and heavily. Gently he brushed away the stones and dirt from the lower part of Seneschal's body until his hand felt the table-like slab of rock. He stopped and knelt, unmoving for a while, listening to the whistling sound of Seneschal's breathing. He leaned heavily on his right arm and began probing with the fingers of his left hand along the underside of the rock edge. He moved his hand down on the floor and groped backwards along the line of the thigh up to the waist. He pulled his hand away and rubbed it hard into the dirt.

Seneschal's eyes opened quite suddenly and then flickered to and fro, restlessly, looking first back into the gob, then towards the coal face, then at Hughes.

Hughes cleared his throat several times and spoke softly.

'Easy does it Vince. Joe's gone off to fetch some trackers from Nines. We'll have you out sharpish. Soon as they come. He'll bring 'em along the return. They'll be here anytime now. We'll tek it steady till they come.'

Seneschal's eyes kept moving, his eyelids fluttering and his focus jumping rapidly from one point to another.

'Bobbie told us you'd had a fall. I've sent him off to get the paddy up. It should be at this end by now. Soon anyway.' Hughes twisted as he knelt and looked back down the face. He shifted from his knees into a squat. He said nothing for a few minutes then spoke rapidly again, still keeping his voice low. 'I couldn't see your lamp anywhere. Still we can look for it after we've got you along to the pit bottom. Paddy train should be here by now. They'll have a doctor to see to you by the time we're there. Pritchard I should think. Or Gorman. Be a bit of a rest for you, I expect.'

He heard the clatter of boots as the men came along the last part of the return road.

'I'll just go an' tell 'em how we're placed, Vince. I'll be back with you in a minute. I'll just get matters sorted out a bit. I shan't be long.'

He scrambled across to the face and went down to meet the men. Cranshaw tried to go past and Hughes thrust him back savagely.

'What's up. Is he dead.'

'Fuckin' squat a minute.'

Hughes knelt down and the four men ringed him in a half-circle. One of them looked back along the return airway and said 'We've got Dickie Smith fetchin' a stretcher from t' main plane. He'll be along in a bit.'

Hughes spat twice into the gob before he spoke.

'He's squashed flat from the waist downwards.'

One of the men dropped the iron bar he was carrying onto the spillage and rubbed his thighs with his hands.

'Christ.'

'Shall we try and shift him.'

'There's no point in maulin' the poor sod about. You wait awhile. I'll go back to him. He'll not be long.'

Hughes crept back up the face and into the gob. He sat down by Seneschal facing the way that the man was lying.

'They're just gettin' set up Vince. They'll not be too long.'

After a few minutes Hughes moved round so that he was facing towards Seneschal.

'Is there anythin' you want to say, Vince.'

Seneschal's eyes were still moving, his gaze veering fitfully from point to point along the line of the gob. There was a low mutter as the men at the return road talked. In about ten minutes Seneschal's breathing stopped for a few moments, then became heavy and rasping, then stopped altogether.

Hughes crawled back to the waiting men.

'I've sat with him. You can fetch him out.'

He went down to the cutter, picked up his jacket, Dudley and snaptin and walked out of the pit.

Half a dozen men were playing peggy stick on the open space at the top of Ings Lane, with a watching crowd round them. When Sam's turn came he laid the one stick across the other, see-saw fashion, with one end resting on the ground. He balanced a small stone carefully on the grounded end of the stick and stood back swinging the pick handle he held in practice strokes. He struck the tilted end of the balanced stick smartly and the stone was levered high into the air. As it came down Sam slashed at it and sent it hurtling away down the lane. Someone shouted 'It's a good'n' but it had been driven slightly downwards and soon struck the ground and pitched to a stop about forty yards away. Sam paced it out, called the distance and came back to the group. The next man took the pick handle and stone from him and stepped forward to take his turn.

Tig Fisher worked his way into the crowd and tapped Sam on the shoulder.

'Comin' for a drink Sam.'

Sam turned and stared at him.

'I've got a deal to offer you so it's worth a pint to me if you'll listen.'

Sam nodded and they walked away from the crowd towards the Club. They found a window seat and Fisher fetched two pints of bitter. He took out a cigarette and left the packet on the table.

'How you doin' then, Sam.'

'Fair to middlin'.'

'Any sign of a job yet.'

'No.'

'Ah'm a bit surprised lad. You were always reckoned a good collier.'

Sam sipped his beer and looked round the half-empty bar.

'You tried all the local pits.'

'I've tried 'em two an' three times. Out as far as Barnsley.'

'Bit rough that.'

'I reckon Patricks has put the word out. I'm wastin' mi time trampin' round pit offices.'

'Owt else goin'.'

'Bits and bobs. I had a two weeks on a sweepin' job at wool factory and I shall get a few days stookin' for Carby when his wheat's ready.'

'You still got your carpentry tools.'

'Aye.'

'Your Dad's weren't they. By but he were a good carpenter.'

'It was all he was good for.'

'He taught thee a thing or two about it.'

'What you got in mind, Tig.'

Fisher took a pencil and a piece of paper from his pocket and put them by his beer glass.

'You know I go in for racin' pigeons a bit.'

'You're usually reckoned to be pigeon mad, Tig.'

'Aye, well. Ah'm ready to tek on a few more but I shall need another hut. Just to t' side of where I've got mi present one.'

'How big.'

'I'll draw it for yer.' Fisher drew on the piece of paper and marked in the size. 'Like that, an' I'll want nestin' boxes, perches and a homin' loft. You can copy them off the hut I've got.'

'Tek a bit o' timber that will. You buyin' the wood for it.'

'Ah well, I've got summat special in mind theer.' He leaned towards Sam and lowered his voice. 'You know them houses this side of Gallons corner that are standin' empty. There's two of 'em as stand by theirselves.'

'You mean behind the blacksmith's shop.'

'That's reight. Well I've had a look round the one nearest this end and they must have put new floorin' in not long before it went empty. Good long laths of timber, just tacked in. I'm thinkin' mainly of the upstairs rooms.'

'You want me to nick it.'

'Well there's no other houses just close by. I could borrow you a rubber-tyred handcart. You wait till late at night, lever 'em up easy, lower 'em out through the window and stack 'em by the wall. Then on to the cart and bring 'em up to my house. We could put 'em round the back and nobody's the wiser.'

'I'd look a bit daft if I met bobby Pace while I was trundling that lot.'

'Go round the top. Up by Lodge Road. He never goes that way.'

'A floorboard meks quite a bit o' noise when it's pulled up.'

'Well go down durin' the day. They're not locked an' anybody can look round. Just loosen 'em a bit while there's plenty o' noise goin' on.'

'How much are you payin' for the whole job.'

'I'll buy the nails and stuff and I'll paint it. I'll not be mingy, I'm offering five quid for the hut by itself.'

'Any bugger goes to rent that house they'll get a bit of a shock.'

'Will you do the job.'

Sam drank some more of his beer and looked at the drawing.

'I'd want to tek some time about it and mek it decent. That hut you've got now is a bit of a bodged job.'

'All reight.'

'I'll get us another pint.'

'Just this one'll do me, Tig.'

'Bugger to that. When I pay you five quid you can buy me one back.'

The four year old trotted behind his stepbrother and the group of older boys. As they walked up Poplar Road and neared the school, scores of children ran in from the streets on either side and Terry dodged to and fro to escape being knocked over as the road became more crowded. Above the noise of talking and shouting he could hear chanting.

Charlie, Charlie chuck chuck chuck
Went to bed with a duck duck duck
The duck it died
Charlie cried
Charlie Charlie chuck chuck chuck.

His bootlace came undone. He scuffed the boot along the ground to stop it coming off and tugged at his stepbrother's arm. Eric Holmes dragged the little lad to the wall at the side of the road, out of the way of the jostling crowd of children and tied the bootlace. He took Terry's hand and pulled him along Lodge Road, through the gates of the school and across to the entrance of the Infants' School. At the door a woman teacher collected children who were coming to the school for the first time and sat them down in the corridor, just outside a classroom. She slapped any who stood up and started to wander away and pushed them back down into the sitting circle.

In the playground outside, a handbell was rung and the children lined up in columns. When the bell was rung a second time they marched into the school. The streets and playground were suddenly quiet and deserted.

The teacher ordered the infants new to the school to stand up. She shepherded them into the classroom and made them sit on small chairs placed about three feet apart in four rows, with their feet close together and their hands palm down in their laps. Standing behind her desk, she clapped her hands and spoke to the children, slowly, in a loud voice.

'Good morning children. Now you must all say good morning Miss Tate. Now all together, say good morning Miss Tate.'

A few of the children murmured 'Good morning Miss Tate' and she made them try it several times till they all said it together.

'Now when I clap my hands like this you must always be quiet and whatever you are doing you must go to your seat, the one you are sitting on now, and sit quietly with your feet together and your hands in front of you.' She repeated this twice and pulled back to her chair a little girl who stood up to go and look at a doll's house at the back of the classroom.

'Now you must all sit quite still and when I come to you, tell me your name.'

She took the attendance register and a pencil from her desk and leaned over each child in turn, marking them present as they gave their name. One or two children refused to speak and she searched their pockets for the slip of paper with their name on it, that parents had been asked to send with them. She went back to her desk and turned to the class.

'When I say now, and not before, you may get up and go and play with the toys that are placed against the walls. You must play quietly and remember to go back to your seats when I clap my hands. When you want to go to the lavatory you must put up your hand and wait till I tell you that you may go. I will get one of the older children from the next class to take you. Remember, you are not to move or touch the toys until I say now.' She stood for a time staring at the children and then said 'Now.'

A few children stood up and the teacher took others by the hand and led them to the toys.

Terry found a cloth book with pictures of trains and aeroplanes in it and sat down on the floor to look at it. For twenty minutes the children played with the toys. Whenever they began to talk to each other the teacher pointed her finger at them and said 'Shush.' Then she clapped her hands. One or two came back to their chairs and the teacher sorted out the rest and seated them. She went round the class to make sure that everyone had their legs together and their hands in their laps.

She fetched a pile of pictures, fixed to large pieces of cardboard, from the cupboard behind her desk.

'Now, I am going to hold up some pictures, one at a time. If you know what the picture is you must put up your hand. If I point to you, you must say out loud what the picture is.'

She held up a picture of an apple and several children shouted 'Apple'. The teacher said 'No, you must not call out, put up your hand if you know what the picture is.' Several children put up their hand and the teacher pointed to a little girl in the front row. The little girl said 'Apple' and the teacher said 'No, say, please Miss Tate, it is an apple.' The little girl just stared at her and the teacher waited a while then asked another child who, after he had been told what to say, said 'Please Miss Tate, it's an apple.' At first the children kept calling out the name of the object in the picture but each time they were told to put up their hands. Slowly they learned to do this and a few remembered to say 'Please Miss Tate' before they gave the answer. Terry said the names of the objects in the pictures silently to himself but did not call out or put up his hand.

As the teacher came to the end of the pile of picture cards the handbell was rung for playtime and there was a clatter of footsteps and chatter of voices as children trotted down the corridor outside the classroom and into the playground. The teacher clapped her hands and said 'Now it is time for your morning sleep.' Three older girls came into the classroom and helped the teacher lay out the small, narrow stretchers that were stacked against the rear wall, one beside each chair. When they left, the teacher stood by her desk and said 'Now you must all lie down on your stretcher, close your eyes and go to sleep.' She repeated this several times and then moved round the classroom pushing the more unwilling children down on their stretchers. Terry allowed himself to be pushed on the stretcher but sat upright. The teacher came back to him and said 'Lie down.' He stared at her and said 'I don't go to sleep in the mornings.' She pushed him backwards and said 'Now close your eyes and go to sleep.' He lay there till the teacher had gone back to her desk, then he stood up and sat in his chair. The teacher said, very sharply 'You lie down Terry Holmes and close your eyes.' Terry shuffled his feet.

'I don't want to.'

'Don't be stubborn. It's morning sleep time.'

Terry sat still and the teacher came across and pulled him on to the stretcher. He sat up again and said 'I only sleep at night.'

The teacher pushed him down and said 'Well just close your eyes and pretend you're asleep.' When she returned to her desk Terry stood up and walked to the door. As he opened it Miss Tate hurried across and grabbed his arm. She slapped him and dragged him back and forced him down on the stretcher.

'That will be enough of that. You will not move again until I tell you to. Now close your eyes.'

Terry closed his eyes and lay still. A few minutes later the hand-bell was rung and children marched in from the playground back to their classrooms. Terry lay with his eyes closed for a while longer. The classroom was quiet save for the creak of the stretchers as one child or another turned over and the scratch of the teacher's pen as she inked in her register. Terry rolled off the stretcher and ran out of the classroom, along the corridor and out into the playground. Miss Tate ran after him and stopped in the doorway to the playground, watching him run out of the school gates and along Lodge Road.

He turned out of Lodge Road and ran nearly the full length of Poplar Road, looking back over his shoulder, flailing his arms and gasping for breath. Near the end of the road he stopped and leaned on the wall, holding his side, his body trembling. He stood there until his breathing slowed, and then walked round the corner and up the hill to the small baker's and confectioner's shop where he lived.

The shop bell rang as he pushed the door open. His mother came through into the shop and looked down at him, over the counter. She said 'What are you doing here.'

'I kem 'ome.'

'What's wrong.'

'They want me to sleep so I kem 'ome.'

'You're supposed to be at school. Eric took you.'

'They tried to mek me close mi eyes.'

'Come here.'

He walked under the counter flap and followed his mother into the living-room. His father had a batch of pork pies set out on the living-room table and was putting gelatin into them. He looked up and said 'What the hell are you doin' 'ere.'

The boy stood behind his mother who said 'He's come back from school.'

'What for.'

'They must have upset him.'

'I'll bloody upset him.' Duncan Holmes came round the table, leaned over the boy and jabbed his finger into his chest. 'What you doin' here.'

'They tried to mek me lie down on a bed.'

'You daft little bugger. Geroff back to school.'

'I don't want to.'

The father pushed the boy half out of the room and shouted 'Never you mind what you want.'

His mother moved and stood between the boy and his father.

'Let's leave it for now, Duncan. See what the school says.'

'I know what they'll say. It'll be truant officers an' all that bloody mularky. He's goin' back right now.'

'He's only four.'

'An' that's too bloody early to start defyin' me.'

'P'raps he's not well.'

'You're not bein' soft with 'im this time. He'll do as I say.'

'I'll take him miself tomorrow. I'll talk to the teacher.'

'He goes back now or I'll leather 'im.'

'You're not to hit him.'

'O aye. I can hit the others all I like but not sonny boy. He's special. Well I'm goin' to teach him a lesson.'

'You're not to hit him, he's not yours.'

Duncan Holmes untied his baker's apron and threw it on a chair. His voice was quiet.

'Whose is he then. That bugger you 'ad five minutes in a ditch with before he went larkin' off. That it then.'

His wife blushed and put her hand to her mouth.

'So long as I graft for 'im, he's mine. I feed him an' that's what counts.' He started to say something else when the shop bell rang and he said 'See to it.' His wife hesitated, then went through into the shop.

Terry was sitting under the table and his father hauled him out and took him through the back door and round into the road. He cuffed the boy and said 'Get back to school and wait for Eric to bring you home to dinner.' The boy walked slowly away down the hill and Duncan Holmes came back into the house.

A while later his wife came through from the shop. She spoke with little hiccuping sobs. 'It's no good Duncan. He's sittin' out there by the road. We can't make him. Let's leave it. Let's. Let's leave it till tomorrow.'

Her husband took off his apron and went out to the boy. He hit him sharply across the arms and legs, pushed him off down the hill and shouted after him 'Next time I'll bloody leather you.' He watched the boy go down the hill and turn into Poplar Road.

Half an hour later a customer said she had seen the boy sitting on the kerb outside the post office and Duncan Holmes went down to him. He took off his belt and hit the boy with it across the legs and sent him off crying, towards the school.

At midday Eric Holmes came back for his dinner and said he had not seen Terry either in the school playground or on the way home.

The father went to look for him and found him in the field opposite the pit gates, playing with an old mongrel dog. He dragged the boy back home, gave him a beating and sent him up to the bedroom that he shared with his stepbrothers, without anything to eat. When her husband had gone to the pub that evening, Cissie Holmes took supper to her son. She sat on the bed and told him that little boys have to go to school and that he would like it once he got used to it and that his father had to make him go for his own good. The boy kept saying 'I won't go to bed when it's daytime.'

Elijah Shears swung his small collier's pick in a tight flat arc and let the sharpened point drop into the grain of the coal face. He levered the blade of the pick outwards and a long shard of coal fell at his knees. Kneeling slightly backwards he swung again and worked another layer of coal off the face. Slowly coal piled up round his knees till some of it was resting in his lap. He laid his pick to one side, shuffled back a yard, cleared the bits that had lodged behind his knee-pads and picked up his shovel. Scraping a space in front of him, to give himself a good bottom, he slid the shovel under the pile of coal and lifted and cast the shovelful gently on the conveyor belt that snaked away down the face. He lifted and cast steadily till the riven coal was cleared then bowed forward for a minute, breathing lightly and flexing the muscles of his back. He laid aside his shovel, took up his pick and moved back closer to the face.

The colliers were spaced nine foot apart along the seventy-yard face and the four-foot high wall of coal gleamed brightly in their lamps. A light fog of coal dust drifted along to the return airway. The noise of picks and shovels and falling coal and the hammering on prop lids overlaid the everlasting rumbling and squeaking of the belt.

The belt stopped and started twice, then stopped altogether, signalling snaptime. The coal face hushed and the voices of the men seemed pitched high in the silence.

Shears climbed over the belt into the gob, found his Dudley and snaptin and sat, legs sprawled out, back against a prop. The deputy passed him crawling down the face.

'You not stoppin' for snap, Parky.'

'Checkin' at loader end, see if we've got enough empties.'

'You worry too much.'

Parks disappeared down the face.

The two men from the stints below Shears crawled up and joined him in his section of the gob.

'Nadden Lije.'

'Nadden Joe. Ned. You happy.'

'We're fillin' off well enough.'

'They should let us do like Frickley. Fill off and fuck off.'

'Never fancied that. Leads to racin'.'

The three men drank heavily from their Dudleys and settled to eating their snap. Further down the face someone peeled an orange and the smell exploded in the warm, stale air.

'Did you go to Mester Cordle's funeral, Ned.'

'I did that.'

'What worrit like.'

'A good do. Ham tea and as much beer as you could sup. An' we all sat round saying what a grand chap he'd been.'

'Asked you because you'd worked for him.'

'Aye. I was in his gang for years when he was a butty at Markham One.'

'What wor he like to work for.'

'Fair enough. He used to complain a lot about how mean the pit's contracts wi' him were and how he were practically payin' us out of his own pocket.'

'All butties talk like that. They're like farmers, always starvin' to death and then buyin' a grand pianner for t' front room.'

'Th'a reight theer. My old man used to mek a point about that. You know that row of shops along the North Road at Broddy.'

'Aye.'

'Well mi Dad used to point out that practically everyone of them was owned by an ex-butty. It's a fact.'

'It's a bad system for pitmen. I'd sooner just be swindled by t' pit than have a middleman tekkin' his cut.'

Shears suddenly chuckled to himself.

'Hey, do you remember old Cordle had a daughter. Bessie.'

'Just about. She died a good while back, when she were young.'

'That's reight. She died in 1919 flu.'

'Did you know her then.'

'I bloody did. She were a mate of my missis's when I first met her. By Christ but she gave me a dodgy time.'

'Tell us the tale then, Lije.'

'Well, tha sees I met Mary, my missis, an' Bessie Cordle, at this day excursion to Brid. Big gang of us went up by early morning train. I fancied Mary straight off and afore long I'd made up mi mind I was goin' to marry her. Christ knows why she and Bessie were such mates. Mary was strict Methodist and proper as you like and Bess was a fast little bitch. Anyway, I'm busy courtin' Mary and Bessie Cordle's all the time tryin' to get me to fuck her.'

'On account of you looked just like the Sheikh of Arabee.'

'No, Ah'm not sayin' that. I don't think she specially fancied me. It were her idea of fun. I knew if I got stuck into her she'd be straight round and tell Mary and that'd be me finished for marryin' her. And Bessie knew I knew it.'

'Why not poke her and then tell your lass she was lyin'. That way you could have the ha'penny and the bun.'

'No. Mary could'a' told I were lyin'. The two lasses were close you know, daft as it seems. I knew if Bessie said I'd been up her that'd be the end of it. Anyroad, she nearly drove me bloody mad. She'd come up to me and rub herself up against me and tell me what she wanted me to do.'

'What were that then.'

'Owt you like to reckon on. She'd offer to suck me off, tell me how she fancied me up her arse. She had me in a right muck sweat.'

'An' you did nowt.'

'I were a saint, Ah'm tellin' you. Worst night were when she caught me in Carky Lane. You'll not believe this.'

'Ah reckon you're layin' it on a bit thick as it is, Lije.'

'Honest Ned, as sure as I'm sittin' here. This night she spots me comin' out of Temperance billiard hall and she follows me down the back lane. I felt like runnin' away but it seemed a bit below mi dignity. I'd got just past Brewster's orchard and all of a sudden she runs in front of me and puts her hand straight down mi trousers and grabs mi cock.'

'Nay Lije. I'll not believe that.'

'It's true. Ah stood there like somebody gone out. I dursent pull away or she might have done me a mischief and she's squeezin' it and I'm gettin 'a hard on and she's sayin' why don't we go into Brewster's orchard and it would only tek five minutes and nobody would know and I could push it up as far as I liked.'

'An' you're tellin' us you did nowt.'

'I stood there prayin' for salvation brother. In t'end she starts cryin', says summat about me and Mary bloody deservin' each other and she buggers off. An' she left mi alone after that.'

'Were she very plain then.'

'Not at all. She were a smart lookin' little lass.'

'An' she died in t' flu.'

'Aye. Not long after I was married.'

Joe Ragg spat into the waste. 'That wor a terrible thing. That flu.' He eased his clogs off and rubbed his feet. 'Did I ever tell you about the two folk I found at Hobcroft Terrace.'

'I've heard tale but 'appen Lije 'asn't.'

Shears shook his head.

'I came off night shift late this one time, after seven, and I'm walkin' past that cottage that stands by itself just before you come to the Terrace. There's little lad standin' by the gate in his night things, roarin' his eyes out. When I asked him what was up he kept sayin' his mam and dad wouldn't wake up. So I went into t' cottage and there's the pair of 'em lyin' in bed, dead wi' t' flu. There's no wonder the poor little bugger couldn't wek 'em up. Willis they were called.'

'What became of the kid.'

'I think relatives took him. He works at British Ropes now, int' offices. Roy Willis.'

'Tall, thin young chap, wi' glasses.'

'That's 'im.'

The deputy came scrambling back up the face and Shears shouted after him.

'We all right for empties then.'

'Just about.'

The three men sat back against the props and dozed for a few minutes till the belt started up again. They stretched, hung up Dudleys and snaptins and climbed back over the belt and into their stints.

The front door of Henshaw's house had an ornamental knocker and Sam stared at it for a while before he walked round the house and knocked on the back door. Henshaw opened it and stood squarely in the doorway. Sam said, very quietly, 'Can I speak to Cynthia, please.'

Henshaw did not move. 'I don't know that she'll want to talk to you.'

Sam looked away and rubbed the side of his temple with his thumb. He took a deep breath and said 'I'd be obliged if you'd ask her.'

Henshaw stayed in the doorway but shouted 'Cynthia.' They heard her footsteps on the stairs.

'Who is it.'

'It's Sam Chard.'

Cynthia came into the kitchen and stood awkwardly by the mantelpiece. She said 'Come in, Sam.' Henshaw moved back only a little, forcing Sam to sidle past him. He left the back door open. Sam tucked his hands in his raincoat pockets and nodded to Cynthia. He cleared his throat and said 'Evenin' Cynthia.' Cynthia half-smiled and said 'Evenin' Sam.' There was silence for a moment then Cynthia said 'What brings you here, Sam.'

Sam shook his head. 'You know why I've come.' He half-looked round at Henshaw and then turned to face Cynthia again. 'I've just heard the news.'

Henshaw, his hand still on the knob of the door, said 'Very good news too.' Mrs Henshaw appeared and stood uncertainly at the door leading into the kitchen. Cynthia spoke loudly.

'We'll go into the front room, Sam.'

Henshaw stepped back into the kitchen.

'No. I shall need the front room. I want to read the day paper.'

Cynthia looked down at the floor and said 'Alright father, we'll talk in here.'

'No. Your mother will be gettin' supper ready soon. She'll need the kitchen.' He moved further into the room so that he was standing halfway between his daughter and Sam. 'Anyway, I don't see there's much to talk about.'

Sam looked at him as he spoke.

'Would you mind very much not chippin' in Mister Henshaw.'

Henshaw stood up straighter.

'Why shouldn't I speak. This is my family. What do you fancy doin' if I do speak. Are you going to try and flatten me like you tried to flatten Patricks.'

Sam waved his arms vaguely and Cynthia said 'We'll go into the garden.' She led the way and Sam followed her down the garden. She turned and stood by the bottom fence. They heard the door slam.

Sam hunched his shoulders and spoke in a flat voice.

'It's true then. You're goin' to marry Roy Brierley.'

'Yes, it's true.'

'Why.'

Cynthia said nothing. She stared down the line of neighbouring gardens.

'Is it because he's a nice fat farmer and his Dad left 'im a nice fat farm.'

Cynthia shook her head.

'It's no good talkin' like that, Sam. There's no point.'

'Well why then. Why are you goin' to marry 'im.'

'Because he'll make a good husband.'

'Is that what you want then. Is that what you're after. A good husband.'

'Why not.'

Sam walked a few steps away and stared at the garden. He shook his head several times then shrugged his shoulders.

'It's time your dad singled his lettuce. They're gettin' cramped.'

Cynthia said 'He's not a very good gardener.'

Sam walked back a few steps and spoke quietly.

'What about me.'

'What about you, Sam.'

'Well am I no bugger at all. Just a passing fancy like.'

'No. You're very important to me, Sam.'

'You used to say you loved me.'

'Try an' see it from my point of view Sam. You would never have married me.'

'You don't know that. I might.'

'No, that's a lie. It was bound to come to an end, Sam. I'm very grateful to you for a lot of things.'

Sam spat and said 'Thank you very much for your kind remarks.'

There was silence for a while, then Cynthia spoke in a low voice.

'We can have a big row if you want to, love. But there isn't any point. We'd only say a lot of things we don't mean. We're both of us proud. Why don't we try and part friends.'

Sam shouted at her 'I am not just your bloody friend' and started to walk away. He stopped, looked at the sky and came back. 'Cyn, I honestly don't understand you pet. All the time you've bin knockin' about with Brierley you've joked about him. You've said he's the youngest chap you know with middle-aged spread and that sort of thing. How he can only talk about his tater yield. Do you really love him more than you love me.'

'That's not the point, Sam.'

'Then what the hell is the point.'

'He loves me and he'll take good care of me.'

'What about me. It's not fair to me.'

'Sam, I don't want to live with my father the rest of my life.'

'You didn't say anything about all this to me.'

'It didn't need saying. We both knew how things stood. It was there between us.'

'I don't know what you mean.'

The girl shivered in the cool evening air.

'O Sam, stop talking like a child. You didn't even stop seeing your other women while you were going out with me. What was I supposed to make of that.'

'Well, you went out with Brierley.'

'We're goin' round in circles.'

Sam pointed a finger at her and raised his voice.

'I know what it's about. It's about me bein' out of work. Well it's not even that. It's because I'm a collier. You're like your bloody father. I'm all reight for a bit of shaggin' now an' again but I'm not to be taken serious. Not enough money to be taken serious.'

Cynthia scowled.

'I'll not listen to this, Sam.'

'You will bloody listen. You will. I'm twice the man that cunt Brierley is. He's fuckin' nowt. An' you know it. What about the things you've said to me. An' the way you hold on to me. You're mekkin' a mistake. You know you are.'

Cynthia screwed up her eyes.

'I'm not. At least he wants me and not a string of women. And he wants to marry me.'

'Well I'll marry you.'

They were both silent for a while, then Cynthia spoke slowly.

'I don't trust you.'

'I will. God's honour I will.'

'Don't say any more, Sam. You're only making it worse.'

'Listen to me.'

'I'm sorry you're upset. I am really. I've a lot of feelings for you love. But we must leave it be.'

Sam started to walk away then suddenly turned and shouted.

'Were you going to bother tellin' me then. About Brierley.'

'I was going to tell you tomorrow night. At the club.'

'By fuckin' hell. That's grand. How were you goin' to do it. Buy me a pint of black an' tan and say "by the way I'm goin' to marry Roy Brierley." Just like that. That's fuckin' considerate that is. Still, you were always fuckin' good mannered, weren't you.' He walked quickly round the side of the house and out of the gate. Cynthia went back into the house.

Sam stood for a long time, staring at the gate. He kicked it and shouted.

'You fuckin' stuck up lot. I hope you enjoy your supper. What you havin'. Fuckin' oysters.'

He stood for a while longer then walked down the hill towards his lodgings. At the corner of Beech Road he stopped, turned and went across to the pub. He bought a pint of beer and said to the barman 'Did you watch Rovers on Sat'day.'

'Aye, they're not doin' bad are they.'

'Fuckin' rubbish. Ten consumptives an' a cripple.'

'I don't see that, they won.'

'Only 'cos t'other team were asleep.'

'I thought they played decent enough miself.'

'Never. What about that bloody centre-half, poncin' about. His job's to stop the fuckers not dance wi' 'em. Anyway he's too bloody fat for t' job.'

'Nowt like. He played a steady game.'

'That steady he were nearly stopped still. Bunch o' bloody deadlegs.'

The barman moved away and started to wash glasses. Sam walked across to a group playing darts.

'Can I join you Nick.'

'Can you wait a bit, Sam, we've just got the two aside.'

Sam nodded, watched them play for a while, went back and put his half-full glass down on the bar and left the pub.

He walked quickly home, hung his raincoat and jacket behind the door and lit the gaslight in the empty kitchen, although it was barely dusk. He stood in the middle of the kitchen looking round then fetched some shelving that he had been making, from the pantry. He took out stain and rags from the table drawer and worked on the shelving.

After a few minutes he left the wood on the table, put out the gaslight and went upstairs to his bedroom. He closed the door and sat on the bed. Then he went over into a corner of the room and crouched down, folding his arms round himself.

As it moved towards pub opening time the union meeting became more restless. Men stood up and walked to the window to look out at the wintry Sunday morning or crossed to where the treasurer sat with his books, to argue about back dues. The chairs had been moved higgledy-piggledy out of their rows and the miners sat with them tilted or turned round so they could lean forward over the chair back. Clouds of blue-grey cigarette and pipe smoke drifted in the air and odd remarks were shouted at almost everything that was said.

The young man stood stiffly, head held back, a sheaf of notes in his hand, speaking slowly and loudly.

'I know Abyssinia is a long way off and you might say it doesn't matter to us what happens to a lot of natives. But I say that it does matter to us because if the fascists get away with it, where will they turn to next. That's apart from bombin' and machine-gunning and massacreeing men, women and children armed with only spears.'

'Do the little kids have spears then' somebody shouted.

'Abyssinia is an act of open aggression an' if dictators like Mussolini get away with it they'll just go on.'

'I thought Mussolini were supposed to be a socialist.'

The young man's voice rose to a shout.

'He's a fuckin' fascist now and every workin' man's in danger.' There was a ragged cheer and the young man quietened and turned over a page of his notes. 'As I've said before—'

'Aye, lots o' times.'

'As I've said before it's not just a matter of Italy grabbin' an empire. It's part of growing fascism and as such it means that where today they're usin' poison gas on helpless natives in Abyssinia, tomorrow they'll be attackin' the workin' class throughout the world. I ask you to pass my motion.'

'Try syrup o' figs' someone shouted, and there was another cheer.

'I ask you to pass my motion as an act of workin'-class solidarity against capitalism. If we mean owt by callin' each other brothers, then the people of Abyssinia are our brothers and they need our support. The trade union movement and the whole Labour movement must fight fascism and make its position clear. It's not just for us to condemn the slaughter of innocent people, it is a matter of our political stand, what we stand for. I ask for your support. Thank you brothers.'

The young man sat down and there was a round of clapping. The chairman tapped his gavel on the table in front of him.

'Right brothers. Young Roberts has put to you, at some length I might say, the motion he wants us to put down for the union conference. An' if you pass it, and in the unlikely event of it being chosen by the platform, then your delegate would have to speak to it. He would be so mandated by you. Bearing this in mind will you now vote upon the motion.'

A stooped, one-armed man at the back of the room called out 'Hoddup Dyson.'

'You have somethin' to say brother Swale.'

Swale stood up.

'I fuckin' 'ave. Reight. Now I don't give a fuck for Musso an' his shits an' you know it. But before we start howlin' about how rotten it is to kill off the blacks and build a bloody empire let's look at usselves. There's old Tindall ovver there as fought in the Boer War, there's me an' Abbott an' a few more 'as 'ave served in India.' He looked around the room. 'There's Taffy Evans was in the Malaya police. Fuckin' 'ell, we're the biggest bloody empire there is an' 'ere we are shoutin' because the Eyeties are grabbin' a bit of bloody sand. What about our empire.'

Somebody said 'It might be your bloody empire. I'm fucked if it's mine.'

Roberts jumped to his feet and shouted 'Just because we're against the invasion of Abyssinia doesn't mean we support British colonialism. It's a political issue.'

The shouting became general.

'Mek 'im Prime Minister.'

'That's tellin' 'im Robbo.'

'Swop it for Lancashire and half a pound of black pudding.'

Two or three began to sing.

Will you come to Abyssinia
Will you come
Bring your own ammunition and a gun
Mussolini will be there
Shooting bullets in the air
Will you come to Abyssinia
Will you come.

The chairman hammered on the table and the noise died down.

'Now then brothers, we've business on the agenda and we're comin' up to time. Now can I tek a vote.'

A small wizened miner over by the door, who had put on his overcoat ready to leave, said 'No you can't' and stood on his chair. 'I have just one thing to say brothers.'

There was another round of cheers.

'Did you know, did young Mester Roberts know, that the Eyeties was promised Abyssinia after the last war. They was promised it as compo for sidin' wi' us in the war.'

Someone shouted 'I never heerd that.'

'It's a fuckin' fact. An' we had a hand in that promise. I'm not sayin' it were right but there it is.'

The little man climbed down off his chair and Dyson tapped the table again.

'Right. Now I'm going to 'ave a try at puttin' this matter to the vote. Everybody in favour of Roberts' motion on Abyssinia going forward to the conference raise their hands.'

Most of the forty or so men in the room put up their hands. 'Against.' Nobody raised their hand and the chairman said 'Carried nem con. Take note Mister Secretary.' George Absalom wrote the result of the vote in his minute book and stood up. He looked towards the chairman who nodded.

'Reight lads. Item on this fish scheme.'

There was scattered clapping and shouts of 'Fresh fish. Fresh fish'.

Absalom spoke quickly.

'I'm glad to say that after a lot of callin' we've got things reight an' the scheme starts up next Wednesday. You've heard enough about it but I'm tellin' you once again so nobody can say they didn't know about it. Early Wednesday mornin' Carby's farm lorry will go off to Hull. Union will pay for t' hire of lorry and driver at cost. At Hull, by our agreement wi' t' trawlermen's association, the driver will tek a load of fish straight from the boat at boat prices, no middlemen. He'll bring it to Carky market where Benny Smith and William Abbott will set up a stall an' sell the fish off at as near as buggery what we paid forrit. Union will pay Benny and Will five bob each a shift for their work but that's unofficial as we don't want to interfere with their dole money. Stall will run every Wednesday mornin', ten till one. Now 'ave you got it straight.'

'How cheap's this fish goin' to be, George.'

'We can't tell exact an' it'll vary a bit we but reckon it should work out not much more than a copper or two a pound.'

'Will there be mackerel, George. I love a nice bit o' mackerel.'

'Wi' your appetite you'd eat my goldfish, if I'd let you 'ave 'em. We get what the boat gives us. There's no pickin' an' choosin'.'

'What you goin' to do with fish left over.'

'We'll give it away rather than let it go bad. But that's just the point. All of us 'as got to support this scheme or it'll not work. If there's a good demand we'll up the size of the load.'

'Worrabout a bit of direct sale from the farmers then, George.'

'We're still dickerin' about that. Local farmers are not so keen.'

There was silence for a few seconds then Absalom said 'owt else', looked round and sat down.

The chairman picked up his gavel and said 'Well brothers, we're nicely on to time' when a tall, soft-voiced man spoke from the window side of the room.

'Easy Brother Dyson, I've something I want to say.'

'You'll 'ave to be quick about it brother, we're into drinkin' time.'

There were calls of 'Hear, hear'.

The man stood up and leaned against the window.

'Six months ago we sold off most of the Welfare Hall furniture and got in a new lot. Now, according to the accounts, we got fourteen quid for selling off the furniture.'

Dyson banged his gavel and cut in.

'Just a minute brother Webb. On a point of order. This is an accounts matter an' the accounts was talked about, approved and passed last week. You should have raised your point then.'

'Aye, very true. But last week you did what you're doin' this week. You kept things goin' till past pub openin' time so nobody would stay an' listen.'

'I resent that Tom Webb.'

'You go on resentin' it Eric Dyson and while you're resentin' it I'll point out that that furniture included half a dozen good-sized tables, a roll-top desk, some bar fittings, quite a bit of glassware and a lot of other stuff, most of it in not bad nick and th'a tryin' to tell me we got just fourteen quid for the lot.'

'I'm not tellin' thee owt except that this is out of order an' Treasurer's business anyway.'

Webb looked towards the treasurer.

'Well Bernard.'

'Nay man. I just keep the accounts. The committee was jointly responsible for disposin' of the furniture. I just enter what I'm told in the books an' add 'em up straight.'

Several men had left the room by now. Webb turned towards George Absalom.

'Well Mister Secerterry. You're bein' a bit of a silent wonder.'

'It's no good mitherin' me Tom. I had nowt to do wi' it.'

Somebody called out 'He's not bloody Absalom, he's Pontius Pilate' and there was a round of applause. Webb turned back to Dyson.

'Well, Mister Chairman, it looks as if you're elected to solve the mystery of the evaporatin' furniture.'

Dyson watched more men drift out of the room.

'There's no fuckin' mystery about it. It were all above board. An' we're not goin' to prolong this meetin' so you can talk a lot of spiteful hot air that's out of order anyroad.'

'Well, now look, Eric, just to help you like, just to give you a clue to start on, suppose I tell you that I've heard say that yon roll-top desk has been seen sittin' nicely polished in the house of a feller called Eric Dyson.'

Dyson stood up and pointed a finger at Webb.

'By Christ, it's fuckers like you make me regret ever takin' this job. When I was just an ordinary pitman coal gettin' on West Sevens.'

'You never filled as much as would blind a gnat's eye,' someone shouted.

Dyson banged the table with his fist.

'Right that does it. There's no quorum and I declare this meeting closed.'

He took his overcoat from the back of the chair and clutching his papers, he walked out of the room. Absalom, the treasurer and most of the remaining men filed out after him. Webb sat on the window sill, his hands on his knees, looking at the floor. A man came over and patted his shoulder.

'Bai gum but that were tellin' 'em Tommy.'

Webb shook his head and said 'You must fuckin' like bein' swindled.' He stood up and followed the man to the pub.

The night grew colder and the half-moon was hidden behind scudding cloud.

The five boys played on the pavement, crowded closely round the street lamp. One of them bent forward at the waist and took tight hold of the railings. Shuffling his feet outwards, he splayed his legs until his back was stretched flat and his head was tucked down into his chest. A boy backed into the road and while the others watched, ran forward and leapt on the back of the boy at the railings, landing heavily, high on his shoulders. He held his thumb out above him, so that the boy he sat astride could not see it and shouted 'Okey pokey finger or thumb.'

The boy bearing his weight shouted 'Finger.'

'Th'a wrong.'

A second boy walked out into the road while the first hitched himself along the back of the boy at the railings until he was almost sitting on his neck. The second boy hurled himself up behind his friend and clung to him, swaying. He crossed his legs under the belly of the boy bent down and thrust his arm out with the thumb cocked.

'Okey pokey finger or thumb.'

The boy playing horse shouted 'Finger' and the lad on his back poked his arm down so that he could see the cocked thumb. The third boy made his leap and landed half on and half off the boy. He clutched at the other two riders to save himself from falling off. For a while the three of them swayed and bounced up and down and shouted.

'Nathen, th'a fallin' ovver.'

'Th'a goin' to brek in two.'

'Gerrup and carry us to Carky pictures.'

The boy clung desperately to the railings and bore their weight. Then the last boy on raised his first finger in the air and shouted 'Okey pokey finger or thumb.' The boy underneath grunted 'Finger' and the three riders climbed off him. The boy whose finger showing had been guessed took hold of the railings and bent forward. The game began again.

The girl was eight years old and she had been watching them, moving a little closer, for some time, before she said 'Can I play.' The boys carried on with their game and she spoke more loudly. 'Please can I play.'

The boys stopped the game and gathered round her. The oldest boy pushed her roughly in the chest.

'Girls don't play okey pokey, Ginny Evers, you ought to know that.'

'I want to play.'

'Don't be daft. A girl can't play.'

'Just this once.'

All the boys shouted at her.

'Get back to your skippin' rope.'

'We've told you before.'

'You'd split your knickers and show your arse.'

'You'd start cryin' if I landed on your.'

'Bugger off.'

The girl stood, head down. After a while the boys went back to playing okey pokey. She stayed watching them and once had to skip out of the way as a boy carrying all four of his friends let go of the railings and toppled over so that the others tumbled, shouting and sprawling, about the pavement.

Then the oldest of the boys stood back to the railings when it was his turn to stoop down and said 'Let's do summat else.'

'What else.'

'We could go to Clip Claps and play boxin' on t' band stand.'

'Y' gormless bugger. It's too dark.'

'Let's have a game of rally can co.'

'There's norrenough of us.'

'Let's get Eric Smith an' is brothers.'

'They're not in. Ah called on t' way down.'

'Worrabout Hawthorn Avenue lot.'

'Ah don't like them.'

The oldest boy shouted 'Ah know.'

'What.'

'We could get some bubble gum from Kidson's machine and go to t' Sally Army meetin' at Ridgehill Hut. Then we could blow bangers.'

'They'll clout us.'

'Yerbut if we're at back we can run out when they come.'

'Ah don't reckon much to that.'

'Come on. It's best thing.'

'Right then.'

The boys started to skip along the kerb and the girl called after them 'Can I come.' They took no notice of her and shouting to each other they went round the corner into Ridgehill Avenue. The girl started to walk after them, then stopped and stood for a while. She shivered, pulled her blazer tightly round herself and walked home.

The cage was about eighty yards down and was gathering speed when the huge piece of ice sheared away from the shaft side. It smashed on the top left-hand corner of the cage and the windsman felt the jar on the drum and stopped the rope. The cage bounced and swung and the four men on the top deck clung to the side rails. It steadied and hung still in the shaft. There was a long silence broken by one of the men sighing as he spoke.

'Ah sometimes wished I could come to work on a bus.'

There was another long silence. The man who had spoken stepped to the front of the cage, stood on one of the cross bars of the gate and leaned his head out so that he could look up the shaft. He held on to the cage top, unhooked his lamp from his belt and shone the light round. He stepped back down on to the deck of the cage. 'Somethin's knocked us out of the guiders.'

'Owt wrong with the rope.'

'I can't see owt. I'll go an' have a look.' He handed his lamp to the nearest man. 'Pass mi lamp to me when I'm on top.'

He climbed on the gate again, leaned out and took hold of one of the bull chains that led from each corner of the cage to the rope. He pulled himself out and on to the roof. The man holding the lamp passed it up to him. The three men inside stood still, heads bent, listening to his footsteps as he moved slowly about on top of the cage. After a few minutes he passed his lamp back inside and his legs appeared below the level of the roof. He found a footing on the cage gate and wriggled back inside.

'We've just come out o' the guiders. Chains are fine an' the rope's still locked into the cap all reight.'

'What they waitin' for then.'

'They'll not know what's happened, so they'll be tekkin' it steady. We'll just 'ave to sit about for a bit.'

The four men squatted on the floor of the cage and chewing tobacco was passed round.

'By but it had me thinkin' just then. About the time Ginger Woods fell down the shaft at Emsall.'

'You cheerful fucker.'

'How did he do that then.'

'They were trying to put this long girder through t' traphole in the top of the cage. Ginger's buggerin' about up there tryin' to guide it in an' all of a sudden cage starts to lower away. Onsetter swore blind he never rang it off and the windsman said he got a signal. Anyroad, it seems Ginger were astride this bloody girder when the cage moved, it cocked up an' flipped 'im over the side into t' shaft. Just as if he were a stone on peggy-stick. An' it's well ovver half a mile down at Emsall.'

'Did his wife get compo for 'im.'

'Norrabit. They said he should have had a harness on before he went on the cage top.'

'Tek you fuckin' hours mankin' about trussed up in harness.'

'Well they didn't reckon on that. Said he were negligent.'

'Poor sod.'

'He come down in two halves.'

'He never.'

'He fuckin' did. I were in t' pit bottom at time. He must have hit the other cage halfway down and it tore 'im in two. There were two splashes as he went into t' sump.'

One of the men tucked his hands under his armpits. 'By Christ it's fuckin' freezin' 'ere.'

'Tha sounds like that song our little kid sings from 'Band of Hope'.'

'What's that then.'

'You know.' The man sang in a high, piping voice.

'It matters not when it snows or freezes
I am safe in the arms of Jesus
Jesus loves me that I know
Jolly old Jesus, fuckin' good show.'

He stopped as a faint sound of shouting came down the shaft. The man who had climbed on the cage top stood up and put his head out above the gate and shouted slowly 'We're all right. It's just out of its guiders. You can start it up slow.' There was more shouting from the shaft top but the words could not be clearly heard. The man came back and squatted down. 'Ah'll 'ave to send 'em a postcard.'

'They'll cotton on in time.'

'Did you hear about that cage do in that Geordie pit.'

'Fuckit. Tell us a joke or summat.'

'No. Listen. This were a good'n. You see this onsetter forgets to pull his blocks away when he signals the cage off. So the cage is sittin' there on the blocks and rope's just coiling on top of it as it unwinds. When he sees this he panics and grabs his lever and pulls the blocks away so the cage just drops down till it's used up the spare rope and it gets jerked to a stop. It's full both decks an' there's about thirty blokes with brokken legs an' hips and Christ knows what. Anyway when they get to check on it they find that the part where the rope's bulled into the chains has stretched that much with the jerk that it's as flat as a penny piece. But the blacksmith who capped it did such a good job that it never pulled loose. So when these blokes get out of hospital they clubbed together an' bought the blacksmith a suite o' furniture.'

'What did they buy for the fuckin' onsetter that let it go.'

'I never heard.'

'A spiked glove to wank 'imself with I should think.'

The cage scraped against the guiders as it twisted on the rope.

'Be snaptime soon.'

'We shall not fill off a fortune this shift.'

One of the men farted and another coughed loudly.

'By the powers, Sid, I think a rat must 'ave crawled up your arsehole and died.'

'They say you can never smell your own.'

There was more confused shouting from the pit top and one of the men went to the gate and shouted back. Another man muttered 'Tell 'em to send us a box o' dominoes.'

One of the men began tapping an iron track rod on the floor of the cage, shifting the rhythm from fast to slow to fast.

'Practisin' for t' Boy's Brigade, Alfred.'

'Do you remember that time when Boothy dumped them tubs into the sump.'

'Give ovver, Sid. Talk about summat else.'

'No it were bloody comical this. See, Boothy were top deck onsetter in t' pit bottom an' this one time he didn't get his lockers in reight and this run of tubs comes crashin' down into t' sump. There's three in the run and then two or three more come toppling over one at a time. Then when last one had come crashing down Boothy leans ovver and shouts down to t' bottom deck, reight cheerful like, "that's the lot, Percy". What he didn't know is that the manager were standin' in t' pit bottom an' he took unkindly to Boothy bein' so cheerful.'

'He sacked him.'

'Didn't even let him work the shift out.'

'Funny that. In the war they used to give us medals for bein' cheerful in the face of fuckin' adversity.'

'Come to think on, Boothy went greengrocerin' after that and made a packet. Lives at posh end of Bessacarr now.'

The cage started to lift slowly.

'Heyup, we're off.'

'What they tekkin' us back up for.'

'They reckon on us bein' loose from t' guiders. If we went down we might swing an' bump the other cage comin' up.'

The men were silent as the cage drew slowly up the shaft. As it cleared the level of the pit top the onsetter put in his blocks and the cage was lowered to rest on them. He opened the gate and let the men out.

The Mayor's New Year's Eve dinner and dance was over and the banqueting hall of the Mansion House was empty save for Sam Chard and Amos Hobbs scavenging among the tables that had been pushed back to the walls. The chandeliers had been switched off and the hall was dimly lit by stage lights reflecting off the waxed dance-floor. Crested plates and cutlery, silver tureens, twisted gilt condiment holders and tiered cake stands were stacked untidily and the shiny damask table-cloths were stained by spilled sauces and bits of food.

Tucking a half-bottle of wine under his arm and spooning from a chased silver dish, Sam walked down the hall to the high balconied windows that overlooked the street. He elbowed the heavy, velvet curtains open and looked out.

'Quiet now they finished New Yearin'.'

Amos peeled the marzipan from a piece of iced cake and ate it.

'What y' think of the Mayor's speech.'

Sam drank from his bottle and sniffed.

'I could 'ardly hear him from our cubby-hole. I gather he thinks well of hisself.' He crossed to a table and put the dish on it.

'So that's caviare. Bit salty.'

'Don't grumble, lad. It's like eatin' gold.'

'An' I get a quid just for helpin' thee put up an' tek down the electricals.'

'That's reight.'

Sam emptied his wine bottle and rooted along the table till he found another, part-full bottle.

'Beats fillin' coal. You know I could tek to wine.'

'Too vinegary for me.'

Amos moved to another table, found a plate of salad and began eating the ham from it.

'What y' think of the band then.'

'Curley Yates an' his bow-tie brigade. Bit blarty with all them saxophones.'

Sam began to walk back up the hall looking at the portraits of former mayors that lined the wall. He tripped over a chair and grabbed the table to stop himself from falling.

'Steady on the drink Sam. Tha'll not be fit to help me clear up.'

Sam finished his bottle and found another. 'Mother's milk this stuff.' He gazed at the picture on the bottle label. 'I like the pictures. Pretty castle on this one. Good lookin' place, France.'

Amos found some cider and poured it into a cup.

'I saw enough of fuckin' France in the War. Never appealed to me. They can 'ave it.'

'How'd you get this job.'

'Ah get it whenever there's a big do wi' a band an' microphone an' stuff. Mi brother-in-law's steward for the Mansion House.'

'Must be nice to have relatives.'

Sam picked at the carcase of a turkey and drank more of his wine. Amos found a half-smoked cigar among the plates and lit it. He coughed harshly and stubbed it out.

'Time we got started.'

Sam said 'No rush' and walked out on the dance-floor, carrying his bottle. He bowed deeply and spoke in an affected voice. 'Ah Lady Muck. How fuckin' fine you look. Those diamonds danglin' from your titties. Dashed splendid. May I have the pleasure of this dance.' He held his left arm in a curve and put his right arm straight out from the shoulder. Still clutching his bottle, he swung into a waltz step, sliding his feet in time with the tune he was humming. He waltzed in larger and larger circles. 'Quite your Ladyship, a delateful assembly. And so jolly when the Mayor caught his chain in his bollocks.'

Amos climbed up on the stage and began slowly dismantling the microphone. Sam changed to a foxtrot, whistling sharply between his teeth.

'And if I may say so your bum reminds me of a rising sun. So sad about his Lordship's constipation. By jove yes, let's give Archibald an extra hundred quid.'

Amos shouted down from the stage.

'Come on Sam. Let's be 'avin' you.'

Sam danced a few more steps then his feet slithered from under him and he sat down heavily on the floor. He took a long drink from his bottle and muttered to himself.

'It's fuckin' money makes the difference mate. That's all they've got. A bit o' cash. An' you'd think God made 'em special. Three balls apiece.'

Amos laid sections of microphone on the edge of the stage and began coiling the cable. He shouted more loudly.

'Come on Sam. Ah don't want to spend the night 'ere.'

Sam lay on his back and sang to the tune of happy birthday to you.

'Happy New Year Amos Hobbs,
Happy New Year Amos Hobbs,
Happy New Year you old fucker,
Happy New Year Amos Hobbs.'

Amos climbed down off the stage, walked across to Sam and pulled him to his feet.

'By the fuckin' powers, Sam. Give over an' start your stint.'

Sam hugged the older man and said 'Right flower, mi old son, what's to be done.'

'I'll pack the stuff up an' you put it back under the stage.'

Sam said 'Tharron' and half-ran to the stage and opened the flap-doors under the platform. Amos pulled the music stands, cables and junction boxes forward and Sam collected them in armfuls, climbed clumsily down and stacked them under the stage. He followed Amos round the hall as the electrician detached the amplifiers from the walls and uncoupled them from their cable. As each one was handed to him Sam trotted away with it.

When Amos reached the far left-hand corner of the hall he found a small untouched jelly and sat down at a table to eat it. Sam wandered off, picked up a part-full bottle of wine and finished it. Then he climbed up on the stage and stood in the centre, arms outstretched.

'Ladeeees and gentlemen. And Amos Hobbs. Your parsnip the Mayor. Lend me your lugholes. I put it to you. Have you, have you ever noticed, have you ever noticed a strange fact. An actual fact. Have you never noticed how when a lass gets rid of a feller, when she gets rid of a feller to tek up with another feller, how fuckin' fast she is. No messin'. Easy as winkin'. Practical like. One minute you are the feller. She's all ovver you. The sun shines out of your arsehole. Next minute. Hey presto. You're no fucker at all. You've just fuckin' vanished. Bloody marvellous in't it. 'Cos she knows what she's after. It's like fallin' off a fuckin' express train. Am I right Amos Hobbs. Am I right. I ask you. Am I right.'

Amos carefully scraped the last of the jelly from the cardboard cup and put his feet up on the chair in front of him.

'You're on about Cynthia Henshaw, aren't you Sam.'

'Give the lad a coconut.'

'Well by all accounts you didn't do too badly there.'

'You reckon not, Amos. You reckon I'm not entitled.' Sam sat down and let his legs dangle over the edge of the platform.

'She was bound to settle down sometime.'

'Ah settlin' down. Now that's the nub that. Settlin' down.'

'Well do you blame 'er.'

'I fuckin' do mi old mate.'

'That's 'cause you're prejudiced.'

'That's reight. Where our Cyn's concerned Ah'm the most prejudiced bugger you've ever met.'

'It's been an' gone an' done with, Sam. There's nowt to be gained by pinin'.'

Sam stared at the far windows. Amos pulled himself to his feet and took down the last two amplifiers. Sam stored them under the stage and Amos dragged the cable across and passed the end down to him. Sam coiled it and climbed out and shut the flap-doors. Amos started to switch off the stage lights and Sam said 'Hoddup a minute, I want to find another drink.' He searched among the tables till he found a nearly full bottle of red wine hidden behind a spray of artificial flowers. Amos picked up the bottle of cider he had been drinking from and switched out the lights. The two men went out on to the broad curving stairway of the Mansion House. It was faintly lit by the rays of a street lamp that shone through the fan-shaped glass at the top of the double-entrance doors.

As they started down the stairway Sam tugged at the other man's arm, sat down on the stairway and took a long drink from his new bottle. He said 'Let's do a bit more callin'.' Amos sighed and sat down three steps below Sam. Sam said 'Give us a fag.' Amos gave him one and lit up with him.

'Dost know, Mester Hobbs, that I was once raped.'

'You're 'avin me on.'

'I was.'

'An' our duck lays mince pies.'

'No. Listen. Listen. It was in t' '21 strike.'

'An she wor seven foot tall.'

'Listen. Durin' t' strike I took a job in Lebrun's quarries, past Hooton Pagnell. You know 'em.'

'I've seen 'em.'

'Well, at that time, there were quite a lot o' lasses worked in the quarries. An' a bloody rough lot they were. Big strappin' lasses, muscles like navvies an' tongues to match. Anyroad, I were more of a shy young chap at that time.'

'I'll believe that.'

'Nay I was. This lass kept on at me. Why didn't I come with 'er an dip it in. I kept sayin' things like there wasn't time and she said there was all'us time for that. In the end I agreed to meet 'er after shift in the bottom quarry that was worked out. When she turned up she'd got three of 'er mates with her. I was in a reight tizzy about this an' I said wouldn't do owt with them watchin'. There was a lot o' shoutin' wi' them laughin' at me and they all grabbed hold of me an' I was raped.'

'You're slow timin' me Sam Chard.'

'God's honour.'

'You're romancin'.'

'I'm not.' Sam drank from his bottle, spilled some of the wine down his shirt and wiped it with his sleeve.

'How could they. Ah mean, what did they do.'

'Well the three of 'em held me spragged out on mi back an' this one, she were called Jean, that I'd said I'd meet, she got mi prick out and played with it till I got a hard on. Then she sat astride me an' fucked me.' Sam took another drink. 'It was just as if she was tossin' herself off on me.'

'An' you couldn't do owt.'

'No. I was frightened they'd scrag me if I thrashed about too much.'

'Wor 'appened then.'

'Well, rest of 'em played about wi' me. Messed me about an' said things.'

'What things.'

'I don't remember. I remember I didn't like it.'

'I reckon you were fuckin' lucky.'

'No I wasn't. It wasn't like you might think.'

Amos yawned.

'Well I wouldn't mind a few lasses playin' wi' me.'

'That's where you're wrong Amos. Ever since then I've reckoned out why lasses don't like bein' mauled about an' forced to do things.'

They drank in silence for a while. Sam stubbed his cigarette out on his bottle.

'You think it were my fault wi' Cynthia don't you.'

'I think you got what you asked for.'

'It's not as simple as that.'

Amos drank the rest of his cider and stretched.

‘Ah’m due down pit this afternoon. We’d best geroff.’

‘What you doin’.’

‘They’re tryin’ out these new shaker pans on Fives. Ah’m wirin’ the motor up.’

‘German idea in’t it.’

‘Aye.’

‘They’ll be no bloody good. You watch.’

‘We’ll see.’

‘Are you puttin’ ’em down the face as well.’

Amos said ‘No, just along the main gate’, and walked down the stairs. He opened the front door by the self-locking bar and stood waiting. Sam sat for a while longer on the stairs before following him down. Amos closed the doors behind them, said ‘I’ll see you Monday with the money’ and walked away up the High Street. Sam shouted after him ‘Happy new year’ and Amos shouted back ‘Aye’.

Sam stood for a while outside the Mansion House, finished his wine and put the bottle down by the gilded railings. He walked down the High Street and stared up at the lighted clock tower for a minute. He fell over, climbing the steel railings that fenced off the corner, picked himself up and walked towards the Don bridge. In front of the grimy columns of the police station a constable watched him closely as he weaved past. Sam turned and came back to him. He smiled at the policeman and said ‘Happy new year.’ The policeman smiled and said ‘Happy new year.’ Sam clapsed his hands behind his back in imitation of the policeman and spoke in a loud voice. ‘Are you married.’

The policeman shook his head.

‘No.’

‘Ah. One of the clever buggers.’

‘You’re married then.’

‘No. I’m one of the clever buggers too.’

Sam weaved his way past the bus station and on over the bridge.

Half a dozen men sat on the flat stone bridge of the stream that ran by the edge of the pit tip, at the bottom of Ings Lane. One of them shouted across to a man sitting on his own on the shallow bank of the stream.

'It's a daft bet, Geordie.'

'It's up to 'im. He can cry off if he likes.'

Above the men rose the high end pylon of the tip. Flat on top of it a big spoked wheel turned, carrying the rope that ran along the spine of the tip supported by eight other pylons. Jutting from the second pylon was a frame and catch and as the huge, box-shaped buckets travelled to it, they were tipped upside down and emptied a stream of slag on the tip. Hanging down, swinging violently at first, they came round the end pylon wheel and were carried the half mile back to the pit yard.

'Do you reckon he'll try it then, Ruben.'

'Likely. Young Dicky Herd's all'us been a bit of a mad bugger. Comes of bein' brought up without a Dad, I should think.'

'Warn't his Dad killed at pit.'

'A good while afore you came here. When Dicky was nobbut a babby. It was just on Christmas. These two blokes got trapped on Old Fours, and on Boxin' Day Simpson took his rescue team down with Tom Herd in it. They got on to the bottom end of the face and there was this gas explosion and the lot came in and all five were buried. Funny thing was they got the two blokes out the next day and there wasn't a scratch on 'em. Herd and the rest of 'em are still down there. They had to close it off.'

The man next to them tapped Ruben Howells on the shoulder.

'Tell you another funny thing about that do.'

Howells turned towards him.

'For years after that Tom Herd's widow would never go past the pit gates. She said she wouldn't go near where he was buried. If she needed to go to Addick or owt like that she'd go right round the top end by Lodge Road so as not to pass the pit gates.'

Howells said 'What's funny about that.'

'Well think about it a bit. She lives in Ridgehill an' Old Fours was a good mile west from the pit bottom. So as near as buggery she's livin' on top of him. Anyroad, she's a bloody sight nearer to him lyin' in 'er bed than she is down by the pit gates.'

'I never thought about that.'

The watery sun failed to warm the chilled air and the men tugged their jackets closer round them. One produced a quart bottle of beer which was passed round. The roar of the slag from where the buckets were emptying grew quieter as they began tipping a wet slurry which moved down the side of the tip like a slow-flowing, black river.

Howells turned to Fred Barthrop and said 'How did this bet get started then.'

'Both pissed I reckon. Geordie starts on about why you get dizzy when you're a kid an' you spin yourself round and round. Summat about liquid in yor earholes gettin' out of kilter. Dicky Herd kept sayin' that he could go round and round wi'out gettin' dizzy an' next thing you know they've got this bloody bet on about Dicky standing on the tip wheel and throwin' his coat down.'

'Where wor this.'

'Half Moon.'

''As nobody tried to talk sense into 'im.'

'They've settled on three quid a side.'

'Does his mam know.'

'I shouldn't think so. She'd go doolally tap if she did.'

Barthrop spat into the stream.

'Best bet I ever saw wor that little haulage lad on forty-eights. Ronnie Flowers.'

'What wor that.'

'Well he bet the road doggy he'd eat this live mouse in a sandwich. For a dollar.'

'Did he do it.'

'He fuckin' did. I saw it. He gets two slices out of his snaptin and packs this mouse in. Poor little bugger's squeakin' away and Ronnie starts crunchin' on 'im, head end first.'

'Was he alright after.'

'He was sick as a dog but he gorr'is five bob.'

One of the men dropped an empty tobacco tin into the water and as it drifted slowly downstream he and another man walked along the bank throwing stones at it.

'It's gettin' more like a pond than a bloody stream.'

'Tip's blockin' a lot of it off. Another year or so an' they'll have to cut round, when it's blocked up altogether.'

'Aye. An' a year after that tip'll come across and bury that willow garth. An' two or three year after that it'll cross field to the railway embankment.'

'They'll 'ave to do summat about it then or pack in the railway.'

'They'll start tippin' on the other side and bury the football pitch an' thy allotment.'

'They're fuckin' welcome.'

Dicky Herd and two more men came down the lane and joined the group on the bridge. Geordie Smith came across and stood in front of Herd.

'If you want to pack it in Dicky, I'm willin' to call it square.'

'Frightened of losin' your money.'

'Have it how you want but let's be clear it's not my idea. If owt happens to thee I'm not tekkin' the blame.'

'Bugger the blame, Geordie. So long as you pay up when I've done it.'

'I'll pay up but if you come down without doin' it, you pay me.'

Howells put his hand on Herd's arm and said 'Think on Dicky. If you fall off that bugger you'll get more than a rupture.'

Herd pulled his arm away.

'I could do that standin' on mi head.'

'You're a cunt Dicky. Nobody'll think any the less of you if you pack it in. Show a bit o' sense.'

One of the other men said 'He's right, lad.'

Herd spoke to Smith.

''Ave we got it straight then. It's up to me to stand up on the wheel while it's turnin'. I take off mi coat an' throw it down and tek off mi shirt an' throw that down. After that I collect me three quid from thee.'

Smith said 'You all heard that. It's his idea.'

Herd buttoned his jacket and flexed his shoulders.

'Right lads, stand back for Harry Houdini. Any of you buggers want a bet. Evens to any amount.'

No one spoke.

'Tell you what. Two to one and Ah'll do a dance on the wheel while I'm theer.'

One of the men said 'Give it up, Dicky.'

'Come on you nesh fuckers. You're that certain I can't do it, let's see your money.'

Herd waited for a moment then walked out of the group and ran up the small hillock of slag around the base to the pylon. He climbed a few feet up the pylon and leaned out, hanging on with one hand and shouting 'Three to one an' Ah'll walk rope tiptoe back to the pit.' He began climbing again, shinning a corner upright and resting for a moment on each cross strut before starting again. He climbed more slowly as he neared the top. The men stood together, watching him closely, heads tilted back.

Herd stood on the highest cross-strut holding tightly to the upright and slowing his breathing. Wiping the sweat from his face with his sleeve, he tucked his head down and closed his eyes as a bucket came banging round the wheel just above him, showering him with bits of slurry and dirt. He stayed there several minutes while two more buckets came round. As soon as the second bucket was clear of the wheel he shinned the upright and, holding on to the frame, pulled himself up and stretched out over the wheel. He gripped the frame tightly and pivoted slowly, balancing on his belly, with his legs swinging out from the side of the pylon and his body poised over the wheel. He hitched forward, let go of the frame and grabbed for the spokes of the wheel. He grunted as he was dragged forward and his legs were thumped and bruised against the frame. He bent his knee and pulled himself on to the spokes so that he lay curled at the centre of the wheel, turning round and round. He lay at rest for a few seconds before pulling himself on to his knees. Sweat ran down into his eyes and he blinked and fixed his gaze on the rim of the wheel. He pulled his right foot forward and jammed the metalled toe of his boot under a spoke near the hub of the wheel and wedged his heel over the next spoke. He brought his left foot forward and did the same, so that he was crouched in a squat, still gripping the spokes with his hands, still turning round and round. For a little while he stayed there, then came suddenly upright, still looking at the one place on the rim of the wheel, his arms outstretched for a moment as he revolved. He felt for the buttons on his jacket, loosened them, pulled the jacket off and flung it away. It caught the air and came swooping down in widening circles. He tore the buttons of his shirt-sleeves off and pulled the shirt over his head. It fluttered away from him. He grabbed for the spokes and went back into a crouched position. Freeing his boots he knelt on the spokes. A bucket came bumping round the wheel. He stayed kneeling, his eyes closed, breathing heavily, sweat running down his chest, while two more buckets arrived and circled the wheel.

The men down below watched the small hunched figure revolving and one of them said 'If he stays like that much longer he'll get dizzy an' fall off.'

Herd opened his eyes and shuffled out to the edge of the wheel. He wiped each hand in turn on his trousers and twisted his head to watch the edge of the frame as the wheel brought him round to it. As he came level he grabbed hold of it. The turning of the wheel stretched his body out and for a few seconds the spokes scraped under him bouncing him up and down as he clung to the frame. His hip slid over the edge of the wheel and he swung downwards, his body thumping hard against the upright, his figure slipping away from the frame. He screeched, scissored his legs tightly round the upright and slid down it till he was sitting on the cross-piece, his arms and legs clinging tightly to the right-angled metal. He sat there for a long time, sobbing, then began to climb slowly down the pylon.

The old men's ward of the town infirmary was long and narrow and the night nurse sat at a table at one end. It had twenty-five iron beds against each wall with a narrow walkway between the two rows. Hanging sixty-watt bulbs, without shades, gave a dim yellow light and the place smelled of piss and carbolic. Rain pattered on the tall end windows and patients snored and coughed and moaned and sometimes cried out.

An old man in a bed near the nurse talked almost all the time, in an eager mutter. Sometimes the nurse would put down the Red Letter magazine she was reading and go and shake him and tell him to shut up but it made no difference.

He had pulled up his ticking nightshirt so that it was bunched under his chin. His body was wasted and covered with bed-sores. His eyes were sunk deep in their sockets. His fingers picked busily at the bedclothes.

'Knew it better than him better than him anytime shine a light and knock 'em out the branches gimmie what it's worth two brace o'rabbits keeps pullin' up mi snares said he'd 'ave me forrit braggin' callin' me pit scum tha dast not tha dast not lost 'is nerve in the wheatfield need a new fuckin' keeper now knew he would lost 'is nerve.'

He touched his face with his hand, feeling it. All the knuckles of his right hand had been broken and were dimpled in. Knotted blue veins bulged as he opened and closed his fingers.

'Put pellets in me 'e said tek his gun to me tellin' all the pub can't catch me you big babby down to the lake net a few up the little gill tell Harry boy come Sunday we'll have us dues give us mi gun fat buck rabbit pheasant feather in mi 'at we'll rattle 'im mi faither before me share an' share alike.'

His knees jerked up convulsively and he opened his eyes and stared at the ceiling. His eyes watered and he blinked. He turned over onto his side and began muttering again.

'Silly fucker mek a little tin god o' t' squire hear 'im a mile off hear 'im tell you pet tell you pet sit down to tea together pretty as a picture me in mi new suit hear the old owl whitterin' old owl me and you old feller me and you.'

Suddenly he spoke loudly.

'I could sneak up and tek his trousers off wi'out 'im knowin'.

He was silent for a while then began mumbling again.

'Better than him waited him out watch yousen Harry lad hear you comin' a mile off blind as a mouldy warp don't nag me Mam tidy up go to see Uncle Jack Buckley at New Miller Dam pop up and both barrels twelve bore right you bugger put pellets in me he said hear a woodcock the more you've got the more you want tellin' all the pub tried for me bang you old bugger run me down into t' wheatfield Ah'm not frit missed by a mile wait him out red as a poppy play tig wi' me black two four six eight hidey-seek in the wheat tell your Mam I'll bring 'er summat for sure where'y bin where y' bin fetch me a penny duck we'll never be short my love promise you.'

Near the far end of the ward one of the old men climbed out of bed, fell over and began crying. The nurse swore and went to him. She pulled the chamber pot from under the bed, gripped him from behind round the belly, hitched up his nightshirt and put him on the pot. When he had finished she heaved him into the bed, pushed the pot back and returned to her chair at the table.

'There's nowt to it moon meks it all look like cardboard put him in his own garden that's it put him in his own garden.'

He pulled his lips back and bared his snaggled teeth.

'Present for his Missis hey Missis Ah've planted your Harry in your snapdragons old braggin' Harry 'ave rabbit stew more the merrier half the time half the time we do crossed knives brek a friendship.'

The nurse stood, yawned and frowned at the old man. She walked to the top end of the ward, sat on the window-sill and lit a cigarette, watching the rain waterfalling down the outside iron staircase into the infirmary yard.

''Ave a try out lad up in that wood like a flash all night an' still work next day see that old dog fox crafty old bugger 'appen tomorrer fixed you Harry boy potted 'im as he come sneakin' through the wheat big old sod to carry round by the crags path turns nearly back on itself lake a shift an' come wi' me our John meks no odds meks no odds lake a shift an' come wi' me.'

The big hall of the Wesleyan Methodist chapel was crowded for the annual performance of the *Messiah*. The choirs of several chapels had been combined and they overflowed the stage so that the pews for the audience had been moved more closely together and people sat tightly packed with their knees uncomfortably drawn up. The heavy, black, cast-iron radiators had been turned full on and the chapel was overheated. The top slats of the high windows had been opened and fog from the outside swirled round the roof beams. To the left of the platform coloured lights gleamed round a large crib and manger long left over from the Christmas services.

As each part of the oratorio ended the conductor waited a while to let the audience cough and shuffle, before pointing his baton at the organist in the loft. There was immediate silence and the next aria or chorus began.

Sam was in one of the side pews, very close to the choir and he saw Cynthia soon after the performance had begun. She was sitting on one of the folding chairs that had been put out near the doors of the chapel. Sam watched her closely. He could not see her husband anywhere in the hall and she did not speak to the people on either side of her. She stared at the platform or down at the programme in her hand and never looked towards him.

When the performance ended the choir mixed with the audience and it took Sam a long time to work his way through the mass of people talking together and across to the door. He soon lost sight of Cynthia. When he reached the door he saw her standing in the wide chapel porch by herself. He stood a few feet from her and they looked at each other. Sam tied his white silk muffler and buttoned his overcoat as people pressed past him, leaving the chapel. One or two said goodnight to him and he nodded to them. He started to go down the front steps, turned and stood in front of her, hesitating before speaking.

'Evenin' Cynthia.'

'Good evening, Sam.'

He pointed to the programme she was holding in her hands.

'What d'y think of it.'

'Not bad. Bass was a bit weak.' She smiled and added 'I thought he was going to run out of puff on "Why do the Nations".'

Sam smiled back.

'Choir gave it some stick on "Unto us a Son is Born".'

Cynthia nodded.

'It was always one of Russell's favourites. He makes them try hard on that.'

Sam looked round and cleared his throat.

'Roy not with you then.'

'No. He's not a great one for music.'

Sam looked back into the hall.

'You come with friends. You're waitin' for somebody.'

'No. I came on my own.' Cynthia stared out at the fog and shivered. 'It's such a nasty night. I was just looking at it. It's near to freezing.'

There was a pause and Sam said 'Can I walk you back.'

'Yes. Thank you.'

Cynthia put a kerchief over her head and they walked down the steps and stood for a moment. Sam put his hands in his pockets.

'Which way would you like to go. Pit or Lodge Road.'

'I don't mind.'

'We'll go top road then. And along Crossfield Lane.'

They walked up Markham Avenue and on to Lodge Road in silence. As they turned into the top road Cynthia put her arm in Sam's. He took her hand and put it into his overcoat pocket, holding it there.

'It's bitterly cold.'

Cynthia said 'Yes.'

As they passed the end of the houses Sam pointed across the field.

'Do you remember when we went down to the newt pond there and you found that little lad putting a reed into a newt and blowin' it up. An' you smacked his ears for 'im 'for bein' cruel.'

'Well he was.'

Sam laughed.

'You kept talkin' at 'im while you were bangin' his head. I don't reckon he could hear a word.'

'I was angry.' She giggled. 'Anyway, you just sat there, not doin' anything.'

'I was admirin' you.'

'No.'

'Yes I was.'

Their footsteps echoed in time as they crossed the top of Poplar Road and turned into Crossfield Lane.

'Cyn.'

'Mmm.'

'Do you still sing much.'

'No. Not much.'

'Sing summat for us.'

'I don't feel like it.'

'Anything you like. How about "Pretty Polly Oliver". You used to like that.'

'No.'

'All right then.'

Cynthia stumbled and they worked their way off the grass round the oak trees that lined the road and on to the metalled path.

'How are you keepin', Sam.'

'Why, are you bothered.'

Cynthia stopped and freed her hand. Sam stood for a moment before muttering 'I'm sorry.' He put his arm round her waist. She put her arm round his waist and they started walking again.

'I'm fair to middlin'.'

'I hear you still 'aven't got a job.'

'No. I went in with Derry Ward for a while. He bought up old sleepers from the pit and we chopped 'em up and bundled 'em to sell for firewood. There wasn't enough in it for it to be worth his while carryin' on.'

'How are you managing.'

'Dole just about keeps me. I'm a lot better off than blokes with families dependin' on 'em.'

'Sam. I don't know if it'd be any good but I've got a cousin runs a little removal business in Tadcaster. I could talk to him for you. He could only say no.'

'Not to fret, lass.'

'No. I know I would be doing him a favour if he took you on.'

'Something'll turn up love. I've got one or two things in mind. Anyway, how about you. You thrivin'.'

'Just so so. It's a quiet life.'

'How's married life then.'

'All right.'

'He's a fine feller, Mester Brierley.'

'He treats me well.'

'Answer to a maiden's prayer.'

'Sam, stop it.'

'What's he like at fuckin'. A proper stallion is he.'

She pulled away from him and slapped at his face catching him across the nose. She stood with both hands stretched towards him like claws. Her voice hissed.

'How dare you ask me that. How dare you.'

'I dare ask you anythin' I want.'

'You've no right.' She started to cry and said several times 'You've no right.'

Sam wiped his hand across his mouth and spoke softly.

'I wanted to know. I just wanted to know.'

Cynthia stopped crying and breathed deeply looking at the ground. 'If you must know – if you – If it's of any interest to you – I might just as well be a barrel with a bunghole in it as far as he's concerned. It would do just as well.'

Sam put his hand out to touch her but she stepped away. He mumbled something and she said 'I can't hear you.' His voice trailed away. Cynthia spoke sharply. 'You satisfied. Does that suit you.'

'I'm sorry. I'm sorry Cyn.'

She shook her head.

'It's not as important as you might think.'

Sam spoke uncertainly.

'Is there anything I can do.'

'What did you have in mind.'

'I don't know. Whatever you wanted. We could meet sometimes.'

'You're saying you want to be my fancy man.'

'If that's what you want.'

'That's what you want. We'd sneak off to Smeaton Woods.'

Sam shuffled his feet.

'You're trying to mek it sound bad.'

'Not enough lasses on your string Sam. A nice married woman would just round up the number.'

'Pet. It's just. I find it very hard, being without you. You see—' He jerked his head to and fro. 'You see I didn't realize how much, how I was goin' to miss you when you left me.'

'That's the difference between us Sam. I knew how much I was going to miss you. So it came as no surprise. I was prepared for it.'

'You miss me, then.'

'That's a daft question.'

Sam reached out and touched her arm.

'If you'll take me back I'll be whatever you want.'

Cynthia smiled.

'You won't you know.'

'I'll try. Sod it. You want me. I know you want me.'

'You're a sweetheart, Sam. But you're like a big kid. You think it's all a matter of what you want. Or what I want. I've got a marriage and I'm going to make it work.'

'When we were together you didn't have to make things work.'

Cynthia turned away and said 'Goodnight, Sam.'

Sam shouted 'Wait a minute' and she stood still. He moved round so that he was facing her. 'If you feel like that, why did you wait for me at the chapel.'

'I didn't exactly wait for you.'

'You did.'

'All right. It was silly really.'

'Why.'

'I wanted to hear your voice, Sam. You have a good voice. I've always liked it.'

'O I am pleased.'

'You're a sarky bugger, Sam. Goodnight.'

She walked out onto the road and along towards the farm at the top of the hill.

The two younger Tyler sisters sat stiffly on the sofa and Jenny, who was sixteen, sat at the table. They had been silent for some time. The carved pendulum wall-clock ticked woodenly. Some girls were skipping outside and they could hear the slapping of the rope and the skipping chant.

My father is the captain of the Lusitania,
The Lusitania, the Lusitania,
My father is the captain of the Lusitania,
On a cold and frosty morning.

The heavy iron kettle rested on the hob which was swung out from the fire and made a low singing sound. A brown stoneware teapot stood in the fender.

Marjorie Tyler turned and knelt on the sofa and looked out of the window. Then she sat down again. Jenny fiddled with the cutlery and the salt and pepper cellars and straightened the table cloth. She stood up and opened the oven door. She unhooked the tea cloth that hung from the corner of the mantelpiece and lifted up the saucepan lid that covered the dinner plate and peered at it.

'It's dry.'

'He'll be mad.'

'Shall we make some fresh gravy.'

Jenny shook her head. 'Bugger 'im.' She covered the plate, shut the oven door and sat down again. Joyce Tyler kept pulling her cotton stockings up to her knees and straightening the coloured tops that turned back over her garters.

Jenny said 'When you hear 'im you two go upstairs. He might not want you. But if he does want you, come down straight away. Don't get undressed.' The two sisters, a year and two years younger than Jenny nodded.

Slowly the room darkened and the girls outside gave up their skipping and ran away up the street. Jenny took the matchbox from the mantelpiece, stood on her chair and lit the gas mantle. It popped, hissed loudly and flooded the room in sheer, white light. Once Marjorie said 'It's him' but the footsteps went on past the house.

They heard him singing 'Roses of Picardy' well in tune but shouting the end of each line. Marjorie and Joyce went upstairs and Jenny stood and faced the rear door of the room. The uneven steps came along the side of the house, the scullery door banged open and shut and Alan Tyler pushed through the living-room door and leaned heavily against the jamb. His jacket was dragged lopsided by the quart bottle of beer in one of the pockets. He blinked in the bright light, belched, slipped from his position and had to prop himself up again, but his voice was steady.

'You goin' to say hello then.'

Jenny smiled and said 'Hello Dad.'

Alan Tyler was a slightly built man, thin featured, with a heavy mop of gingery hair. He grinned at his daughter and said 'Come and give your Dad a kiss love.' Jenny came slowly round the table and stood in front of him. She gave him a quick kiss. He laughed and still propped in the doorway, took her breasts in his hands and squeezed them hard. Jenny winced and he pulled her closer. 'A proper kiss mi little love.' She kissed him and did not try to move away until he let go of her breasts.

He pulled off his scarf and jacket and dropped them on the floor. As he shuffled across the room Jenny picked them up, hung them behind the door and put the bottle of beer on the sideboard.

Tyler bumped into the chair and swung it clumsily away with his foot. He slumped heavily before the set place and Jenny fetched the dinner from the oven and put it in front of him. He pushed the dinner round the plate with his fork till one of the potatoes fell on the tablecloth.

'It's bone dry.'

'I'm sorry.'

'Yer mother was no kind of fuckin' cook but she could do better than this.' Tyler chewed on a piece of the meat and Jenny picked up the teapot and stood holding it.

'Do you want any tea Dad.'

Tyler looked round the room.

'Where's the other two.'

'They're upstairs Dad.'

'Get 'em down.'

Jenny went to the bottom of the stairs and called up.

'Dad wants you.'

Marjorie and Joyce came quickly downstairs and stood in the doorway to the living-room. Tyler messed with his dinner for a while, then turned to look at them, grinning.

'And how are mi little beauties.'

The two girls stood stiffly, heads down.

Jenny went back to the fireplace still carrying the teapot.

'Would you like some tea Dad.'

'What you bin doin' at school then.'

Marjorie stuttered slightly and said 'Lessons, Dad.'

'You goin' to be clever, Marjy.'

'Yes Dad.'

Tyler sprawled his legs out in front of him and looked intently at Joyce.

'You look just like your mother, Joyce, A pretty bit. So when is it your turn to run off with some bastard, eh.'

Joyce began to snivel.

'Run off with some travellin' salesman with a big prick, I reckon. That right Joyce.'

Jenny put her hand on the tea caddy on the mantelpiece and said 'I'll make you some tea Dad.'

'Shut your mouth, I'm talkin' to our Joyce. Well sweetheart.

You started openin' your legs for the lads yet. You humpin' 'em like your mother used to.'

Joyce turned and put her face against the wall.

'Well, answer me then.'

'No Dad.'

Tyler suddenly turned to Marjorie.

'You learn songs at school, clever lass.'

'Yes Dad.'

'Well sing us one.'

'I can't Dad.'

'You will you know.'

'I can't Dad. I can't remember.'

Marjorie started to back out of the room. Her father hooked his right finger at her. 'Come here.'

She stood for a few seconds, then came towards him.

'You know when I smack your little bare bottom, that meks you sing doesn't it Marjy.'

Marjorie mumbled but the words could not be heard.

'Do you want me to take your knickers down and mek thee sing our Marjy.'

Marjorie began stammering again and said 'Please Dad.'

Tyler came slowly to his feet, leaned forward, slapped her lightly on the cheek and said 'Now sing you little cow.'

Marjorie started to crouch down and as Tyler slapped her harder Jenny came forward and swung the teapot against the side of her father's head. He staggered forward, tripped over a chair and fell heavily against the sideboard. He turned clumsily over, holding his head, his legs tangling under him. Staring at Jenny, he muttered 'Bitch' and lunged towards her. Jenny hit him with the teapot again and it broke against his head. He sat down and howled. The three girls backed to the walls of the room, watching him. For a while he sat on the floor clutching his head, then he put his hand in front of him and stared at the blood on it. He pointed at Jenny and said 'I will fuckin' kill you.' He stood up and started slowly forward. Joyce ran from the wall behind him and kicked him hard in the nape of the knee. He dropped to his knees and began swearing without stopping. Joyce ran at him again but he swept his arms sideways and caught her ankle, toppling her over and dragging her towards him. Jenny picked up the poker from the fender and slashed it across his elbow. He let go of Joyce's ankle and held his forearm, leaning back and screeching. Jenny shouted 'Marjy kick him, kick him' over and over again. Marjorie stepped closer, stood still for a second, then kicked her father in the crotch. Tyler dropped forward and lay stiffly, his arms between his legs, face down, his breath whistling. Mumbling he forced himself up on to his feet but Jenny swung the poker across the side of his leg and he fell backwards. Joyce kicked at his head and the heel of her shoe caught his mouth.

The girls stood bowed over him, gasping. Slowly he came into a sitting position. Blood made a red mask of his face. His words were slurred. He held his fist out towards Jenny and said 'You wait, you just wait.' Jenny stared at him and lashed the poker at his fist. Tyler squealed and rolled over, hiding his hand under his belly. He kept saying 'You've smashed mi fuckin' hand.' Then he began to whimper.

They could hear someone shouting in the street. Jenny put down the poker and went to the front door and opened it. Old Harwood, from the house across the street, was leaning over their front gate and shouting. Several neighbours stood at their front doors.

'Has he hurt you. Shall I send for somebody.'

Jenny's chest heaved up and down and she shook her head.

'Are you all right love. The noise. Has he hurt you.'

Jenny spoke hesitatingly.

'I'm all right.'

'Has he hurt you.'

'No.'

'Do you want anything.'

'We hurt him.'

Harwood dithered at the gate for a moment, then said 'Are you sure you're all right.' Jenny said 'Yes' and he started to walk back across the road. Jenny shouted after him 'We made a good boy of him.'

She shut the door and went back into the living-room. Her father was still crouched over, his right hand hidden under him. Jenny said 'Pull 'im up.' The girls stood looking at him and Jenny shouted 'Get hold of his hair.' Joyce gripped her father's hair and pulled him so that he came on to his feet. Jenny stood directly in front of him and shouted at him.

'If you ever do owt to any of us again we'll all set on you. We'll kill you.' She stared at him for a moment, then said 'Go to bed.' For a long time he stood, swaying. In little steps, he shuffled across to the open door and slumped down on the bottom stair. Jenny went over to him and said 'Get off to bed.' He crawled up the stairs.

Jenny shut the stairs door and came and sat down on the sofa. Her two sisters sat down on the floor.

There was a long silence. Joyce started to giggle. Jenny said 'It'll be all right.'

The long, low, upper room of the grain store smelled dry and musty and both men sneezed from time to time, their noses tickled by the heavy dust hanging in the air. The only light came through the yellowed glass of a dormer window and Sam had to cant his head to see the wedges that held the tie-beam into its curved slot in the side timbers. He muttered 'Hod it up' and Zack Dobson moved to the loosened far end of the beam and took hold of it. Sam propped the near end on his shoulder and began tapping and levering the wedges free with a claw hammer. Bits of rotted wood broke away with the wedges and Sam grunted as he humped the beam upwards, clear of its slot. They lowered it to the floorboards and rolled it away to the back of the room. Sam cleaned out the curved slot and they began to hoist a new beam into place. The far end by Dodson fitted neatly into its slot but Sam's end was too broad and they failed to force it into place.

They lowered the beam to the floor and Sam began to shave it with an adze. Twice they tried it again and each time Sam thinned the end a little more till, on the third try, it slid neatly in. Sam tapped new wedges under each end of the beam forcing it up against the sloping rafters and the centre strut from the roof. He pulled and pushed on the new beam, testing its fit, then went and sat on the grain sacks under the window. Zack joined him and offered him a bottle of beer.

'Try a swig o' this, I brewed it misen.'

Sam took a long swallow, wiped his mouth and passed the bottle back.

'Not bad. Bit yeasty.'

'All'us is when you brew your own.'

Sam rolled himself a cigarette and one for Zack.

'When's Carby comin' to admire us work.'

'He'll be here shortly.'

'What's it like, farmin' for 'im.'

Dobson loosened his belt and rubbed his eyes which were reddened by dust.

'He's t'only bugger I've ever worked for. He's all right I suppose. Not what you'd call a Santy Claus.'

'Your lad's his tenant, in't he.'

'Nick. Aye.'

'How's he gettin' on.'

'Fair to middlin'. Place he's got doesn't drain well and he's not enough acreage to really mek it pay. Aside from that his wife's a poorly sort of lass.'

'What's up wi' her.'

'She's frail really. All'us has bin. She's got six kids runnin' her ragged besides the farmwork.'

'Whose lass is she then.'

'Toby Smith's. Him as was pit saddler.'

'Sounds like a bad sort of do.'

'Aye. She's got that sort of gaunted look. I reckon she'll not see forty.'

'We wear the poor bitches out. There's no wonder they look old afore their time.'

Sam paced slowly down the room examining the butt ends of

the beams beyond the four ones they had put in. He took out a penknife and gouged away bits of timber.

'Half these buggers 'ave got rot in 'em Zack.'

'T'ole place is mouldy.'

'There's not a lot o' point puttin a few new bits in and leavin' this lot.'

'Place must be nigh on a couple of hundred years old . . .'

'I'll have a word with Carby when he gets 'ere.'

'You'd be wastin' your breath. It'd be like paperin' the roof wi' pound notes to him.'

Sam walked back and sat on the grain sacks. A light wind-blown rain pattered on the tiles as the two men gossiped.

They heard the door of the lower storeroom thud to and Carby slowly mount the stairs. He was an old, heavy-boned man, several inches over six feet and he had to stoop under the beams as he came towards them. Nodding to each of them in turn and muttering 'Afternoon' he peered at the new timbers and thumped on the rafter supports with the side of his fist. 'That'll do.' He sucked noisily on a mint toffee and pointed vaguely in the direction of the farmyard. 'There's just the one other job. Puttin' that dry wall by the barn back in fettle.'

Zack Dobson got to his feet but Sam remained sitting and said 'There's just one point about this roof Mister Carby.'

'Aye.'

'You've another half dozen beams wi' rot in 'em.'

'I know that.'

'They need strippin' out an' replacin'.'

'They'll have to wait a while.'

'It's not good policy to leave bad timber in, Mister Carby.'

'Is it not then.'

'No.'

'How long do you think they'll last.'

'Well they'll last a few years but—'

Carby cut in and said 'Aye, an' I'll perhaps be dead in a few years an' mi son can fret about 'em. I'll leave 'em to him in mi will.'

'The rot'll spread back along your side timbers and infect what we've just done.'

'Will it now.'

'Bound to.'

'Well you just leave me to worry about that and you start on the wall.'

Carby moved back towards the stairs and Sam said 'I don't enjoy leavin' a job half-done.'

Carby turned round and stared at him.

'I didn't bring you here for your enjoyment, Sam.'

'It's a matter of doin' things properly.'

Carby spat the last bit of his mint toffee on the floor.

'It's a matter of this bein' my farm and you doin' what odd jobs I want you to. Now I'd be obliged if you'd get out to that wall and start graftin'.'

Sam shrugged his shoulders.

'If I'm not to be let do mi work reight, I'll not bother.'

Carby stood in silence for a moment before taking his purse out of his back trouser pocket. He walked across to Sam and thrust a ten shilling note into his hand.

'That'll set us straight for the roof. Now you can be on your way.'

Dobson shuffled his feet and Sam held out the ten shilling note.

'If you're goin' to mek the job a nonsense you can have your money back.'

Carby pushed Sam's hand away and said 'Don't talk so fuckin' soft.' He stamped down the stairs and slammed the door behind him.

Sam put the note in his pocket and went over to the window and stared out of it.

The cocker tunnel had been driven forward from the end of the abandoned coal face. It was two foot by two foot large and had already been driven eighty feet. Stan Cowan and Cyril Harris squatted by the entrance sorting out their tools. Harris lay down on his belly and shone the beam of an electrician's light along the tunnel.

'Bugger seems to be holdin' up alright.'

'It's a fuckin' waste of time. We'll never find coal out this way. I told Briggsy yesterday. There's never bin coal further out than Elevens.'

'You leave that to the engineers. So long as they pay us by the foot I don't care if we drive this fucker to kingdom-come.'

'My Dad all'us said there's more coal under this pit than where we are. He said they should tek the shaft down another couple of hundred yards and try there. He said we're just rivin' at odds an' ends up here. He used to say we're piddlin' about above an ocean of coal.'

'Thy Dad had a mouth as big as thee.'

Harris hitched his lamp to the back of his belt, held a short-pointed steel bar in one hand, gripped the nozzle of a compressed air-pipe with the other and wriggled into the cocker tunnel. A little weight had come on at the mouth and he had to force his way through the first four or five feet till the going became easier. Cowan wriggled in after him pushing a shallow-sided wooden sled in front of him. The sled was loaded with two-foot wooden props and lids, a two-pound hand hammer and a Dudley. He pushed through the narrowed entrance and as he came into the slightly wider part of the tunnel he leaned over the sled and tapped Harris on the legs.

'Hey, Cyril.'

'What.'

'Dost know summat.'

'What.'

'This tunnel puts me in mind of a lass I used to fuck.'

'What you talkin' about.'

'Well, she were just like this place. When you started to go into 'er she were reight tight and you had to push like billyho to get anywhere, but just inside she sort of widened out a bit and you slid in a treat.'

Harris grunted and slithered further along, stopping from time to time to check the props which were spaced eighteen inches apart along the tunnel. When he came to the end he turned on to his side, hung his lamp on the last set of props and twisted the nozzle of the compressed air hose that he had dragged in with him. A sweet, rubbery tasting flow of air hissed through, blowing a light dust round the cramped end of the tunnel. Cowan muttered 'By but it smells foisty' and emptied the wooden sled, laying the props and lids along the right-hand wall of rock.

Harris jammed himself across the tunnel with his knees and shoulders and began breaking up the end face with the crowbar. He worked from the bottom upwards, spitting as the dust dried out his mouth. Each jab of the crowbar brought pieces of rock tumbling off the end face till the pile was so high that it blocked his spearing movement. He lodged the crowbar behind a prop and lay down on his side, legs straight out and his back tight against one wall. Using his arms as a scoop he pulled the pile of loose rock down towards his feet. Cowan reached forward and pulled the riven rock on to the wooden sled, packing it into a tidy heap and then squirming backwards out of the tunnel, pulling the sled after him. Clear of the tunnel he stood upright, hoisted the sled in his arms and emptied it into the tub which stood a few yards away, at the end of the track. He went back into the tunnel pushing the sled in front of him. By the time he reached the end Harris had hacked down another pile of rock and they refilled the sled for Cowan to drag out. When he came back to the blind end of the tunnel for the eighth time Harris said 'I think we'll do a bit of proppin'.' Cowan stared at the space just ahead of the last set of props.

'Ah reckon this bugger's solid enough to stay up wi'out props.'

'Aye and there's many a fucker could 'ave that carved on 'is gravestone. Pass 'em along.'

Cowan dragged forward three short props and two wedge-shaped lids. Eighteen inches forward of the last set of props they set two upright against the walls and one balanced across the top with the narrow end of a wedge-shaped lid tucked between each side prop and the roof prop. Their bodies snugged close together, Harris held the props steady while Cowan took the hand hammer and slowly tapped the lids in, forcing the top prop tight against the roof. When the wedges had been driven hard home Harris tugged at all three props checking that they were firm. He lay back against the end of the tunnel and said 'Pass the Dudley up. We'll 'ave five for the King.' Cowan passed the Dudley and when it was returned took a long drink for himself. He rested on one elbow and wiped the sweat from his face with the front flap of his shirt.

'What y' think of our new king Cyril.'

'Young Neddy.'

'Aye.'

'I think fuck all of 'im.'

'They say he's got a lot of sympathy for workin' man.'

'If I'd got as many bawbees as 'e has I could afford to 'ave sympathy for every fucker.'

'Be fair, Cyril.'

'Be fair, be fucked. He farts about wi' yachts and racehorses in his top 'at and you tell me he 'as sympathy with the working man.'

'Well he was born to money. It's not his fault.'

'He's welcome to enjoy it but he can keep 'is big gob shut about how sorry he is for everybody.'

'You're a cantankerous bugger, Cyril.'

'No Ah'm not. I just don't like buggers who're well off tellin' me how their 'earts bleed for the poor.'

'You watch. He'll get summat done for us.'

Harris closed his eyes and for a few minutes the two men rested quietly.

Cowan stretched himself and rubbed his stomach.

'By but I've got a bellyache.'

'It's drinkin' stout. Bad for the gut. You should stick to bitter. Briggsy'll be down later on, to see what sort of stuff we're goin' through.'

'We'll be goin' through stone forever and ever amen. It's like I said. You'll never find coal at this level past Elevens.'

'You let him worry about that. They don't pay you for geology.'

Harris turned on to his side, picked up his crowbar and began to hew at the rock. Soon Cowan was wriggling his way up and down the tunnel shifting the sleds of rock. In an hour he had filled the tub and he trammed it down to the junction and brought back another empty. Going back in he saw that one of the props near the opening had split. He shouted Harris back down to join him and they replaced the prop and went back to the head of the tunnel. After another two sleds of rock had been taken out they put in another set of props and came out of the tunnel for snap-time.

They ate and drank in silence and shared the plug of chewing tobacco that Harris provided. Cowan undid the belt of his trousers and stretched into a half-lying position.

'I know what I mean't to ask thee, Cyril.'

'What's that.'

'I'm tekkin' Kath to t' Grand Theatre on Satt'dy neet. Would thee and thy missis like to come wi' us.'

'What's on.'

'Sandy Powell's main thing but they've got some good acts. There's a magician they say is clever and a lady contortionist. Dick Price says she's made of elastic. He reckons she could bend ovver backwards an' suck 'erself off.'

'I'm not bothered. If it were a good play it'd be different.'

'Suit yoursen.'

'Anyroad, we shall need some kip Saturday night. We're on early turn Sunday.'

'Fuckin' hell. I forgot to tell thee.'

'Tell me what.'

'Ah'm lakin' the Sunday shift.'

'Christ Almighty. Who am I supposed to get to work this bloody thing wi' me.'

'Ah'm sorry Cyril. Ah meant to mention it afore.'

'Why are you not workin'.'

'You remember me tellin' you I was puttin' in with Greg Bates an' his brother to buy a whippet. Well they're pickin' it up on Satt'dy and we're givin' it a try-out at Highfields track on Sunday mornin'.'

'You're a fuckin' mess Stan Cowan. You know they're givin' us rate an' a half for Sunday.'

'If it were owt else I'd brek it off lad, but Ah promised Greg.'

'Tha promised me.'

'Aye well. I didn't think on at time.'

'You'll do owt bar graft you will.'

'Nay it's just that A've niver 'ad a share in a whippet afore.'

'You'll die fuckin' poor you will.'

'It's only the one shift.'

'It's not the bloody first time. When we took this fuckin' contract you knew it was a weekends as well job.'

'Keep your hair on.'

'I reckon a bloke that won't stick to his job an' work his proper time is not worth botherin' about. You've got a family to think about and all you can do is pratt about wi' a bloody dog. It's time you acted like a grown man, Stanley and not so much bloody indulgin' yourself.'

'Here endeth the third lesson.'

'I sometimes wonder why I have you for a bloody mate at all.'

Cowan rolled on to his feet, buckled his belt, picked up the crowbar and wriggled into the tunnel. Harris followed him in pushing the sled with a new load of props. Cowan stopped, lay still and looked back at Harris.

'It's because no other fucker would put up with thy naggin'.'

Although it was well after midnight and the bride and groom had left long before, the house was still crowded with guests. They crammed the kitchen and the big front room, sat on the stairs and stood around on the patch of grass at the top of the back garden. When more beer was needed someone had to force their way through the mass of people sitting on the floor, the fender edge, tables, chair arms and sideboard tops, to the barrel propped on the kitchen sink and carry the slopping pint mugs back. A young girl in the front room started to feel sick and was passed over the heads of the folk packed in the kitchen and out into the garden. Talking was pitched loud to carry over the sound of Ernie Rice playing the piano in the front room and the voices which roared in a slow, heavy singing of 'Love's Old Sweet Song' or 'Daisy' or 'Whispering'. Food was loaded on trays in the pantry and people grabbed at it as the trays were hawked to and fro. The bride's father sat swaying drunkenly on the front doorstep repeating his wedding reception speech to the half dozen people who were leaning by the front garden gate, shouting to people in the house. A young boy sat astride an upstairs window sill pretending to fall out into the garden and grabbing the frame to stop himself each time. Wedding presents were handed round and people argued over how much they had cost. The piano stopped while someone played a simple form of the 'Poet and Peasant' overture on a trumpet and was loudly clapped. A skinny young man played 'Keep the Home Fires Burning' on his mouth organ and people sang songs so that they could hear him play. There were shrieks of laughter when a man stood on the board placed over the front table, turned his collar back to front, pinched his nose and gave an imitation of the parson, changing the words of the service and ending with love, honour and obey till shaggin' wears us out. Cigarette and pipe smoke eddied through the house and the roar of talk was endless.

'They'll be well bedded down in Blackpool bi now. Bashin' the mattress up an' down a bit.'

'Funny though. He's such a pretty lad and so finicky about 'is clothes and 'abits, for a long time I thought he were a bum-boy.'

'Nay. He courted a few before Margaret Ann. Sally Mitchell for one. And she'd 'ave kept 'im busy.'

'They're goin' to live in Farrow's old house then.'

'Aye. It should do 'em nicely. I remember when Crossley's built it. A good house.'

There were cheers as a lad in a black suit and dicky bow-tie put on his tap shoes and climbed up on the boarded front room table.

He nodded at the pianist who began to play 'Kitten on the Keys', thumping out the chords heavily while the lad tap-danced, holding his arms wide to keep his balance.

Willie Hankin's voice was hoarse with shouting.

'Ah tell thee there'll be a fuckin' war. Wun't surprise me if this bloody thing in Spain din't set it off.'

'Well they'll 'ave to do wi'out me. I did my stint in t' last fuckin' lot. It'll be bloody Germans an'us again. Thee see.'

'We're not that fuckin' soft.'

'Politicians are soft enough for owt. Annit'll be a worse bloody mess than last time.'

A tray of cheese, biscuits and black pudding was passed into the corner to the three men sitting by the front door. One of them patted the black pudding and said 'No lie. I once seen a bloke eat a yard o' that and drink a pint o' beer wi' it in five minutes. For a bet. Five bob. Slavin's pub.'

'Nay. It's too bloody rich.'

'Well he did it.'

'Ah'll bet tha can't do it.'

'Ah'm not sayin' I can.'

'I know fuckin' well tha can't.'

'Tha can't be sure.'

'I can you know.'

'Beer 'ud help. It'd wesh it down.'

'Well fuckin' try it then.'

'Well I'd want summat forrit.'

'A florin says tha can't.'

'Right then.'

'Kenny, you be judge.'

Kenny Smith laughed and spanned off a yard of the black pudding, topped up Barthrop's glass to a full pint and took out his watch and wound the spindle. He dropped his hand and shouted 'Go.' Barthrop began to gobble the black pudding pausing now and then for a gulp at his beer. He was more than halfway through it when his ruddy face went pale and sweat beaded his forehead. He stared at the other two men for a moment then lurched round and forced his way out into the front garden. Smith shook his head.

'Silly bugger. He's lost his florin and med himself sick into t' bargain.'

There was a crash as somebody dropped a tray of glasses on the pantry floor. A cheer went up from the guests.

Sam Chard was sitting in an armchair at the back of the kitchen, a slight tow-haired girl lounged on the side of the chair with her arm round his shoulders and Diddy Adams half-squatted in front of him, shouting above the noise.

'Come on Sam. Sat'day. Four of us. A meal at the Barrel, Donny races and round the market place pubs in t' evenin'. We'll 'ave a right time.'

Sam shook his head.

'Ah come on feller.'

'It's not on Diddy.'

'Ah've said I'll pay for you.'

'You won't you know.'

'Look. I'm well set just now. I've bin Sunday workin' for a month.'

'Forgerrit.'

'Don't worry about the money. I'll cover it all.'

Sam flushed and shouted 'Shut up about fuckin' payin' for me.'

Diddy started to say something and Sam leaned forward, grabbed the lapel of his jacket and back-handed him across the face. The lad jerked backwards and cocked his fist. Then he laughed and said 'I'll set Arthur Patricks on to you Sam Chard.'

Sam blinked and put his hands on his head and half-grinned.

'O Diddy lad. You'll never know what that was like. It was like hittin' a fuckin' oak tree.'

The girl leaned across and kissed Sam and whispered 'I still love you, Samuel.'

Sam pulled her on to his knees and said 'You think that meks it all right.'

'Course it does.'

'You bloody women. You think you're God's gift.'

'Well aren't we.'

Sam laughed and said 'Yes.'

The crowd in the front room had begun to sing 'Onward Christian Soldiers' conducted by a stooped old man who leapt around the table top as he waved his arms. Someone kept shouting from the kitchen 'You're a fuckin' blasphemous lot.'

Joe Ragg had the other man pinned against the jamb of the door and he kept tapping his chest with his finger.

'Your fuckin' lot looted that house. We hadn't gorr'im buried in the bloody ground and you lot were round there like bloody locusts.'

'We only took what Charles said we could 'ave when he went to hospital.'

'Be buggered to that. When I went round wi' t' furniture feller it were like a flamin' empty house.'

'Get your hands off me. We just took one or two bits an' pieces as were promised to us.'

'You include a bloody sideboard in your bits an' pieces. You din't even leave his war medals. You ransacked that bloody place.'

'We took just what was rightly due. Anyroad, why drag that up, it's all bloody ancient history now.'

'I wonder you din't 'ave the shroud off him when we took him to t' cemetry.'

The little lad was fetched from the bedroom in his pyjamas and everyone in the front went quiet while he sang 'Two Lovely Black Eyes' in a squeaky voice. Sixpences were pressed into his hand as he was taken back to bed.

The tall woman by the fireplace squeezed her own arms in front of her.

'She looked lovely in that long dress. Like a princess.'

'Well at least she had one day all to herself.'

'Don't you think they'll get on then.'

'Not while men are men, love.'

'They're young yet.'

'I thought the bouquet was too big though. Her being tiny.'

'His family looked a bit sour. They might at least 'ave put a good face on it.'

'It's funny you know. I use to swear blind I'd never get wed. I saw what mi mother went through and I had it all worked out. No man was going to have me for his skivvy. I was goin' to live mi life my way. An' then I was just like all the rest, off down the aisle.'

Two or three people in the front room started to shout for Sam and he told the girl to hang on to his armchair and struggled through to the piano.

'It's thy turn Sam. Do us summat.'

Sam mimed patting his hair straight and shyly twisting his tie. 'What d'ye fancy.'

Someone shouted 'Recite us summat.'

Sam climbed on the table and knelt down on one knee. He sipped at a glass of port that someone passed to him and held up his right hand. The room quietened and Sam recited 'The Burial of Sir John Moore at Corunna' in a clear, steady voice. There was clapping and cheering at the end of it and Sam worked his way back to the kitchen and the armchair. The girl snuggled down on his lap and said softly 'Cynthia Henshaw as was hasn't come to the reception then.'

Sam screwed up his face and said 'We tek it in turns to avoid each other.'

The girl kissed him and Diddy Adams looked up from where he was sitting on the floor and said 'Can I come an' sit on your lap Sam.'

Sam said 'Bugger off' and cuddled the girl.

Outside, in the darkness of the ginnel that ran between the house and its neighbour the man tried to hold Eileen Evers but she pushed him away and said 'Stop slawmin' all over me.' The man folded his arms and spoke sharply.

'You're a right contrary bitch, Eileen.'

'And you're conceited. Just 'cos I won't let you.'

'You let me do all sorts. You'll let me fingerfuck you but when it comes to doin' it properly o dear me no.'

'There's a price for that.'

The young man said nothing and Eileen turned away and went back round the house and into the kitchen. As she stood by the pantry door the young man came into the kitchen, forced his way across to her and shouted at her.

'You're like them women in the Three Legs pub in Donny. They charge a price for lettin' you fuck 'em.'

Eileen spat at him and he turned round and left the house, pushing people out of the way. The elderly man next to Eileen said 'Steady love, half your spit went ovver me.'

In the front room a heavily built Scot called Kenna had mounted the table. He clutched his beer mug to his chest and swayed gently as he sang 'Goodnight Sweetheart' in a near falsetto voice. The crowd shouted for more and he went on to recite poems by Burns. After a while people shouted for him to shut up and give someone else a chance but he kept on reciting.

George Absalom came into the kitchen from the front room pulling two men along with him. They worked their way over to where Sam was sitting. Absalom winked at the girl sitting on Sam's knee and chucked her under the chin. He sat on the arm of the chair and pointed to the other two and said 'Sam, I want you to tell these two buggers about that time when you let that run of tubs go straight into t' pit bottom. I've promised 'em it's a good tale.'

Sam kissed the girl in the nape of the neck and said 'Can't you see I'm busy, George.'

Absalom sighed and said 'Can I tell 'em then, they shunt missit.'

Sam said 'If tha wants' and the two men bent close to Absalom who talked with jerky arm movements, bunching his fist or splaying his fingers to mark points in the story.

'Sam were nobbut a lad then, you'd be what, fourteen.'

'Fifteen.'

'An' he's put to lowerin' full tubs down to t' cage side as they come off the district. It were gravity haulage at that time. You just dropped enough lockers in the wheels to part hold 'em and let 'em slide down the slope. Well Sam's new to this an' e' keeps overdoin' his lockers and bringin' runs to a full stop so they've all got to push to get 'em started again. An' this road doggy gets fed wi' this an' he keeps naggin' Sam to speed 'em up and mek a bit sharp wis 'em. He were called Wilfred summat.'

'Wilf Fletcher.'

'That's reight. He used to nag like an owd woman. Anyroad, Sam's still bein' a bit ower cautious an' puttin' in too many lockers an' stoppin' the tubs altogether. So come the grand finale Wilfred meks a big speech at Sam, screamin' an' shoutin' at him an' howlin' on that he's got to get the buggers movin'. Sam looks at 'im an says all quiet an' polite "You want the buggers movin' Mister", an' Wilfred bawls "I fuckin' do, move the sods." An' afore any bugger fathoms what's 'appenin Sam walks ovver to this run of tubs, pulls all the lockers out, gives em' a shove an' they're off down to t' pit bottom runnin' free. Well you've never seen owt like it. When pit bottom fellers hear this lot thunderin' down they start runnin' up t'other slope like blokes with squitters who just spotted a lav. T'ole bloody run sides off at water slit turn an' starts smashin' round pit bottom. Ah'm not kiddin' you, place looked like the battle of the bloody Somme. An' Sam's standin' there wi' 'is Sunday school face on saying "Ah've got 'em runnin' for yer Mister."'

The two men chuckled and one said 'You mad-headed bugger, did they give you the sack.'

Sam grinned.

'Fletcher were a funny old bugger. If you stood up to him he was all right with you. He told pit bottom manager t' lockers had broken.'

One of the men took their glasses, scrambled across to the barrel perched on the sink and brought more beer back.

In the front room Len Thomas had begun to play a different tune on his accordion to the one Ernie Rice was playing on the piano and there were cheers and shouting and scuffling till they agreed about what they were to play.

Standing on the patch of grass at the back of the house the man shook his head so strongly that his shoulders swayed.

'Dickens teks too long to get to t' point. You've got to bear in mind as he were writin' at a penny a line. That's why you get all that describin' things that don't matter. Now Rider Haggard. He's the feller. He dun't hoddup the story. He keeps it goin' on so you keep goin' on with it. Half time wi' Dickens I'm waitin' for him to get on wi' it.'

The man standing behind him put a hand on his shoulder and said 'What about Ragged Trouser Philantropist then.'

'Well that's different. That's just politics.'

'It fuckin' isn't. He meks you feel sorry for his people. My wife read it to our kids and they cried.'

The man sitting on the grass, almost under their feet, pointed up at them with his beer mug.

'Edgar Wallace. He's my feller. I read one called *The Green Pack of Cards* or summat like that. An' there's this bit where this bloke blackmails this young lass into tekkin' her clothes off and lettin' him do it to her. An' there were no beatin' round the bush. You knew he were 'avin some an' enjoyin' it. I'm surprised they let that bit in.'

On the stairs Diddy Adams was trying to talk to two girls but they sat with their arms round each other, whispering and giggling and after a while he went back into the front room.

Peter Tate was stepping over people on his way through the kitchen and out into the garden when Sam caught his arm and said 'Nadden Peter.'

Tate looked down at him and said 'How are you keepin' Sam.'

'Managin'.'

'I heard your recitation. You did it well.'

'Who you workin' with now.'

'Bailey's gang.'

'That fuckin' lot couldn't shovel snow.'

'Aye well, there's not a lot of option.'

Sam muttered something that Peter could not hear then said 'Whereabouts you workin'.'

'West Tens intake. Weight keeps comin' in at an angle and knockin' the props out. So we're tryin' to straighten it up.'

'You should notch your props into your roof timber, like the old Welsh miners do. Makes 'em hold better.'

'Aye. I'll praps tell 'em that.'

Neither of the two men spoke for a few moments then Tate said 'Tek care o' yoursen.' Sam nodded and Tate went out into the garden.

Two girls had taken a gramophone out on to the little front lawn and were dancing to a record of 'Red Sails in the Sunset'. The group round them clapped as they imitated a pair of ballroom dancers, swaying and dipping with one bending the other other steeply backwards. The one dancing as the man spoke in a loud, mockingly gruff voice.

'Does tha cum 'ere often.'

Her partner piped 'O yes, I'm so terribly fond of the sprung floor.'

'Has ta cum alone.'

'O no, I've come with my Mummy.'

'Will tha let me 'ave a bit after t' dance.'

'A bit of what my good man.'

'A bit of that theer 'ere.'

'I'll ask my Mummy.'

'Ah don't want a bit wi' your Mam.'

The girls fell over and sat on the grass, tittering.

The sound of 'If You Were The Only Girl In The World' came loudly from the front room and Sam and the girl on his lap joined in the singing.

The mild spring evening was darkening and a light breeze tossed the dog roses that grew along the hedge. The girl sat astride the large root of a tree that had grown into the hedge and the two boys sat together, a few yards away, feet dangling into the ditch. The taller of the two boys was whispering to the other. He nudged him and put his arm round his shoulders.

'Honest. If I tell her to, she'll do it to you.'

'How often has she done it to you.'

'Lots of times.'

'Where do you do it.'

'When mi Mam and Dad are out we go into the front room and do it there.'

'Did they ever catch you.'

'Never. If we 'ear the gate open while we're still doin' it, I go to t' lav and she pretends now't happened.'

'How did you know she'd want to do it.'

'Well tha sees a lass at school told her how boys toss theirselves off and she asked me if I did it. An' I said yes. And one time I asked if she'd like to see me do it. An' she watched me do it quite a few times. An' she said could she play with it an' I let her and she started doin' it all the way for me.'

'Do you tek your trousers off.'

'I just open mi buttons.'

The smaller boy looked towards the girl and whistled to himself.

'I don't know. I don't know if I'd like her to do it.'

'Go on. You'd like it. I'll bet you anythin' you'll like it. It's better than wankin' yourself off.'

'That's what you say.'

'Honest.'

'How does she know how to do it.'

'Cause she knows.'

'Like how hard to do it.'

'You tell 'er. If you want her to go faster you just say to her to go faster.'

'I'll bet she dun't really want to do it.'

'Yes she does.'

'You're 'er brother. That's different.'

'No it isn't. Anyroad, if I tell her to do it to you, she'll do it.'

'What if she dun't want to.'

'Well let me ask 'er.'

'I'm not sure I want 'er to.'

'Yes you do.'

'What if I ask her miself.'

'Alreight.'

'No, you ask 'er.'

'You just wait.'

The taller boy went and joined his sister, sitting astride the tree root with his head close to hers. The other boy walked further away and took a ball out of his pocket and began bouncing it. He tried to pass his leg over the ball while it was bouncing and missed his catch. He ran after the ball and put it back in his pocket. He walked to where the hedge joined a fence and tried balancing on the top rail but twice had to jump down as he started to topple over. He hung upside down on the fence, righted himself and sat on the top rail. He took out a comic and held it close to his face but it was too dark to read. He put it back in his pocket and sat whistling till the other boy shouted.

'Colin. Come up here.'

He walked slowly back up the hill and stood next to them. The taller boy grinned.

'I told you. Maggie says she will.'

There was a silence for a few moments. Maggie's brother said 'You will won't you.'

Maggie nodded. Colin looked at the girl and spoke loudly.

'You want to do it. What he said.'

Maggie said 'Yes.'

Maggie and her brother climbed off the tree root and stood looking at Colin. Maggie's brother said 'Let's go under the bandstand at Clip Claps.'

Colin shook his head.

'You're not comin'.'

'Yes I am.'

'No.'

'It's my sister. You'd never have asked 'er. I fixed it up for thee.'

'I don't care.'

'Why can't I come.'

''Cos you can't.'

'Why not.'

'Why do you want to come.'

'I'll not do owt. I'll just watch.'

'No.'

'If you don't let me I'll tell Maggie not to do it for you.'

Colin spoke to the girl.

'Will you do it.'

Maggie said 'If you want me to.'

The boy pushed his sister in the chest and said 'If you do, I'll tell Mam and Dad.'

Maggie stepped back from him and said 'If you do tell 'em, I'll tell about what you and me do.'

The boy shouted at Colin.

'I'll bloody well come if I want to.'

'No you won't. I'll fight thee.'
'Thee an' whose army.'
'I slotted thee at Carky Park.'
'Thee 'it me when I wasn't lookin'.'
Colin took off his jacket.
'Well tek thi coit off then.'

Maggie's brother started to walk down the hill. He shouted back 'Tha not worth fatin'.' A little later he shouted 'Tha needn't think Ah'm knockin' about with thee again. Ah'm not friends of thee.'

Colin put his jacket back on and stood watching the boy go out of sight down the hill. He said 'Do you still want to do it.'

Maggie said 'Yes, and shall we go to Clip Claps.'

'No. I don't want to go where he says.'

'Where shall we go then.'

Colin stared at the sky and folded and unfolded his arms.

'Shall we go into that barn in Naylor's yard.'

Maggie nodded and took his hand.

They walked up the hill to the large, green-painted gates of Naylor's farmyard. Colin looked around, felt the padlock on the gates and said 'You can stand on my back and hang down on the other side and drop. It's not far.' Maggie grinned. She jumped and caught the top of the gate with both hands, pulled herself over and dropped down into the yard. Colin followed her. The dog that was chained to the stone warehouse started barking and tugging at its chain. Colin said 'It'll be alright. I know it.' He went across to the dog, patted it and rubbed its muzzle and kept saying 'There Black, there's a good lad, good old Black.' The dog quietened. Colin went back to the girl and they tiptoed into the Dutch barn on the left of the yard. Colin went over to some unbaled straw, lying in the far corner and said 'Is this alright.' Maggie sat down on the straw and Colin sat beside her. After a minute Colin put his arm round her shoulders and said 'Are you cold.'

Maggie slipped her arm under his jacket and said 'No, it's warm in here.'

They sat for a while, then Colin said 'Will you let me feel you.'

'If you want.' She pulled up her frock and held the elastic band of her knickers away from her belly. Colin slid his hand down and rested it lightly on her cunt. After a few seconds Maggie put her hand on top of his hand and forced his middle finger into the slit. She took her hand away and closed her thighs tightly. She pulled him so that he was half-lying against her.

He said 'Do you like that.'

'Yes. It's like when I feel myself.'

'Do girls feel theirselves.'

Maggie giggled.

'Course they do.'

'I didn't know girls felt theirselves.'

'You don't know much.'

'I heard this joke once about nuns and candles.'

'What was that.'

'Well this bloke made all these candles out of spunk and sold 'em to this place where all the nuns were.'

'Why did he make candles out of spunk.'

'I don't know. Anyway, in nine months all the nuns had babies.'

They wriggled down on the straw until they were lying nearly flat. They could hear the dog whining and pulling at its chain.

Colin raised himself on his elbow and said 'Mi hand's goin' numb.' She opened her thighs and he slid his hand out and opened and closed the fingers several times. He said 'Do you want to feel me now.' Maggie put her hands behind her head.

'In a minute. I want you to do somethin' first.'

'What.'

'First put your hand back down there.'

Colin said 'I'll use mi other hand' and he crawled over to her left hand side and slid his hand down on her cunt. She shook her head and said 'Further down.'

'What do you mean, further down.'

Maggie said 'You are slow' and slid her hand down on top of his. She forced his hand further between her thighs and put his middle finger into her arse. Colin started to pull it out but she held it tightly.'

He said 'What are you doin'.'

Maggie said 'Never you mind. Just move your finger in and out a bit.' For a moment Colin did nothing and she said 'Go on.' He began to move his finger a little way up and down in her arse and she took her hand away and put both her hands back behind her head. Colin stopped and she said 'Don't stop' and he began to move his finger again. She closed her eyes and said 'Push it a bit further in.' Colin moved his body slightly away from her and slid lower down so that he could push his finger further in. She said 'Faster' and he quickened the sliding of his finger. She closed her eyes and began breathing very rapidly. Colin looked up at her. Her face darkened. Suddenly she grunted and grabbed hold of his wrist and held it still. She said breathlessly 'You can stop now.' Colin leaned slightly away from her, took his hand out and keeping it hidden by his body, wiped his finger on his trousers. He lay back and like Maggie, put his hands behind his head. He spoke in a half-whisper.

'I've never been with a girl before.'

'Do you like it.'

'Yes. Well once Jacqueline Millard let me see hers and I showed her mine but we were only kids.'

'I've only been with mi brother. Do you think he won't be friends of you again.'

'Course he will. He always wants to knock about with me.'

Maggie sat up and said 'It's your turn now. I'll come the other side.' She started to climb across him and suddenly sat astride his belly. 'Am I too heavy for you.'

'I could carry three like you.'

She leaned right over, looked down at him and grabbed his armpits. He squeaked, held her wrists tightly and shouted 'No, you mustn't. I can't stand bein' tickled.'

She said 'I'll let you off this time' and rolled off him and lay resting on her elbow.

Colin said 'What do I do.'

'You don't do anythin'. Just lie back.'

Maggie leaned across him and carefully undid his fly buttons. She pulled his prick out and cupped his balls in her hand. She looked at it.

'Do you come.'

'You mean with spunk.'

'Yes.'

'Only a bit. Well not really.'

'You haven't got much hair.' She began stroking his prick. Colin lay very still with his eyes shut. She stroked it for a minute but it stayed slack. She stopped and looked at Colin and said 'Is anythin' wrong.'

He opened his eyes and said 'No. It's just that I'm not used to it. To you.'

She stroked it again, and took the knob end between her finger and thumb, slowly jerking it up and down in small movements. It began to stiffen. She kept jerking it slowly until it was stiff and upright then slipped all her fingers round it and pulled the foreskin gently back, moving her hand up and down, a little more quickly. Colin stretched out very stiffly and muttered something she could not hear. Maggie propped herself up on her left hand and leaned right over him, watching his prick very closely and tightening her grip on it. His body began to buck under her and she churned his prick more quickly and deeply. He rolled on to his side and she followed him, leaning right over still jerking his prick, until he brought his knees up sharply and trapped her hand. She nursed his prick as it went soft.

Maggie stretched her body till her face was close to his and said 'Are you alright.'

Colin said 'Yes. It's just that it was a lot quicker than when I do it.' She kissed him on the cheek, wriggled her hand from his crotch and lay down. Colin sat up, buttoned his trousers and lay down alongside her. They were quiet for a few minutes.

She said 'Did you like it.'

Colin said 'A lot' and she sighed.

She said 'Tell you something.'

'What.'

'You know about our Dennis saying to you that he'd ask me to do it to you, if you wanted.'

'Yes.'

'Well I told him to.'

'How d'y' mean.'

'I told Dennis to ask you if you wanted to. But he wasn't to say that I'd told him to.'

'Why did you ask him to.'

''Cos I fancied you.'

'Honest.'

'Course.'

Colin reached down and put his hand under her skirt and began rubbing her thigh. She let him for a few seconds then said 'That's enough.' He stopped and sat up, crosslegged, looking down at her. He spoke loudly.

'Would you like to go to the pictures. Wi' me.'

'All right.'

'When.'

'When do you want.'

'Tomorrer night.'

'All right.'

'I'll see you outside pictures at six.'

'Why don't we walk to Carky together.'

'Mi mates would laugh at me if they saw me goin' to the pictures wi' a girl.'

Maggie stood up and said 'It's time I was off 'ome.' Colin stood beside her and she said 'Brush me down.' He brushed loose straw from the back of her frock and she pulled bits from her hair. She walked to the farm gate and Colin followed her. They climbed over the gate and into the road. Maggie started to walk up the hill. When she was about twenty yards away Colin ran after her shouting 'Hoddup a minute.'

She turned towards him and said 'What for.'

'If you like, we could meet at the end of Briar Road at half past five. An' walk to the pictures. Together.'

'All right.'

'Shall we go back there again after.' Colin nodded towards the farmyard.

'We'll see.' Maggie turned and walked up the hill.

Colin shouted after her 'See you then.'

Sam finished strapping up the rucksack, tied his raincoat across the top of it and put it by the kitchen door. His landlady stood at the kitchen table, shoulders hunched, making a pile of sandwiches and sniffing from time to time into her handkerchief. She wrapped a second pile of sandwiches in greaseproof paper and said 'Will that be enough, Sam.'

Sam smiled.

'Last me a week that lot, Agnes. You're a sweetheart.'

Agnes Jones sniffed again, went to the sink and began scouring out the meat tin. Sam went into the pantry and fetched his carpentry tools from under the slate shelf. Except for two wood saws and two planes his tools were all fitted into a big, folded sheet of soft leather, tied with plaited thongs. Sam opened it out. It had been made by a pit saddler and each tool was fitted into its own shaped pouch. He ran his hand over the hammers, chisels, bradawls, fret saw, brace and bits, set square, spirit-level, ruler, oil stone and other tools and then folded it up again and tucked it under his arm. He picked up the saws and planes and said 'I'll be back in a minute, love.'

He went out into the garden, stepped over the low fence and into the neighbour's garden. The back door of his neighbour's house was open and he could see Frank Durdy sitting at the kitchen table. Sam knocked on the door and went into the kitchen. Durdy was sitting in his shirt and trousers, eating his dinner. He grunted at Sam. His wife was lodging a large iron kettle into the firegrate. She said 'Morning Mister Chard.' Sam nodded to her, put the saws and planes down and unfolded the sheet of leather with its fitted tools on the pegged rug in front of the fire. He stepped back and leaned against the sink.

'Right Frank. You've all'us said you fancied mi tools. What'll you offer for 'em.'

Durdy turned in his chair and looked down at the tools, picking bits of food from his teeth with his forefinger. He knelt and pulled a few of the tools from their pouches and ran his fingers over the sharpened blades and the oiled wood. He moved back into his chair and stretched his braces with his thumbs.

'Three quid.'

Sam frowned at him.

'Christ. You'll never die poor Frank.'

Durdy mopped grease from his plate with a piece of bread and ate it.

'Tek it or leave it.'

'Come on lad. They're worth eight an' Ah'll tek five.'

Durdy shook his head. His wife coughed and said, quietly, 'They look very nice, Frank.'

After a while Sam said 'What about it, Frank.'

Durdy rubbed his hands up and down his chest and yawned. 'It's not a question of what they're worth. It's what they're worth to me.'

Sam folded his arms, whistled tunelessly for a minute, then said 'Alreight, I'll tek it.'

Durdy looked towards his wife.

'Fetch it from t' box.'

While his wife went upstairs he inspected the saws and the planes. His wife came back with three one-pound notes and he handed them to Sam. Sam pocketed them and said 'Thank you very kindly, Frank.' He turned to Missis Durdy and said 'Good day to you Missis.' She said 'I'm sorry' and Sam walked out of the house, back over the fence and into his own kitchen.

Agnes Jones was standing by the fire holding a pint mug in her hands.

'Would y' like a cup of tea, Sam. I've just mashed.'

Sam smiled at her and she poured the tea, mixed in sugar and condensed milk and passed it to him. He took it and stood at the kitchen door, looking out at the garden. He sipped the tea for a while before he spoke.

'Get Marshall or somebody to manure yon left-hand side. Soil's skimpy.'

Agnes muttered 'Yes Sam.'

'And don't bring in too much coal at a time. You'll hurt yourself. Just half-fill the bucket.'

He drank the rest of his tea in silence and put the cup into the sink. He put the two packets of sandwiches into his jacket and moved to the door.

'I shall have to be movin' love.'

Agnes put her hands out towards him and said 'You will write me a letter sometimes.' He took her hands.

'Course I will. An' you tek care o' yoursen.'

She began to cry and he put his arms round her and stroked her head.

'Now Agnes. Young Harper promised to move in next week an' he'll mek you a grand lodger. I've picked 'im special for you 'cos he's so young and handsome.'

Agnes mumbled 'I wish you were stayin'.'

'You let him do the top windows. I don't want you hurtin' your back.'

'I've tried to take good care of you.'

'An' no one could 'ave done better, love. I've bin as snug as a bug in a rug. Now give us a kiss.'

She kissed him and hugged him to her. Sam picked up his rucksack, touched her face and went out of the kitchen, round the side of the house and into the street. He walked quickly to the end of Beech Road then slowed as he turned up the hill.

As he walked past the miners' club, two young boys ran across towards him, the older one clutching a cap full of marbles and the other shouting 'Mester Chard, Mester Chard.' Sam stopped and waited till the two boys reached him. He smiled at the boy who had shouted to him and said 'Danny Walker in't it.'

The boy spoke breathlessly.

'Yes, Mester Chard. Mester Chard me an' Sidney Goodlad is goin' to chock a hundred and twoer an' will you chock it forrus Mester Chard to see tharrit's fair.'

Sam pursed his lips and said 'Are you sure you want to chock that many' and the younger boy said 'Aye, it's all I've got.'

They sat down on the edge of the kerb. Sam put his rucksack to one side and took the cap full of marbles from the older boy.

'Right lads, we'd best count 'em first. Hundred and twoer. It is a big chock.'

Emptying the marbles out onto the kerb, he began grouping them in tens. 'You've each put in fifty-one then.'

Danny Walker waved his hands as he spoke.

'That's reight. Ah wanted to put a bolly in against eight prits from 'im but he says 'e won't 'ave that.'

The other boy said 'Just prits, no mibs and no bollies.'

Sam said 'It's easier wi' just prits.' He finished counting. 'We're agreed then, there's a hundred and two 'ere. Now let's get it straight before we start. I chock 'em an' if an odd number roll off then Danny wins an' if it's evens Sydney wins. Agreed.' Both the boys said 'Yes' and Sam said again 'Odds for you Danny, evens for Sidney.' He put the marbles back into the cap and said 'Now hutch up a bit and give me room.' The boys moved back a few inches and Danny put two of his fingers in his mouth and held them tightly with his teeth. Sam said 'Ready' and the boys nodded. He turned the cap over quickly, banged it down on the edge of the kerb and pulled it away sharply. Nearly half the marbles rolled off the kerb into the gutter. Sam said 'Just wait a second to be sure they've finished rollin.' No more marbles moved and Sam slowly counted those in the gutter. There were forty-six. Sam looked up and pointed his finger at the older boy. 'They're yours Sidney.'

Neither of the boys spoke and Sidney Goodlad hurriedly scooped all the marbles back into his cap and stood up. He looked at Danny Walker and said 'It were fair' and started to trot down the hill.

Sam shouted after him.

'Aren't you goin' to give him a few back for loser's luck.'

The boy stopped and looked at his cap full of marbles.

'I won 'em fair.'

He ran off down the hill.

Danny took his fingers out of his mouth and muttered 'It's not fair. He all'us wins. That's twice he's skint me. It's not fair at all.'

Sam shrugged his shoulders.

'Well tha shouldn't play with him.'

'It dun't mek no difference. Ah'm always beaten. Everybody beats me. Our kid bested me an' he's got hundreds o' prits an' he won't give me any.' He started to cry. Sam rubbed the boy's head and Danny pushed his hand away and shouted 'Ah don't see why I shouldn't win, just for once.'

'You 'ave to take your luck as it comes.'

The boy put his head on his knees and sobbed. Sam took a penny out of his trouser pocket.

'Hoddup greetin' a minute. How much do prits cost.'

The boy stared at the penny still crying.

'Paper shop sells new ones in boxes, fourteen for a penny but there's a lad near Gallon's Corner will sell y' twenty-four for a penny.'

Sam held on to the penny.

'Now listen to me. You're to go down to this lad an' get yourself your twenty-four prits. But you're not to play chockin'. You can lose 'em in no time at all chockin'. Play hit an' span or summat like that and you can only lose one at a time at worst. Are you listenin'.'

The boy said 'Yes Mester Chard' and Sam gave him the penny.

'Now geroff.'

The boy stood up and rubbed his sleeve across his eyes. He trotted off down the hill and shouted back 'Thank y' Mester Chard.'

Sam stood up, dusted his trouser seat and hoisted his rucksack on to his back through one strap. He walked up the hill, by the butter cross at the top, down past the wall that ran by Captain Dorman-Davis's house and on towards the dike.

Near the bottom of the hill he came level with the gate of Bletcher's joiner's and saw Bletcher working in the yard. The old man had his workbench outside the shed and was planing a coffin top. His unbuttoned shirt-sleeves flapped in the light summer breeze. From time to time he leaned over the coffin lid and smoothed it with his hand. Sam leaned on the gate and said 'Mornin' Mister Bletcher.' At first the old man failed to hear him but when Sam spoke more loudly, he turned and came slowly across to the gate, peering closely at him. His face wrinkled into a toothless smile.

'It's Sam Chard.'

'That's reight Mister Bletcher.'

'And how's the world treatin' thee, Sam.'

'Fair to middlin'.'

Sam pointed towards the coffin lid on the workbench. 'Looks a nice bit o' wood that.'

Bletcher put his plane on top of the gatepost.

'Best oak.'

'Who's it for.'

'Nixey Cook. Lived on Markham Avenue. Did y' know 'im.'

'Only bi sight. What'd he die of.'

'No idea. He were all'us weakly.'

Bletcher spat and pointed to the coffin standing against the side of the shed.

'Look at it. Best oak, brass fittin's. He never 'ad two ha'pennies to rub together an' he'll be buried wi' all t' swank there is. An' 'is family'll be near beggin' afore the year's out.'

'Spent all his burial club money on it.'

'Every bit I should think.'

'It's a nice mornin' for work.'

'It is that. Breeze just nicely sucks your sweat away.'

Bletcher looked more closely at Sam and pointed to the rucksack.

'You on your travels then.'

'I reckon so. There's not a lot for me round here.'

'Things is thin.'

Bletcher screwed up his eyes and tapped Sam on the shoulder.

'Did you know your faither used to work for me once.'

'No, I never knew that.'

'O aye he did. When he were only a young feller. He worked nobbut a few weeks here. Before he set up on his own.' Bletcher slapped sawdust from his waistcoat and took out his pipe and filled it. He offered his pouch to Sam. Sam shook his head. 'He were a good carpenter, Sam.'

'He was held to be.'

Bletcher lit his pipe and sucked noisily on it.

'A feller of uneven temper though.'

'I remember that.'

Sam shifted the weight of his rucksack and took his foot off the bottom bar of the gate.

'I'd best bi goin' Mister Bletcher.'

'If you must.'

'Watch yoursen then.'

'And thee Samuel.'

Sam walked across the dike bridge and away up the slope towards the Great North Road. He looked back and saw Bletcher was still standing at the gate, puffing on his pipe.

When he reached Five Lane Ends Sam walked fifty yards down the Great North Road and stood on the grass verge, holding his thumb out as traffic passed. After a few minutes a canvas-topped lorry stopped just below him and he ran to it and opened the cab door. There were two men in the small cab with an old border collie sitting between them. The driver shouted over the noise of the engine.

'Where you after.'

'Nowt special. Where you goin'.'

'Brum.'

'That'll do me fine.'

'You'll 'ave to ride in the back.'

Sam nodded, slammed the cab door and ran round to the back of the lorry. He dumped his rucksack over the tail-board and climbed in after it. Settling his back against the side, he stretched his legs out and thumped on the floorboards. The lorry started away with a grinding of gears. Sam rested his arm on the tail-board and watched the fields go past as the lorry pulled up the long slope past the Red House.

The pit siren sounded for the beginning of the afternoon-shift and other pits, farther away, hooted in ragged succession.

Jean Stubbs
Kit's Hill 95p

Set in the bleak, harsh countryside of Lancashire on the eve of the Industrial Revolution, this is the fascinating story of the Howarths; of Ned, the rugged Yeoman farmer, consumed with a passion for a girl above his station; of Dorcas Wilde, the beautiful and spirited girl who married him in the face of family hostility. We share their joys, fears and heartbreaks, from a splendid country wedding feast to the devastation of cattle-plague and the horrors of primitive surgery.

John Broderick
The Waking of Willie Ryan 90p

Willie Ryan, an old man locked away unjustly in an asylum for twenty-five years, returns unexpectedly to his hypocritical family and to those responsible for his confinement. Perceptive and clear sighted, he confronts intolerance and bigotry, born of a reactionary Catholicism and outdated morality. Set in a rambling Irish village this is the powerful story of an anarchic individual's lust for revenge against a village wallowing contentedly in its myopic prejudices.

Dick Francis
Trial Run

Ex-steeplechaser Randall Drew is sent to Moscow to investigate the identity of the mysterious 'Alyosha' who is threatening a royally connected candidate for the Moscow Olympics. The brief is vague, and the opposition invisible...

You can buy these and other Pan books from booksellers and newsagents; or direct from the following address:
Pan Books, Sales Office, Cavaye Place, London SW10 9PG
Send purchase price plus 20p for the first book and 10p for each additional book, to allow for postage and packing
Prices quoted are applicable in the UK

While every effort is made to keep prices low, it is sometimes necessary to increase prices at short notice. Pan Books reserve the right to show on covers and charge new retail prices which may differ from those advertised in the text or elsewhere